D1506947

Lesser Creatures

Also by Amy Pirnie

Let Heaven Fall

LESSER CREATURES

Amy Pirnie

CARROLL & GRAF PUBLISHERS
New York

Carroll & Graf Publishers
An imprint of Avalon Publishing Group, Inc.
245 W. 17th Street, 11th Floor
New York, NY 10011-5300
www.carrollandgraf.com

AVALON
publishing group incorporated

First published in the UK by Constable,
an imprint of Constable & Robinson Ltd 2007

First Carroll & Graf edition 2007

ISBN-13: 978-0-78671-892-4
ISBN-10: 0-7867-1892-7

Printed and bound in the EU

For Freddie

Chapter One

'Catch!'

Sue Bennett tossed her car keys to Anil who caught them with his usual deftness.

'Get it back in time. I'm meeting someone at the Min. of Ag. At four,' she told him.

'To be dished the real dirt or palmed off with the official version?' Anil asked, his eyes dark with mischief.

He walked away whistling, throwing the keys high from hand to hand as Sue's phone rang.

'Gerry!'

'I must be quick, Sue. Richard said to contact Morton Hospital, a Dr Nanda.'

'Morton, Hampshire?'

'That's the one. They've been working on a private project, anti-malarial, and the results are nearly ready for publishing.' Gerry spent some time outlining for Sue the years of careful research, the impact on the profitable drug scene.

'Thanks, Gerry. I owe you.'

'No, you don't. Just give Dr Nanda one of your usual good write-ups and some rich man with a conscience will get out his cheque book.'

'What about rich women?'

'My dear Sue, very few women who become rich do so by having a conscience. Just think of Lucrezia –'

A huge hand lifted Sue, her chair, her desk, and slammed them back down. A violent, rolling wall of noise echoed around the newsroom. It was punctuated by glass disintegrating, the crash of falling objects and screaming quickly stifled. Bemused, Sue looked at her phone, the line now dead.

'What was that?' she asked Jonah as he lumbered towards the source of the disturbance like an old dog ready to retrieve.

'Bomb.'

Sue shook her head to clear disbelief. In the immense space of the newsroom there was no panic. An exodus was already under way, innumerable fire drills proving their worth.

A small group huddled in a corner. 'Pull it out gently,' she heard. There were gasps of dismay and crouched bodies leaped away from spurting blood. Sue hurried across the glass-littered aisles and knelt by the victim. Sandy Jackson's face was contorted with pain. Above his knee an artery had been sliced by flying glass.

'It's OK, Sandy.'

Her crossed thumbs met on the wound and she pressed with all her weight. It was no good worrying about splinters of glass still in the leg. Sue knew she must get the bleeding under control as fast as possible. It took time but the pumping stopped, Sue unsure if it was the result of her struggle or because Sandy had lost so much blood.

'Just relax,' she told him, trying to sound confident, even cheerful. 'We'll soon have you ready to be moved. Anyone got a tie?'

One of the political team held out a striped grey and pink affair, and Sue wondered how she could keep pressure on the artery and manage a tourniquet at the same time. While she gnawed at the problem an authoritative voice with North Country overtones ordered everyone out of the building and Sue was vaguely aware of the small crowd dispersing. Hands came against hers, the thumbs ready to push.

'Let me, Sue. You tie the knots.'

Sam Haddleston, the *Journal*'s editor, was as blood-soaked as Sue by the time the tourniquet held and they could sit back on their heels.

She checked the time on her watch. 'We've got ten minutes, then I must release it and let the blood flow as normally as possible.'

'Or I lose my leg?' Sandy groaned. 'Thank God you two aren't practising on other parts of my anatomy or I'd be singing soprano.'

'Aren't the twins enough for you to be going on with, you randy devil?' Sam asked.

'We need a paramedic – and soon,' Sue said quietly to Sam as Sandy was diverted by pain which waxened his skin.

'Julian's tried phoning but all lines are either down or engaged. He's looking for a computer still up and running – failing that he'll keep searching for a usable mobile until he gets on to the emergency services. Gavin's liaising with them as they arrive.'

It was typical of Sam, Sue thought, that he sent his deputy editor to safety while he searched the wreckage of the building for casualties. Sandy was holding his breath, trying to lessen agony.

'Every team coming in will be concentrating on the site of the explosion,' Sue told Sam. 'Can't you hurry one up here?'

Sam ran for the door, jinking rugby-fashion around obstacles. When he disappeared from her view Sue felt horribly alone and exposed.

Sandy's grip was loosening. 'So, what will they do when they get here, these paramedics?'

'Improve on my handiwork for a start.' She smiled at him. 'A sterile dressing instead of Paula's tissues.'

Sandy tried to grin. 'But they're from Harrods.'

Even as Sue watched, Sandy's fresh young face was shrivelling, his eyes sinking into their sockets. He had already lost too much blood for safety and it was time for Sue to loosen the constriction of tie and pencils. The flow was necessary if the tissues of his leg were to survive, but more blood gushed away. She pictured veins collapsing, making it impossible for paramedics to get a line in and transfuse liquid. If they did not arrive in the next few minutes Sandy's heart would simply stop beating.

Sue tightened the tourniquet until the flow of blood stopped. Sandy groaned, turning the sound into, 'Sue, I'm so cold.' She held his hands as she looked around the once-busy room. Without glass the windows allowed through a strong wind which whipped paperwork into scurrying masses dancing on desks. Sam had cleared all the staff but a jacket had been left behind and Sue used it to cover Sandy.

'This should get you off nappy changing for a day or two,' she teased as she tucked it round him.

'Will I see them again? Brenda and the girls?' Sandy's voice might be faint but his fear was not.

With all the warmth she could muster Sue held his cold fingers and nodded, not trusting herself to speak. If help did not come quickly Sandy must die and there was nothing she could do to prevent it happening.

'Mr Haddleston, you must allow me to decide priority,' a strange voice insisted.

'I know, I know!' Sam shouted. 'I can spell triage too – but this is urgent.'

With relief Sue saw the longed-for equipment materialize from the paramedic's satchel. The man tutted as he bent over Sandy, then his movements became swift, sure. With Sue's help clothes were cut away and after an interminable search a needle bedded into an accommodating vein and fluid dripped in at regulation speed.

'Keep him as warm as you can while I see to the wound,' Sue was ordered after she had given the last time for easing the tourniquet.

'That gives me three minutes,' the man told her.

The expensive and blood-soaked tissues were lifted, the edges of the cut skin and artery examined and a dressing ripped from its sterile wrapping to be fixed firmly against

10

the damage. The bloodstained glass beside Sandy's leg was noticed.

'You really shouldn't have removed that,' they were scolded.

'We didn't,' Sam snapped. 'When can he be moved? I've made sure everyone else is out of the building.'

The uniformed man looked at his two assistants and recognized concern for a friend. 'You did a great job – just be patient a little longer. If you can find a blanket, that would be a great help,' he said and Sam ran.

Sue stayed beside Sandy, massaging warmth into his hands, reassurance into his mind, until Sam returned and they could wrap his chilled body in a woollen cocoon.

By the time a stretcher arrived and Sandy was ready to be moved, Sue was exhausted. She picked her handbag from the drawer of her desk and made her way to the stairs, following Sam as he carried a corner of the stretcher.

Only when she was outside did Sue see the extent of the devastation. The foyer of the *Journal* building lurched drunkenly, devoid of glass. Fire engines closed off the main entrance and car park while a fleet of ambulances was being filled with people she must know. White bandages obscured faces and enveloping blankets transformed friends into shuffling invalids.

By the car park exit were two long, black plastic bags, full and zipped shut. Sue shuddered and was distracted by a policewoman's question.

'Sorry?' She frowned at the girl.

'Were you injured?'

'Me? No.' She followed the PC's gaze and saw her own clothes drenched in blood. Nausea rose and she fought it. 'A friend was.' Sue watched while Sandy was loaded into an ambulance. Doors slammed and a siren rose to a howl as the engine roared away.

The real chaos was on the far side of the police barriers. Spectators attracted to a scene of carnage were being jostled out of position by reporters from all the news media. Sue could see a multitude of cameras sniping at the *Journal*'s misery.

The PC touched her arm and she turned away, hearing behind her a screaming of metal as firemen pulled away loose debris, followed by the sound of concrete dropping and disintegrating. She became aware of, 'Routine questions, if you don't mind, madam,' and gave her full name, address, the way she travelled to work, the registration number of her car.

A line of taxis moved past. Kate Jeffries was in one, her arms around a sobbing girl. Shocked faces looked back at Sue, the day's events numbing expressions. There was the warmth of a firm grip on her arm and she turned to see Sam.

'Pippa's number?' he demanded. Blood had dried in the tight, fair curls where he had run his fingers as he planned and organized. 'Pippa's number,' he said more gently and waggled a mobile phone. 'I want to make sure she's in.'

'Of course – but I can help here.'

A fleeting smile softened the bleakness in Sam's eyes. 'Thanks, but I've a paper to get out. You can work from home and I want anything possible to fill the gaps. You'll give a touch of normality we badly need. Pippa?'

Mechanically, Sue listed the digits and in seconds Sam was talking to Pippa, reassuring her as he insisted she be there when Sue arrived home. Another ambulance shot away and more taxis rolled. Sam waved one to a stop and helped Sue in. 'As soon as I've got things set up I'll be calling, so have your best efforts ready to go.' Flash bulbs popped. 'We've got the front page right here – and the editorial,' he added bitterly as he shut the door of Sue's taxi and watched it driven away.

It was slow going past the police cordon, reporters from other papers pressing against the window and shouting questions, taking photos. Once clear of the hassle the driver sped towards Islington, Sue catching anxious glances from him in the mirror. She decided he must be worried she would throw up but she was too numb to do anything but stare out of the window, seeing nothing.

Pippa must have been watching from her window. She was on the pavement and embodied all that was safe in jeans and a bright green sweater as she waited for Sue to stop trying to pay the driver.

'No, miss, the *Journal* foots the bill. No questions asked as long as we get you all home on the double. You've got a good guvnor,' trailed behind him as he drove off.

Pippa's hug was almost Sue's undoing. 'First thing a shower and a bin bag for those clothes,' she said as they walked in the front door. She chatted on, leading Sue upstairs. 'I've got your spare key – didn't know if you'd been parted from your handbag,' she added as she let Sue into the flat.

The phone was ringing and Sue went to answer it.

'Shower first,' Pippa said and pulled Sue towards the bathroom. 'I've had my orders.' She was taller than Sue, big-boned, with strong, feline movements. 'Your answering machine can cope until you feel more human.'

Sue was allowed no peace until she stood under the benison of hot water, which sluiced away the stains of destruction as heat penetrated and fought the shivering deep inside her. It took a long time.

When she was ready to leave the comfort of the bathroom Sue found Pippa had dealt with her clothes. Even the shoes had been tossed into a bin bag already out of sight.

'You won't want any reminders – and you can always claim off the insurance if you're desperate,' Pippa said with a grin. 'Go and sit by the fire and I'll make some coffee.'

'I must talk to my parents!'

'Did that as soon as Sam called me. I said you'd want to talk the second you were human again. Your mother even told me what to give you for lunch but coffee first, I think.'

Lunch? It was as though an interminable day had passed but Sue stared at the clock on the mantelpiece and saw what a short time had elapsed since she had left for work. So much had happened, but trying to make sense of it all she realized her mind had recorded sights, sounds, thoughts, even emotions, in a jerky and disjointed framework.

Pippa handed her a steaming mug, the heat of the china warming Sue's fingers and steadying them as she sipped. Whisky hit the back of her throat. 'You'll have me an alcoholic!'

'Hardly. Just get it down you.'

Sue sipped again, this time feeling the medicinal bite hearten and soothe. Pippa talked as she heated soup, beat eggs and laid a tray across Sue's knees.

'I can't eat this.' Sue's throat had tightened against the idea of swallowing and she was almost ready to cry.

Pippa sat beside her and in a gentle voice talked of inconsequential things until Sue had dealt with most of the soup. As she took away the tray Pippa was glad to see her friend lay her head back on the cushioning of the couch and close her eyes. Short, dark hair was drying to a shine but Sue's facial bones were exposed, flesh tight against them with the tensions of the day. There were dark shadows beneath her eyes, stark against the whiteness of her skin. For all her size Pippa moved quietly as she cooked and Sue rested.

'Scrambled eggs and soldiers?' Sue smiled at the nursery dish.

'Your mother's orders.'

The tightness was back in Sue's throat. So much concern for her and yet she was uninjured. 'Sandy,' she began, then tears rose. 'The twins aren't a year old yet. How will Brenda manage if anything . . .'

'Sam told me what happened when you were on your

14

way home. If Sandy survives it'll be because of you. Sam also warned me you'd look a mess. He was right there too.'

'It was Sandy's blood. He lost so much, so quickly.'

'And now he'll be stitched up and having transfusions with half Fleet Street asking him how he feels.'

'Wapping.'

'I know – but it doesn't have the same ring to it.'

Pippa's smile undid some of the knots in Sue's muscles and she made an effort to eat her lunch. When she could force down no more the tray was whisked away. She recognized the weariness of despair creeping through her body. Tears misted and stung and Pippa was holding her.

'Let it come, Sue,' she said gently.

It was not a storm of weeping, just reaction to the intense anger, frustration, fear Sue had endured. 'Why?' she asked when she sat upright and blew her nose.

'I don't know. Little men wanting to be noticed? It could be Al Qaeda getting through the security ring – or another group. Just because there's almost an official peace in Ireland doesn't mean everyone agrees with it – or wants it. The big boys there have become respectable. They're interviewed on TV, fly to Washington, just like regular politicians. One jealous idiot carrying a grudge . . .'

'Is that all it takes to rip the *Journal* apart?'

'Why not? Who else has been as tough on terrorists as Sam? He's done his damnedest to separate the maniacs from normal peace-loving Muslims and you said yourself, no one worked harder persuading the White House to stop money flooding from the States to finance the Irish bombers.'

'So today was the price of freedom from nutters of all kinds?'

'Perhaps.'

'It won't stop Sam. Tomorrow's editorial will blister harder than ever – oh God, I forgot. I promised to have work ready.'

Sue made for her desk, switched on the computer and became immersed in a search for topics she could write up quickly. Engrossed, she did not see Pippa's satisfaction as she pulled the bag of blood-soaked clothes from its hiding place and returned to her own flat.

One article complete, Sue was starting on the next when she remembered her parents and picked up the phone. In seconds she heard her mother's calm voice and Sue made an enormous effort to sound normal, almost cheerful, as she talked to her mother and then her father.

'I haven't had the radio on. Is there any more news?' she asked him.

'So far, all we know is that there are twenty-seven in hospital, most with minor cuts from flying glass.'

She remembered the body bags. 'How many dead?'

'Three.'

'Have any died since reaching hospital?'

'Not so far.'

A nodule of ice in Sue began to melt. Sandy was still alive and might go back to his twins one day.

'You're sure you're all right, poppet?' The question was lightly asked but it demanded the truth.

'Yes, Dad. I'm fine – really, I am.'

'Good. I'll let you get on.'

By the time Sue had finished the second of her articles she was ready to talk and dialled Miles's number. She pictured him as she waited for him to answer, remembering a day when they had picnicked. Miles had spent much of the time laughing but there had been a moment when he had gazed at her. He wanted to say something but hesitated, always careful to keep his distance as he waited for her to progress from her loss of Colin, widowing her so abruptly.

'Sue?' His anxiety was almost tangible. 'I tried ringing you but could get no answer.'

As she spoke and reassured she heard him sigh with relief.

'What are you doing?'

'Working. The *Journal* will be on the streets as usual tomorrow.'

'How?'

'If our presses are down we'll get time on others.'

Miles's chuckle was warm in her ear. 'The traditions of the Blitz live on. When can I see you? Tonight?'

'No, not tonight. There's someone I must go and see in hospital.'

'I could come with you.'

Sue imagined his expression, his grey eyes bright, expectant, one eyebrow quirked. 'It's kind of you but I must do this on my own.'

Ending the conversation, Sue was about to write up the feasibility of studying DNA in Egyptian mummies when she remembered she had no car at her disposal. Public transport did not appeal and it would mean a phone call and a taxi. Tomorrow, she reminded herself, she must get the keys back from Anil but now she must concentrate on the mummies.

'Mrs Bennett?' It was a man's voice on her intercom after her doorbell had rung.

'Thank you. Coming now,' she said to the taxi driver.

It took a little time to set the alarm and double lock the door of her flat. Sue ran down the stairs. The sooner she could see Sandy still alive and improving, the sooner she could relax and sleep.

Habit made her check the spyhole in the front door. The driver looked very respectable, perhaps an office manager made redundant and changing direction. Sue registered strong, regular features and greying hair, but as she swung the door open she was surprised when two men barred her way.

'Susan Bennett?'

It was the voice she had heard moments ago. The owner had a solid look to him, emphasized by his height and the width of his shoulders. He offered a card and Sue looked up, puzzled.

'I'm Detective Superintendent Ashford, Mrs Bennett, and this is Detective Inspector Eden.'

She read the information on the warrant cards, checking each man's photo. The younger officer was tall, fair, and gave the impression of someone who spent what time he could in a gym.

'May we come in?' the senior man asked.

'I'm on my way to a hospital – I've a taxi coming.'

Superintendent Ashford pursed his lips. 'I took the liberty of sending it away. May we come in?' he asked again. 'We do need your help and the doorstep is hardly the right place.' His brief smile was merely polite and did not reach his eyes.

Sue was annoyed, her visit to Sandy being thwarted, then common sense prevailed. The police had a job to do. 'Of course. I suppose it's about the bomb?'

Ashford nodded and Sue led the way upstairs, hearing the inspector shut the door firmly and check it was locked. Once inside the flat Sue shut off the alarm and ushered the men into her sitting room, still warm from her afternoon's occupation. They made no comment on the way Sue had blended cool pastels and comfortable furniture, nor did they notice the few original paintings she and Colin had chosen with such care. She watched them settle, wondering why two ranking policemen from Special Branch needed to visit her.

Superintendent Ashford wasted no time. He asked Sue to recall what had happened that morning. She told them of the phone call from Gerry and the line going dead.

'Before that, Mrs Bennett?'

It was the inspector who asked. She turned to her questioner, seeing a firm jaw and thoughts shuttered from her. Sue's memory went back to the normality of the newsroom.

'Paula – Paula Caulfield was doing some research into over-fishing. She came to check if we should use the Crown of Thorns.'

'Great Barrier Reef?' Inspector Eden asked.

She was surprised at his knowledge. 'That's right. Over-fishing may have upset the balance there and the starfish are decimating the coral. The build-up of the starfish is allowing it to spread to other regions.'

'Interesting,' Ashford said. 'And then?'

'Then Anil came to put up a good case for borrowing my car. His was in for repair and I'd asked him to check out a report of a factory's effluent leaking into the Thames. He was to interview residents nearby. I gave him my keys.'

'When did you decide to let Mr Naib use your car?'

The hard edge to the question startled Sue. 'Time? I don't know. Nine thirty, ten, thereabouts.'

It was the inspector's turn. 'Was he in the habit of driving the vehicle?'

'Habit?' Sue thought hard, trying to remember. 'Twice, maybe three times.'

'In how long?'

Both men were intent on her answer.

'Since he started working with me – six or seven months ago.' Sue began to be irritated. 'What's all this about? Surely, with all that's going on two such experienced men as you should not be checking how often my car – the *Journal*'s car, come to that – has been driven by somebody else. Why don't you ask Anil? He'd remember the occasions much better than I can.'

'I wish we could, Mrs Bennett.' The superintendent leaned forward. 'Unfortunately, Mr Naib was killed when he used the electronic key to open the door of the car you drove to work this morning.'

Sue heard little of the insistent voices as she tried to absorb what she had been told. Anil could not be dead, the explosion happened too soon after he had left the news-room. He always stopped to talk to Julia in reception and Anil would never have missed an opportunity to spend time with her, yet someone had been killed. The detectives' attitudes made that one fact real.

'Are you sure it's Anil?'

'Yes.'

19

Inspector Eden's certainty convinced Sue. She closed her eyes, picturing the scene in the car park. In her mind she watched the driver approach the door but it was not Anil. Shocked, she looked at Superintendent Ashford with dawning horror and met unexpected sympathy. This was why Special Branch officers were in her home. They needed to know who had planted the murdering explosives and had the unexpected chance to talk to the intended victim.

'I was the one to be killed,' Sue whispered. 'But why?'

There were no answers, only questions which went on for hours. Sue opened her mind to them, replying as accurately as she could. Other police came and went, some in uniform. Permission was asked for a search and Sue saw her computer and disks packed up for checking as well as papers, tapes from her security cameras, even the notes she had left herself on her fridge door.

Part of her wanted to protest until she allowed logic to have its way. If the bomber had succeeded she would have been in a million pieces and the police would have had the freedom of her home. She let them take what they wanted. Anil was owed that, at the very least.

At one point Sue lost control, refusing to answer any more questions until she knew Sandy's condition. Superintendent Ashford accepted her desperate need and nodded to his junior. A few minutes of Inspector Eden's efforts and she was handed a phone.

The specialist in charge of Sandy explained the operation which had been performed, the need for an arterial graft to replace the tattered blood vessel Sue had fought in the newsroom. The surgeon realized her understanding of the technicalities and talked of the methods used as well as the materials. The details helped to convince her Sandy had been repaired. With transfusions and time he should be ready to be discharged in a few days, she was informed officially.

It looked as if she might be the cause of Anil's death. Sandy's life redressed the balance a fraction – but it was not enough. 'Why me?' she asked for the umpteenth time.

'First thoughts were, of course, one of Bin Laden's disciples but that had to be discounted.'

'Why?'

'There was no evidence of a body in the car. Al Qaeda specializes in martyrs and in turn that system ensures the explosion is more directly controlled.'

'So who else? The Provisionals, the Real IRA, have been quiet for a while now.'

'Agreed, and we've been aware for some time of splinter groups, here in London, determined on the old ways. They want the glory of English deaths by bombing and to hell with any peace the politicians may be trying to arrange.'

'This was down to them?'

'Maybe not,' Inspector Eden said slowly. 'The sophistication is well out of their capability. It's obviously been a new tactic to get the explosives in place. Use an unsuspecting driver and a car not likely to be checked. The odd thing is,' he said slowly, 'there was really only enough material for one death to be guaranteed.'

There was the quiet of exhaustion in the room, the aftermath of interminable questions and answers.

'Whoever it was, what did they hope to gain by killing me? Was it completely random?'

Ashford shook his head. 'I doubt it. A blast at the *Journal* would ensure maximum publicity for the bombers but if it was you slaughtered in the process, that's two fingers up at the editor.'

'Sam?' Sue was horrified by the idea. 'I know he's very anti-terrorist, especially the IRA. His brother was killed in Belfast.'

'He also has a chauffeur who's ex-army and checks the car regularly. Besides, it would hurt him more if they involved you.' To Sue's puzzled look Ashford explained, 'We've had Mr Haddleston under observation for his own safety. You pop up quite frequently in our reports.'

21

'Sam's a friend – nothing more!' she protested.

'That's in our reports, too.'

'How absolutely ghastly for you!'

Kate Jeffries pecked at a cheek and swept on into the flat trailing the latest heavy-duty perfume. Behind her Pippa and Ken searched Sue's face for signs of distress and found only weariness.

'Were you able to help?' Ken wanted to know. He had been a detective in the Metropolitan Police before he qualified as a solicitor and became Colin's friend. 'I'm sorry, I should have asked how you are?'

'Fine,' Sue said and smiled, feeling muscles complain at the attempt. 'Really. It just went on for so long. I even began to wonder if they'd bed down for the night. As it is a couple of them are in a car parked across the road.'

'They certainly know how to make a mess.' Pippa was annoyed on Sue's behalf as she lifted cushions, beating them with unnecessary vigour before tidying the couch.

'You should see the kitchen!' Kate shouted. 'Didn't their mothers teach them anything?' There was the sound of cupboard doors being opened and closed. 'Where do you keep the gin?'

Sue chuckled at the idea of a frustrated Kate. 'Top shelf, cupboard nearest the door.'

'What did they take?' Ken asked when at last the sitting room looked fairly normal and Pippa was washing up discarded mugs.

'Everything. Even my diary.'

'Darling! You need that for work,' Kate protested.

'I'll manage. I expect my contacts will be understanding when they hear the news.'

'That's not the point,' Kate said. 'By the way, is your phone working again?'

Sue was surprised. 'I didn't know it was out of order. It explains why no one called me.'

'Sam's been going berserk trying to get through, it's why

I'm here. He rang while I was in the bath and insisted I come right over and find out how you were. I thought he'd go into orbit when I told him you had the police crawling everywhere.' She smiled benignly at Pippa and Ken. 'Fortunately, these two took me in and kept me entertained.'

Ken leaned towards Sue. 'Did the police say who they suspect?'

She shrugged her shoulders, a tired gesture. 'Probably not Al Qaeda – more likely to be London-based IRA. Who else?'

'That's what I don't understand,' Ken said with a frown. 'According to the TV news there were no claims of responsibility, nor was there a coded message to any of the media.'

'He's right,' Kate said, helping herself to more gin. 'First thing Sam checked while he was sorting out the front page. Not a whisper from anyone to a paper or TV station, certainly not the police, here or in Ireland.'

'How odd,' Sue said slowly. 'Al Qaeda would want to glory publicly in the devastation – then it's a major tactic of the IRA to phone in a warning with just too little time for the police to clear everyone out of the danger zone.'

'So, why have the bombers kept quiet today?' Pippa asked quietly. 'What's so special about the *Journal*?'

The doorbell at seven thirty the next morning was an unpleasant reminder of reality. With no chance to renew her video tapes Sue could not check her visitor until she used the front door spyhole.

'I hope you had a chance to sleep?' she asked Superintendent Ashford.

'I'm sorry if we woke you but it is a matter of urgency.'

She looked at his companions, recognizing Inspector Eden but not the uniformed woman PC, nor a very young detective, his suit suspiciously new.

'You'd better come in.'

Sue went ahead, apologizing for the fact she was still in her bathrobe.

'While you dress I'm sure DC Perrott will make us all some tea.' The superintendent was being very urbane for such an early hour.

Sue nodded agreement, trying not to smile as she explained the lack of milk. 'There's a shop on the corner,' she added helpfully. 'Perhaps you'd better not send someone in uniform.'

'No, you're right. DC Perrott can go,' the inspector decided. 'Is there anything else you need?'

Peace and quiet were Sue's silent wishes but she settled for, 'Toilet rolls. Mine all got used last night.'

A speedy shower later Sue climbed into jeans and topped them with a blue and white striped shirt before pulling a comb through her hair. She was unaware of the impression she made on her guests. There was fresh colour in her cheeks and her short dark hair swung like silk, free of her oval face with its small features and dark brows winging away above hazel eyes. Superintendent Ashford could see why one of the toughest editors in London was in hot pursuit of this particular science reporter.

'Something's happened,' Sue decided.

'Intelligence reports before and after the explosion. They all dismiss both Al Qaeda and an IRA initiative.'

'If it's not them, then who?'

DC Perrott was at the door. The PC let him in and he headed for the kitchen and his chore, so it was to a background clattering of mugs that Superintendent Ashford assessed Sue and her stamina.

'We had to proceed yesterday as though old-style Provos were behind the blast and using you as the conveyance. Today we have to find the real reason. We have to assume you were the intended target, not because of your association with Mr Haddleston, but because you've upset someone. Very badly.'

'Me? It's absolutely ridiculous!'

24

'Is it? Journalists, some very fine women among them, have been gunned down for what they've written – or could write.'

'But I don't do that sort of stuff. I'm not political, I don't work with the crime team –'

'But you did get involved, and not so long ago. Rocket?'

Suddenly, Sue could not breathe. There was a memory of fingers tight around her throat.

'I'm sorry to rake up past events but he did try to kill you.'

'It can't be him.' James Rocket had died while on remand, charged with the attack on Sue.

'Perhaps his friends want to settle an old grudge against you and your husband?'

His words reverberated in Sue's mind. Colin had been quietly gathering evidence against a group of paid killers and been murdered when Rocket pushed him under a train. Sue looked at her hands, nails scratching at a mark on her jeans. Colin, she begged silently, help me. As she thought of him, some of the calmness which had been Colin began to pervade her and common sense surfaced.

She faced the policemen resolutely. 'You know perfectly well that any of Rocket's cronies need cash before they'll kill. Then they have to see the victim die – it's part of the deal. Really, Superintendent, do you think for a moment anyone who was on the same level as Rocket could have put together a heap of explosives, planted them without being seen and then detonated the whole thing with some offbeat electronic wizardry? A baseball bat or a sharp knife is more their idea of sophistication.'

'What about the articles you write?' Ashford asked. 'Have you trodden on any corns? This effluent business – could the factory owners be involved?'

'Hardly. The Thames is constantly monitored and the pollution has probably already been picked up by the Rivers Authority – they do all the dirty work of regulating and prosecuting. Anil was to interview people living nearby. We'd had complaints coming into the office and he's very good at sorting out fact from hysteria – he was.'

'In the past, have you upset any Greens?' Eden asked.

'There's always someone waiting to be upset but I've not had much aggro that way. No threatening phone calls from a pressure group – not that I can remember.'

'I've got our people going through past articles of yours to see if names match up with what we want in our computers. It'll be a long job, I'm afraid, and we need you on call until it's completed.'

'House arrest?' Sue tried to joke but she was weary in spite of the early hour.

'Protection, we like to think.' Ashford forced a smile. 'We've not released the names of those killed. When we do, and the organizer of all this realizes they've made a mistake, you could be at risk again. Until then, we have a few hours' start on him.'

Sue remembered talking to Gerry. 'Or her. A woman without a conscience is a very deadly animal.'

'I agree, which is why I'm asking you to stay here and not go out. If you're not seen our quarry might think he – or she's – succeeded and to all intents and purposes we're simply investigating the life of someone killed in the blast.'

Sue shivered, ice crawling across her back. 'When do you go public with the names?'

'When your friends in the media get too persistent for our commander,' Ashford told her.

The morning dragged on. DC Perrott was sent out shopping for food for the team, Sue raiding her freezer to augment the sandwiches he brought back.

'You're doing me a favour,' she said as stew, vegetables, rice, were eaten with gusto. 'My mother stocks my freezer to bursting point and it needs cleaning out.'

There was no time for Sue to start that particular chore. The sound of an argument in the streets below drew

Ashford and Eden to the window. After a terse message to the PC on duty at the front entrance Sue heard someone running swiftly up the stairs. There was another exchange at her front door before Sam strode in and went straight to Sue, holding her shoulders while his gaze raked her face.

'Were the articles yesterday that bad?' she asked.

There was a quick grin for her. 'Who's in charge?' Sam asked the assortment of police officers.

Ashford introduced himself. 'You told my man downstairs you had vital information?' He waited for Sam to explain.

'A Professor Turnbull got hold of me this morning.'

'Turnbull?' Sue was surprised.

Ashford turned to her. 'You know him?'

'I last visited his labs three or four days ago.'

'What's his speciality?'

'Carcinoma – cancers. It's part of his brief to devise ways of marking cancer cells loose in the blood. He's a first-class cell biologist, particularly the cell membrane.'

Understanding began to dawn in Ashford. 'Does he use animals in his research?'

'Yes – but he's very well organized and the regulations are strict.'

Sam was grim-faced. 'Someone objects.' He pulled a folded sheet from his pocket and handed it to the superintendent. 'Turnbull had an e-mail this morning. He faxed me a copy after we talked.'

Ashford read the missive, then handed it to Sue. It was simple, stark.

Your friend Sue Bennett died yesterday. Tomorrow it could be your wife or even Gemma. You know what we want.

Chapter Two

By the time Sue's flat was almost empty she was ready to scream. The questioning, bad enough the first time round, became insistent, her answers examined for every innuendo.

No, Professor Turnbull was not a friend.

On only three occasions had Sue visited his lab at the university.

Each time she had been checked on entry, issued with a pass and interviewed Professor Turnbull in the presence of his secretary.

Of course it was possible the interviews had been recorded, Professor Turnbull was nobody's fool.

No, she had never met Mrs Turnbull, or her daughter, Gemma.

The logo of an equal sign across a Z was new to her. If it stood for Animal Equality it was the first she had heard of it.

What the terror group wanted from the professor, she had no idea: she could only assume it was to make him stop using animals in any of his experiments.

Professor Turnbull's aim was simple – to devise one or more tests which would mark cancer cells in a blood sample, thus making early diagnosis of the disease simple and swift.

Sam had been banished but insisted on returning in the

evening, wanting to stay on after the police left. Sue fed him a risotto from the freezer, made coffee and small talk and longed for solitude, silence, but he was concerned for her and unwilling to leave. It was easier when she could get him talking of the efforts being made to restore the *Journal* to its usual routine. Insurers were consigned to the devil and builders scathed for being slow to move and get the *Journal* independent again.

The presses had suffered least damage. They were housed in a solid framework because of the normal vibrations of printing and would be rolling in a day or two when all the electrical connections had been checked. It was the flimsier offices which had been wrecked by the blast and where most of the casualties had occurred. Sam listed for Sue the staff who had been hurt, taking it as a personal affront they had been injured while working for him.

'Anil?' Sue asked, after she had heard of the plight of the families of Barker, the security officer, and Peacock, the courier, men who had filled the body bags she had seen.

Sam stood and paced, his steps short, restless. 'It's so bloody unfair! His parents just sit there, not moving, not crying. His brother was ready to lead a riot against every Irishman he could find – but now? With no one knowing who planted the bomb?'

'Animal Equality – whoever they are.'

Sam was cynical and it showed. 'If they're using the "All animals are equal" battle cry, they should remember the next stage. "Some are more equal than others" – and look where that leads.'

There had been silence in the room, the flick of flames in the gas fire soothing, hypnotic.

'The bombers certainly consider themselves more equal than you or me – especially me,' Sue said bitterly. 'To them I'm no different from one of Turnbull's rats, my death just as useful.'

'It was, but they'll have moved on. My bet is there's already another target in their sights.'

'Are you saying that to cheer me up?'

'No.'

Had Sam protested vigorously, Sue might not have believed him. 'Anil was enough?'

'It would be the publicity that was important. I doubt it really mattered to them who died – as long as someone did.'

Sue gazed at the flames, her eyes aching. 'Why?' she whispered.

'To get the reaction they wanted. If they had to kill and maim . . .' The muscles of his face were taut, pulling bones into a profile of anguish. 'The arrogance of evil.'

She knew Sam had faced its consequences with his brother's death in Crossmaglen as well as the destruction and fatalities at the *Journal*. 'Is that all it is? Bloody-minded arrogance?'

'To plan mass murder? It's the ultimate in selfishness.'

Sue shook her head. 'No. Pippa explained it once. If you're selfish you see the other person's point of view but choose to ignore it. It's when you're self-centred you see no one's needs and wants but your own.'

'So, total self-centredness –'

'Is total evil.' Sue was cold in the warmth of her home.

Sam leaned towards her, would have held her, seeing how tired she was. 'Don't forget these animal rights fanatics will claim they're acting for beings with no voice, no vote.'

Sue frowned, wanting to express herself clearly through a fog of weariness. 'I've watched and listened to so many of them. A small but healthy core does genuinely care about animals and their welfare. Those protestors can see when there's something wrong and might not have much idea how to put things right but they mean well.'

'Not all?'

'No. For the hard-line activists, animals are an excuse.'

'They're like any other kind of terrorist? The urge to kill

comes first. The cause – politics, religion, whatever – comes a long way second?'

'Exactly. I'd guess the people behind Animal Equality want to be seen to be in control and they choose fear to get their way. If it means the slaughter of other humans they can do it as easily as a farmer deciding which chicken is lunch, or which rabbit he'll shoot to scare off the rest.'

'Mm. An idea for an article. Mass murderers regarding their work in the same way as a slaughterman in an abattoir.'

'It's why appeals to the better nature of terrorist groups never work. All the anger against them, all the protests, have as much effect as the bleating of sheep and calves on their way to a butcher's slab.'

'You realize your theory explains why the Nazis set up and ran death camps so efficiently?'

Sue lay back against her cushions and closed her eyes. 'As far as Animal Equality's concerned, Anil merely took my place in the queue.'

Sam's thoughts were racing. 'The legislation in place to tackle terrorism – I must get Clive and his team going through it thoroughly to make sure it includes animal rights extremists.'

Almost asleep, Sue nodded slowly. Sam saw the depth of her exhaustion and gave her a quick kiss as he said good-bye. She closed the door behind him, leaning against it until she heard the front door slam, and some of her tension eased. Walking through her flat to the sitting-room window she pulled at a curtain and watched Sam drive away, the occupants of a car across the road stirring a little as he passed. Her guard was in place.

In spite of tiredness, sleep was a long time coming and thoughts were unpleasant companions. Twist and turn as she might, Sue could not escape the fact that she had been named in the letter to Professor Turnbull. She was the one who had been marked out to die but it was Anil in pieces in a mortuary.

Through the long hours Sue was at one moment flooded

with the relief of still being alive, the next suffused with guilt. Anil was so young. He had had such talent, so much to give. As morning approached she faced the harshness of the days to come, but could she ever learn to live with the reality that his death had saved her life?

Two days passed. Pippa's cheerful visits were an aid to sanity and Sue's solitude was punctuated by phone calls, mostly from her parents and Sam. She kept herself busy at the computer ferried over from the *Journal* along with her back-up disks, sending copy to Beth who would be wearing the brightest of her rugby shirts and calmly sub-editing in a makeshift newsroom.

Routine helped fill the hours, items on swallow populations threatened by modern building methods, or invisible organo-phosphates covering fruit unwashed but free of pests.

The news of Anil's death had been released but there was little information on Sue's car. Radio and TV news suggested the bomb had been planted on site by an intruder. Daily papers had followed the idea, Super-intendent Ashford doing nothing to dispel the public's perception of the incident.

Sam would not agree to Sue visiting the Naib family in case the bombers were watching their house. The police echoed his concern but did allow her to be driven to the hospital and see Sandy with a healthy colour.

His wife, Annie, cried as she held Sue, thanking her for being with Sandy when he needed help so badly. Tears were quickly dried and followed by laughter at the antics of the twins, wriggling happily in the arms of every nurse possible.

'Sue, what info have you got on noise?' Sandy asked when everyone was busy with his daughters.

'Stacks. Any special emphasis?'

'The staff in here have been marvellous but sleep is impossible. I'm going off my trolley with the racket which goes on morning, noon and night – especially night. I thought, Sam willing, I'd try a write-up on noise pollution.'

'It's a great idea, Sandy. Noise is the nuisance least legislated against and most all-pervading. It can also drive you out of your mind.'

'Don't I know it! It's helped me understand Annie better. She's been so determined to get back to work as soon as she can. I must admit I wasn't too happy with that idea but I can see now that however much you adore your babies, having the same sounds all day and every day, you do wonder where your marbles have gone.'

'The treatment here must be doing you some good in spite of the din. Not only does your leg improve, your attitude is becoming much less chauvinistic,' Sue teased. 'How is it, by the way – the leg?'

'I want to scratch. Apart from that it's fine. I walk a little but the nurses stop me putting too much weight on it.'

'When are they likely to throw you out?'

'A few more days. Sam's making arrangements for me to work from home and he's insisted on ordering a wheel-chair for the office. He's been terrific.'

Sue was glad Sam had got Sandy looking forward to normal life so quickly. 'I'm working from home as well. We can chat by computer when I send you the data I have on noise.'

They sat in quiet companionship, then Sandy studied her. 'I can't get much up-to-date gossip lying here but I do know Anil was going off to use your car when he was killed. Was it you they were after?'

Sue nodded and examined a crease in a sheet.

'Do you want to talk about it?' he asked quietly.

'There's nothing to tell. Some group decided a killing at the *Journal* would publicize their campaign.'

'Bin Laden's boys? IRA?'

'Neither. Animal-friendly fanatics. They wanted to use my car – and me.' Sue tried a smile. 'I just hope they're not of the "if at first you don't succeed" variety.'

Annie produced two bottles from a roomy bag adorned

with elephants and bears. The twins sucked and were silent.

'Do you think this gaggle will try again?' Sandy asked.

'You mean, will they have another pop at me?' Sue looked down at her hands. 'Police psychologists say the choice of me wasn't personal and the group's objective has been achieved. They'll know by now I'm watched day and night so they won't risk their necks. When all's said and done, bombing from a distance is a coward's method.'

'You don't sound convinced.'

Sue hesitated. 'When your name's been at the head of someone's death list, it feels hellishly personal.'

'I'm just glad you were in the office and not in the car park when I needed help.' Sandy held out his hand and Sue grasped it, feeling strength flow from him.

London dusted off Wapping and carried on as usual, though Sue was still monitored round the clock by Special Branch. At times it irritated her but she concentrated on her work, using it to drive away all other considerations.

One by one, units at the *Journal* joined in the daily routine until the huge newsroom hummed again, even if the smell of fresh paint was overpowering. It was not long before Sandy limped to Sue's desk and perched on a corner.

'Welcome, stranger. Where's your wheelchair?'

Sandy grinned. 'Parked at my desk. I'll use it when salient bits begin to ache.' He looked around the newsroom. 'It's good to be back.'

'We missed you.'

'Thanks. I'll be glad to see my girls tonight but I'm determined to enjoy myself today. I've had the go-ahead for a noise pollution campaign but you've got to explain this melanin business before I go any further. Sam thinks it's political dynamite.'

'Certainly explosive – if it's handled wrongly.'

'What is?' Jonah asked. The senior crime reporter, he

34

stood like an elderly beagle with his paws on Sue's terminal. Yellowish skin hung in folds and breath wheezed in and out of damaged lungs but his bald pate shone and his eyes were bright with interest.

'A theory coming out of research labs,' Sue explained. 'The presence of melanin in the ears affects the level of sounds able to be detected.'

Jonah groaned. 'You bloody scientists are at it again. Why can't you do things in English like the rest of us?'

He lumbered away to the coffee machine as Sandy responded to demands from his damaged leg and went in search of a comfortable chair. Left alone, Sue listened to familiar sounds and was reassured. Phones rang and were answered quickly. Keyboards were in use, the resulting copy, diagrams, photographs, tailored to fit ordained space.

In the centre of the room Cary Mitchell was the target for Kate's spleen. The two engaged in a daily battle which served to sharpen their verbal claws, and from a safe distance Sue gathered that today Kate disliked one of the subjects in Cary's gossip column.

'She's very newsworthy at the moment,' he insisted.

Kate was incensed and her hair, a halo of fire, quivered. 'She's using you and the *Journal* to turn herself into a horizontal celebrity when she's nothing more than a tart!'

'Maybe she is but she's also very well connected.'

'You mean her clients are. She's signed up with some sneaky little PR man no one's ever heard of, Cary. Instead of having to slime around and stick up cards in phone boxes – his usual practice – he gets you to write her up and increase her price and his commission. It's bloody pimping!'

Cary's well-bred tones wore away at Kate's loud sallies until coffee was suggested and they trailed off amicably. Sue watched them go, glad some things had not changed.

Even Anil's desk was covered in papers but it was no longer Anil sitting there. His replacement was a girl Sue had not found as easy to work with as Anil. Karin Meacher had plain features and sharp, pale blue eyes; her dry, mousy hair was scraped back and held by a leather slide and habitual black dragged all colour from her face. It was a pity, Sue decided at their first meeting. The girl had fine skin marred only by the grimness of her expression.

There was a whisper of wheels and Sandy grinned from his wheelchair. 'This is great for getting around. If I can only get it fitted with a keyboard and VDU there'll be no stopping me.'

'I'm sure Sam will oblige if you ask him nicely.'

'No taking the mickey, if you please. I've come to check that disco stuff with you.'

As Sandy made notes, Sue explained the effect of excessive noise. The pain it caused could be alleviated by opening the mouth and moving one's body with the beat. Flashing lights added an hypnotic effect and raised the level of sound which could be endured. The resulting dry mouths and throats made bar sales soar.

Sandy decided he was in the wrong job. 'I should be running discos for a living.'

'And go deaf permanently?'

'OK, OK. Since you insist, I'll stay a poverty-stricken journo. Now, I think I'll start with the major breweries.'

'You won't get far questioning their methods of making money.' Sue wrote swiftly. 'The first one is a leading ENT specialist,' she said as she handed Sandy a note. He read it.

'And the other?'

'A psychologist who's done a fair bit of good research.'

'Sue, you must have the memory of an elephant!'

She grinned at him. 'I guessed you'd need the names sometime so I checked them this morning.'

Sandy wheeled away and Sue bent to an assignment for the next day's issue. She was not left in peace for long, her phone shrilling and Maimie, Sam's secretary, calling her to his office. When she opened the door she was surprised to see visitors already there.

'Superintendent Ashford, has something happened?'

The policeman was on his feet with old-fashioned courtesy. He shook his head. 'Nothing drastic. This is Sergeant Webley.'

The sergeant, a tall and very attractive woman in her late twenties, was dark-skinned, with the same sharp intelligence and awareness Sue had come to expect in Ashford's team. They shook hands, assessing each other as Sam prowled, made uneasy by this reminder of Sue's danger.

'I'm here to see if you can help us,' Ashford said when they were all seated.

'If I can, of course.'

The superintendent weighed his thoughts for a moment. 'In your capacity as a science reporter, I assume you've attended animal rights demonstrations?'

'Most papers cover them, even if they earn little space in the columns.'

'We've had difficulty tracking down the Animal Equality organization, mainly because it's so small. As far as we can gather there are two significant members, but we only have the name of the leader.'

'Two! Is that all?' Sam's fingers curled as he queried the number of people who killed *Journal* staff.

Ashford's expression was grim. 'It's enough, sir.' He turned to Sue. 'We have a video of a demo outside labs in Bristol and I'd like you to take a look at it. See if you can identify anyone.'

'The bombers?'

'Let's try it, shall we?'

Ashford nodded to his sergeant who produced a cassette from her bag and handed it to Sam. Within seconds images were on the large screen in the corner of the room and Sue frowned as she concentrated on the flying figures. It was a short film and when it ended, Sue's brow was still furrowed.

'Anyone?' the sergeant asked her.

'There are women I see at quite a few of these events. They're genuine and each has a valid point which should be followed up. Mostly, they're normal, sane individuals who wouldn't hurt a fly.'

Ashford was not so sure. 'Try telling that to a young copper who's just been clouted by one of them,' he advised and gave the order to run the film again.

After the third showing Sue caught her bottom lip between her teeth. 'It's odd. I'm sure I've seen . . .'

'Who?' Ashford's quietness encouraged her.

'It wasn't Bristol, I'm positive about that. If I could only remember where.' Sue had a sudden longing for an elephant's memory.

Sergeant Webley passed Sue the video handset. 'Can you isolate the individual puzzling you?'

Sue used the controls until she was as certain as she could be and put the image on 'hold'. The others peered more closely at the screen. A man had his arms raised and most of his face was hidden.

Ashford gazed at Sue. 'You recognized none of the women as being especially fanatic?'

She shook her head. 'They all scream a lot on these occasions – it's part of the herd behaviour. I mostly look for the ones not so involved emotionally. They're there for the power thing so I guess they see themselves as the controllers. What they are, in fact, are predators.' Sue smiled wryly. 'They aren't usually the ones who get arrested.'

Ashford pointed to the screen. 'Did this man qualify as a predator?'

'Not really.'

'Yet you remember him and can recognize him well enough to place him in another situation?'

'Yes – but he was wearing a white coat then.' Sue was angry with herself for not remembering where.

The superintendent was prepared to accept any help he could get. 'Well, Mrs Bennett, if you could identify any of the women you put in your controller group, I would be most grateful.'

There were two. A middle-aged woman with piercing eyes in a long, narrow face, her unkempt hair swirled by

38

the wind. The other was a much younger woman, quiet, her face a mask of secrecy. Sue sat back in her chair and sensed satisfaction in the police officers.

'One of them?'

'Perhaps not the bomber but possibly part of the set-up. Perhaps we could go back to the man you spotted?'

Sue found him again, his features still indistinct.

'Pity,' Ashford said, 'his face would have been useful.'

'I can try a photofit or an e-fit?'

'Did you see him clearly enough for that?'

'Not then, only when he was wearing a lab coat.'

'How can you be sure he's the same one?'

'I'm a zoologist,' Sue explained. 'When you spend large chunks of your degree years watching different species of animals, you learn to identify individuals by their movements.' She pointed to the screen. 'It was the way he hopped about I recognized. He has an odd, bouncy step and I'd seen it before – the exact pattern. That time, he had a face.'

'And with luck we get our second target.'

The driving force behind Animal Equality Ashford and his team already knew. She was the smaller of the two controller women Sue had seen at Bristol.

Andrea Passmore was the product of a very comfortable home and had attended an extremely expensive girls' school until she was expelled. Embracing vegetarianism with an unholy zeal she had tried to join reputable animal rights organizations but they had all sensed in her the need to upset their status quo. Although she had become known as a nuisance, until now her partner had been in the background and invisible.

'Could he have seen you at the demo?' Ashford asked Sue.

'It's possible. I wouldn't have been in hiding and I'd have had a photographer with me.'

'Who?'

'Probably Pete Tym. We'd have been part of the press scrimmage and indistinguishable from the rest.'

'And then our unknown male spotted you on a trip to a lab and could put a name to you, as well as the paper you represented.'

'Was it as simple as that?'

'When we find him, we can ask,' Ashford promised.

'Can you tell me if they've planted any other bombs?'

He decided to trust Sue. 'Three others, small affairs. One each in Bristol, Cambridge and London.'

Sue remembered the blasts. 'They were responsible for those labs being wrecked?'

Ashford nodded.

'Animals were killed or so badly injured they had to be destroyed,' Sam added.

'Wanton slaughter,' Ashford agreed. 'Letters were sent to the Yard with the Z and equals sign logo, claiming the attacks were intended to free the animals from the tyranny of scientists. Sergeant Webley got as close to them as anyone but the only identity we could get was Passmore's. That young lady has no practical skills and so is not the actual bomb maker. Until today we had no idea who might be working with her.'

Sue was curious. 'The bomb in my car. How long had it been there?' she asked the superintendent.

'Your guess is as good as mine. It's likely you'd been carrying it around for some time – a couple of days, maybe.'

She was silent, reviewing the people she had been near. Celia's children came to mind, their innocence threatened by her friendship. 'Could it have exploded before reaching the *Journal*?'

'Possibly not. A chunk of Semtex is fairly safe until it's detonated and the mechanism under your car was very sophisticated.'

Sue shivered. 'It could have gone off any time I opened the door.'

'Specialists tell us the detonator would have been activated only minutes before the blast. Then the next time the key was used . . .' Superintendent Ashford opened his hands and raised them.

'Someone saw me drive in and then they set off the damned thing?'

'That's how it would have appeared to have happened.'

Sue was silent, forcing back imagined horrors and a rising scream. Furtively, she tried to hide her panic and the trembling in her fingers.

Only the policewoman noticed. 'They won't have another go at you,' she assured Sue. 'Thanks to your help we can complete identification and get a full alert out on the pair of them.'

'The girl's noticeable but the man's a very insignificant sort of person and can hide anywhere.' It was only the springing step which had stayed in Sue's memory and to which she could link his features.

'We'll get them,' the sergeant said.

Sue believed her. 'You already have plenty of information about the girl, Passmore?'

Ashford inclined his head. 'We think she's the real intelligence of the group.' His face darkened. 'We also know she'll use any means to get what she wants.'

'Which is?'

'Animals to have the same rights and legal protection as you and I. They're very vague about details but there has been a virulent communiqué comparing money spent on human medical care with the outlay for sick and injured animals. Fancy sharing a hospital ward with beds full of pigs and goats – all on the NHS?' There was a chill in Ashford's attempt at humour.

Sue had her own priorities. 'I'd have more respect for them if they campaigned where real harm is being done.'

'Such as?'

'The appalling conditions in which some Canadian breeders keep pregnant mares.'

'Why?' Sergeant Webley wanted to know.

'HRT. It can be produced in the lab but far too much

being used in Britain comes from the urine of pregnant mares.'

'From Canada?'

Sue nodded. 'Yes. Most breeders are OK but there are a few who need stringing up. Let Animal Equality tackle them and see what happens.'

The sergeant was realistic. 'It would be far too dangerous for them. They want other people to suffer and die for their adopted cause – not themselves.'

'It's more than that with these far-out pressure groups,' Ashford said. 'Their aims and demands have to be totally unrealistic.'

Sam understood. 'Nothing changes, does it? Anything reasonable or logical would take discussion, compromise, common sense at the very least.'

'Quite right, Mr Haddleston, but an impossible demand which can never be met by the authorities?'

'Naturally. It opens up the way for very drastic action – action which was always the intention and for which their opposition can be blamed. It means they feel free to bring about destruction of whatever is the supposed cause of hatred.' The bones of Sam's face were white, his skin and muscles tense. 'In our case responsibility for the attack on Sue and the *Journal* can be laid at the feet of anyone but Animal Equality.'

Sue was thoughtful. 'Perhaps the bombers do have a conscience, however minute.'

'How do you work that out?' Sam wanted to know.

'They don't want the blame?'

'A good point, Mrs Bennett, but we have to ask ourselves what it is they're really after?'

The answering silence was disturbing.

'To be noticed without being seen,' Sam offered at last.

Sergeant Webley was not so sure. 'I think, in this case, Passmore and her helper simply enjoy killing – at a distance.'

Sue tried to picture the two fugitives and the life they must be leading. It would be easy to find a bolt-hole in

London, neighbours not bothering with transients. 'For what they're doing they'd need money – quite a lot. Have they got it?'

The superintendent straightened in his chair, denying his own tiredness. 'I doubt it. The boyfriend's an unknown quantity. There's cash in Passmore's family and her father keeps paying her an allowance, but we've got a watch on her bank accounts and she'll know it.'

Sue remembered an article Jonah had written in a bitter moment. 'Bombing's an expensive business.'

The sergeant was interested in Sue's train of thought. 'If they need ready money they may use more orthodox methods to get it. That's when they stop being unpredictable fanatics and become ordinary crooks.'

Sue saw the implications. 'It means they'd then be moving into your territory.'

'And will be more easily spotted,' Ashford assured her.

An evening with Miles helped. He had sensed Sue's need to escape masses of people and she found herself in Chelsea, walking into a Japanese restaurant. They were welcomed and led to a table. Swathed in immaculate white napkins they watched their chef wield knives to advantage as warm rice wine soothed and loosened knots of tension.

The dining space was quiet, dark, pools of light illuminating each steel cooking area and the adjoining stretch of polished wood at which they sat. Sue felt safe, cocooned by deft service and entranced by visual art arriving on her plate. Flavours were subtle, conversation easy, and she allowed herself to relax.

Miles was an undemanding companion, happy to sit beside her and talk of small matters. A glint of blue fire distracted Sue and she noticed at a nearby table a woman who was expensively dressed and very attentive to the much older man at her side.

'My God, those earrings!' Sue whispered.

43

A huge gold-edged comma hung from each ear, the centres diamond-studded so that light glimmered and flashed.

Miles grinned. 'Envious?'

'No way! I couldn't afford the insurance. Besides, a few years of wearing them and her ear lobes'll be down round her ankles.'

'I don't think she'll have them that long. My guess is her sugar daddy trades a bit too far away from the law for comfort.'

'You should know.'

Miles worked for a firm of accountants brought in when executives feared financial assets were being illegally diverted. A silent waiter poured wine for her as Sue glanced at the woman's companion. Suddenly, she felt again the warm wind of an African plain and in her memory saw the dry landscape. There was the impala she had watched killed by a lioness, her mate and their cubs arriving for the feast. A movement in the long grass had caught Sue's attention and she turned her binoculars to focus more clearly. Hyena prowled and one in particular had stared straight at her before its eyes slid away to the carcass.

'You're right,' she said, 'but he'll be difficult to catch.' A spoonful of sorbet arrived and her palate was fresh again. 'Where did you take James at the weekend?'

'Deepest Surrey. We walked quite a way, I suppose. Lunch was in a rather nice pub in the woods – you could imagine it having been there for centuries. James loved the old beams and the ancient rifles hanging on the walls. If he'd had his way we'd still be there. I insisted on a nice, healthy walk and when we got back to the car he was exhausted. He was out for the count the whole way home.' Miles frowned, concerned for his son.

'It all sounds normal.'

'I don't know. Perhaps I'm imagining he's not sleeping enough.'

'I'm sure he is, although he may have been too excited the night before – glad to be spending the day with you.'

'I expect you're right – you usually are.'

She laughed and caught a look of envy from the woman with the costly earrings who had been watching Miles's every movement. Sue guessed the lady might sigh with regret but she would turn a smiling face to the man who could afford most.

Miles was certainly younger and more attractive than the diamond-provider. He had pursued Sue from the moment of their first meeting but she was too newly widowed to allow anything but friendship. He understood and waited for her to leave the past behind, enjoying her company until she was ready for more.

As they were ushered from the restaurant Sue was aware of activity in a nearby car. For a moment she froze then Miles took her elbow and the warmth of contact released her fear. White paper was hastily folded and dumped in the back seat as her two police guardians finished their less elegant supper. They gave Miles a thumbs-up and prepared to follow his car back to Islington and Sue's flat.

The teasing was only to be expected once Sue's colleagues discovered that she arrived for work every day in Sam's car. She tried explaining that George, his driver, collected her from Islington only after he had left the editor at the newly built main door of the *Journal* building.

'He's very loyal, that George.' Kate Jeffries was perched on Sue's desk.

'Any special reason?'

'Not that I know of. George insists he's always at Sam's front door by seven thirty.'

'Is that a problem for you?' Sue wanted to know.

Kate's gaze was intense. 'Would he have been there all night? Sam?'

'I expect so,' Sue said and waited for data on tuberculosis to appear on her screen.

'You can tell me, Sue.'

Kate had a disarming smile but Sue knew her in this mood. She was hunting a story. 'Check with the police. They watch me in and they watch me out. Anyone who visits me is recorded somewhere, along with the time they leave. The police can tell you I sleep alone.'

Kate eased away her expensively clad rear. 'It was worth a try,' she grinned, then leaned on Sue's monitor. 'Is it getting to you?'

Sue looked up, surprised by the question. The shutters had gone from behind Kate's eyes and genuine concern was exposed. 'Thanks, Kate. I'm OK.'

'You're sure?'

'I'm still a bit numb. It helps.'

The older woman touched Sue's hand in quick sympathy and went in search of juicier prey.

Determined to follow up a conversation with her friend Gerry at the London Hospital, Sue set herself the task of phoning hospitals which ringed airports, checking on the incidence of tuberculosis each encountered. Three had disturbing levels to report and it would mean Sue visiting specialists in the disease. Anil would have loved this sort of assignment, she remembered. Sue made herself put aside all thoughts of the engaging and happy young man as she delved into the statistics of a disease associated with Victorian death lists and Swiss sanatoria.

'Busy?' It was Jonah, his shirt collar open and the knot of his tie sliding over his paunch.

'TB. It's coming back in a drug-resistant form.'

'Great,' Jonah said. 'What've I got to do about it?'

'If you're on a plane and someone in your section has a very bad cough, make sure you get a check-up when you start spluttering.'

'It's that easy to catch?'

Sue nodded. 'It's cheaper for airlines to recycle air in the cabins instead of using fresh.'

'Thanks very much! I think I'll head for Bognor instead of the bloody Balearics next time my missus insists on a holiday. Hate the damned things anyway – holidays.'

'You're one of the not insignificant percentage suffering stress when you take it easy in the company of your loved ones,' Sue told him with a demure smile.

'And the same to you,' Jonah retorted. 'Now then, remind me about the chemical twaddle of the date-rape drugs.'

'You mean Rohypnol and GHB?'

'Do I? One of our stringers phoned in. The police in her neck of the woods have pulled in a guy using it on a few dollies who've objected.'

Sue was furious. 'So would you if you'd been put to sleep for hours and raped continually!'

'OK, simmer down. I only came to check up on the details.'

Sue regretted her outburst, knowing Jonah's opinion of rapists. He would willingly watch them swing from a gibbet. She called up the data on her screen then printed out a copy for him.

'What's this?' he asked as he frowned. 'Gamma hydrox –'

'Gamma hydroxy butyrate, which is GHB. Then there's Flunitrazepam which is Rohypnol and that one's chemically related to Librium,' Sue read out for him. 'The trouble is, they're now well known and far too easily available and exploited.'

'As Watty used to say, "Water I put in my whisky, other buggers drown people in it."' Jonah was silent, remembering a good friend. 'This Gamma stuff and Rohypnol, good for what they're designed?'

'Very.'

Jonah ambled off deep in thought and Sue was making notes when the internal phone buzzed. It was Maimie with a summons, hidden meaning in the tone of her voice.

Sue was not surprised to see Superintendent Ashford in Sam's office, nor Sergeant Webley.

'We've traced our man – or rather we've identified him, thanks to you and the director of the lab where you eventually remembered him working.'

Sam settled Sue in a chair next to him and Ashford gestured to his sergeant.

'Dennis Gibson, aged twenty-six,' the girl began in her clipped, well-educated tones. 'An only child, parents stable but rather old-fashioned. Father's just retired – he was the senior clerk in quite a large law firm in Exeter. The mother's never worked since she married. Gibson did well on the academic side at his school – one of the better comprehensives. He was a loner. No friends, no clubs, no sports. Computers seem to have been his only hobby.'

Sam scowled. 'The classic set-up for some major obsessions.'

'You could be right, sir,' the sergeant agreed. 'He went on to university, one of the newer ones, and got an upper second in some form of chemistry. A big food and drugs conglomerate in Norwich took him on and he did well in a quiet way. Bosses said he was ambitious but rapid promotion wasn't on the cards for him. The modern habit big firms have of psychological profiling showed up some strange attitudes. He was sidelined and I think he knew it.'

'At twenty-six?' Sue was astonished. 'I think I'd have resented it too.'

'You can imagine the effect on him of meeting Passmore. Another lone oddball but this one with the fire of rebellion. It warmed a cold corner of Gibson until he became alive, providing the practical talents Passmore needed.'

Sam scented a story. 'How did they meet?'

Ashford shrugged his shoulders. 'We assume at a demo of some kind. There'd been one or two at the lab where Gibson worked. Another branch of the conglomerate does research using animals but that's in central France and not so easy to get at for the welly brigade.'

The office was quiet.

'That's not what you came to tell us, is it?' Sue's level gaze demanded the truth.

'No,' the superintendent admitted. 'The machinery at the Yard's been in motion. Gibson and Passmore have been profiled – from the criminal aspect. It's been decided they're no longer a threat to the *Journal* – or to you, Mrs Bennett.'

'So?'

'Your protection is to be scaled down.'

Sam started arguing. When it became clear the order had come from the top he outlined plans of his own for Sue's safety until a bubble of anger exploded in her. Two half-wits had not only killed Anil as they maimed and murdered indiscriminately, they had imprisoned her. Since the bomb Sue had not been able to get into a car and drive to an interview or to see her parents. She could not even get into a cab without someone fussing. Every detail of her life had been under scrutiny, even a walk to the chemist for some aspirin logged and reported.

The surveillance might be reduced because of decisions taken by yet more faceless individuals but now Sam was intent on making up the difference. For too long the mindless activities of terrorists had kept her isolated from the real world and helpless.

It was time to fight back.

Chapter Three

'You look more like you. Has anything happened?' Pippa asked as she poured coffee.

Sue cradled her mug. 'Some of the watchdogs are being called off.'

'That wouldn't explain it.'

Sue looked out of the window. It was the same view as from her own kitchen but a storey higher. For Islington it was a quiet street, the tall, stately houses once homes for important families. Divided into flats they were mostly filled by people like Pippa and herself. She saw the old lady from number 35 making sure the front door held before she turned to her little dog and chatted to it as they walked slowly along the pavement to the nearest tree.

When she had been stalked by Colin's killer there had been a period during which Sue had refused to leave the safety of her home. Watching movements in the street below had become so compulsive that she had seen shrubs in the tiny gardens grow, bloom and die away.

At night her dreams had been filled with a terror pushing aside grief and every waking moment had been filled with panic. Part of the fear which kept her imprisoned was that she must face life without Colin, the idea so raw it had bled into her mind. She had survived that hell and believed nothing could be any worse, yet her new dreams were of body bags and beyond them Anil's back as he walked towards her car. Too many mornings she had woken crying, 'I'm sorry, Anil.' It had to stop. Even ghosts needed their peace.

'Well?' Pippa had waited with her usual serenity.

'I've just decided not to stay locked up any longer.'

'Is that wise?'

'Probably not – but what's the alternative? Let others think of me as a helpless female they can toss around as they please? Start that and every Tom, Dick and Harry would believe they had a God-given right to use me.'

'Sam won't be pleased.'

'He doesn't own me!'

'No, he'd just give you the world on a plate if you'd let him. Then there's Miles. He'll have his own ideas for looking after you.'

'Not to mention my parents. They'd like me to go and live with them in Dorking until the police have got the bombers.'

'Makes sense.'

Sue nodded. 'Last time they all helped, no one more than you.' She smiled at Pippa but there was sadness in her eyes. 'Last time I was the one who shut myself away.'

'And now?'

'Now, it's other people doing it.' Sue's expression became mutinous. 'I don't want to be cooped up like some sad little mongrel in a dogs' home, waiting to be freed or killed. It's human minds doing this to me and my mind's the same as theirs – if not better. They might be playing some damned game they've dragged me into but I'm not putting up with it!'

'It all sounds very grand but what will you actually do?'

'Start looking for them myself.'

Pippa was horrified. 'Sue! For Pete's sake! It's dangerous.'

'So's crossing the road. No, if I'm to stop feeling hunted I have to become the hunter.'

'There's a certain logic in that, I suppose.'

Sue gazed at her friend. She was large and tawny, and her green eyes were filled with anxiety. 'I doubt I'll get anywhere near them – but I have to try.'

'Sue, you must be careful. Remember, they tried to kill you.'

'And might have another go?' Sue swirled coffee dregs and watched them spiral. 'That part seems unreal. Oh, I know I should have died – I've seen the letter to Professor Turnbull. Sergeant Webley's even done the psychology bit and explained Passmore may have been jealous of me because Gibson talked of my visits to the lab where he worked. I can take it all in, understand it. I just can't believe it.'

Pippa leaned towards Sue. 'You'd better believe it,' she said then laughed, a throaty chuckle. 'I sound like a third-rate film.'

'The whole thing's got that sort of feel about it, as though events have no link to reality – but Anil's dead because of me. That's real.' Tears rose and were sniffed away.

Pippa poured more coffee and sipped her own. 'How will you go about finding the bombers?'

'I've been thinking about that. Jonah did a piece on explosives.'

'Not a commodity you can get at the corner shop.'

'Exactly. As far as I can remember he said if you know the handlers you can just about trace every ounce of it.'

'Won't the police have done that?'

'Their way – but they have to go by the book.'

'Sue!'

'It's OK. I've a resource Superintendent Ashford would like to be able to use.'

'The *Journal*?'

Sue shook her head, her smile bleak. 'Cash.'

'But you can't use the money Colin left you!'

'Why not? There's more than I need – and it's my sanity at stake.'

Next day there was a flurry of news items which needed Sue's expertise. The pressures of the newsroom kept her busy and her mind away from Animal Equality. She was sorting through her disks when Andrew Carroll leaned on her monitor. He was tall and thin, his eyes bright blue behind his glasses.

'Why double-hulled tankers?' he asked.

'They're ecologically the safest but also the most expensive to build.'

'How come safest?'

Sue surprised him with bacteria feeding like kings on modern lubricating oils and having the ability to erode steel, propeller shafts eaten away to a third of their size and quite useless. Andrew began to picture such organisms between two hulls of a tanker and went off to pester major oil companies, leaving Sue to pick up a notebook and make her way to the library.

She was, as always, fascinated by the past copies of the *Journal* on microfilm, even if her eyes occasionally demanded a rest from the constant flashing of words and pictures. There were pages in abundance on bombs and explosions. In the past Ulster had the lion's share of the space but now there was modern warfare, aircraft detonations, gas mains, demolitions of all kinds to be considered, then rejected.

An old article on Colonel Gadaffi's training grounds held Sue's attention and she read at speed, finding it an excerpt from a book. A print-out did not take long and she was searching again. Nothing of what she wanted was in the second half of any *Journal* so issue after issue was checked quickly.

'Got it!'

'You OK?' Beryl, the librarian, asked anxiously.

'Yes, thanks.' Sue waited for the article to emerge from the printer.

The phone rang and Beryl dealt with it. 'Sue! Mr Haddleston wants you in his office. Urgent, Maimie said.'

'Tell her I'm on my way.'

Sue always walked quickly and had time to open a drawer in her desk and stow away the results of her research. In a far corner of the newsroom there was an exclamation and she looked up, seeing heads turn her way, hearing whispering. There was no time to solve that little mystery. Maimie had said 'Urgent.'

Sam was pacing. 'Come and look at this.'

She sat in front of the screen he had swung towards her.

'I had a phone call, an informant on the spot. It's just being confirmed.'

Explosions in Oxford Street, she read. They had occurred simultaneously in the meat sections of two major stores. Both food halls were littered with casualties and there was no idea yet how many had died.

'It's them, isn't it? Animal Equality?'

'Almost certainly.' Sam was grim, punching a fist against an open palm. 'I'd like to get hold of –'

'No warning?'

'None – but I bet someone's had a letter or will get it tomorrow.'

'It would be their style.'

Sue sat back and closed her eyes. Sam was behind her and put his hands on her shoulders. She felt the warmth and knew he needed to touch her, be reassured she was safe. It was difficult to accept the bombers had changed direction, and in the vacuum they left Sue was strangely unsure of herself. For a moment she leaned into Sam's caress and was glad he was there.

'So, can I have a car again and go and see the Naibs?'

'I'm not sure about the car.'

'Suit yourself. I'll get one of my own.'

Sam saw the independent tilt of Sue's head. 'OK. You can have a *Journal* car and I'll make sure you get a mirror on a stick to go with it. You've got to promise to check every time before you get in.'

'Don't worry, I'm not an idiot. I'll alter the range of the camera on the front door and park the car where it can get filmed all night.'

He wanted to drop a kiss on the top of her head but

knew he must not. If ever Sue turned to him he wanted it to be because she chose to do so.

With a lithe twist Sue was out of her chair and ready to leave. 'I've work to do and you've got at least the first three pages for tomorrow.'

'Poor devils,' he said, 'out shopping and then bang.' His anger was a crackling force. 'The sooner the bastards are where they can do no harm, the better.'

Mrs Naib opened the door. There was white in her hair and her eyes were sad. The fresh blue of her sari with its gold edging told Sue of the struggle to live normally.

'I'm so sorry,' she said. 'For Anil and that I didn't come straight away.'

Tears rose and Mrs Naib held out her arms. The two women held each other, their grief for the lively, lovely boy uniting them.

'Your letters have been such a comfort, my dear Sue, and Mr Haddleston is so very kind.' Mrs Naib led Sue to the stiffly elegant sitting room. It could have been anywhere in the well-to-do Home Counties except for the pictures on the walls and a slight aroma of sandalwood. 'He brought us your letters and your flowers but said you were a target. The murderers would expect you to come and see us and might set a trap for you.' There was the faintest of smiles. 'It was very odd to think of my home as a watering hole where tigers might wait in the shadows for deer.'

The women were quietly sharing memories of Anil, bringing him to life again, when the door burst open. A young man, very like Anil, strode to his mother.

'More bombs! Oxford Street! There must have been casualties but no one will say how many.'

'Anwar, we have a guest,' he was chided.

The young man gazed coolly at Sue. 'Mrs Bennett,' he said at last, inclining his head in a bow which almost escaped civility. 'Is it safe for you to come out of hiding?'

'The police guard which restricted my movements has

been withdrawn. Naturally, your mother was the first person I wanted to visit.'

'Before your own parents?'

'Yes. Even before my own parents.'

It was obvious he did not believe her. 'Have you come to tell my mother you wished the death we mourn had been yours?'

'Anwar!' Mrs Naib rose to take her son's arm and lead him from further rudeness.

'Mrs Naib – please. Anwar has only said what I've been thinking since Anil died.' Sue turned to face the young brother whose hurt ran so deep. 'You're right. I'd have given anything that Anil had not died in my place.'

His disbelief was tangible. 'Your life?'

'Had I been the first to go to the car, what would I have known?'

'The choice of fate was not yours to make, Mrs Bennett,' a deep voice said behind them.

Sue turned and met the compassionate eyes of Anil's father.

'Mrs Bennett, may I call you Sue? Anil spoke of you often. He admired you tremendously.'

Mr Naib, as tall as his son had been, was a distinguished figure immaculate in good tailoring, his silk tie perfectly knotted. He held Sue's hand and accepted her condolences.

'It was common practice for you and Anil to travel together to your assignments?' The lines on Mr Naib's face were freshly deepened but his upright carriage showed his natural pride.

'Yes. Anil was a great help when we had to investigate. He would listen to an interview and come in with some very perceptive questions which helped get at the truth.'

'Ah, the truth. Why did Anil go on his own that day?' Mr Naib asked the question gently, expecting honesty.

'He asked to do the interviews. There were three people to see and no need for two of us to go.'

Anwar was restless. 'Did you suggest he took your car?'

56

'No. Anil explained his was in for repair and asked to borrow mine.'

'How fortunate for you!'

'Anwar!' Mr Naib was angry but he controlled himself and turned to Sue. 'I must apologize for my son. He and Anil were very close.'

'I understand.'

'Do you?' Anwar challenged.

'Yes, Anwar, I do. My husband was killed, deliberately, less than a year ago.' She watched the boy's skin pale as he realized his harsh words could have offended unfairly.

'Anil told us of your loss and your fight to bring the murderer to justice.' Mrs Naib was a gentle woman but there was a sudden, fierce light in her eyes. 'I hope the same fate awaits those who took Anil from us.'

'Believe me, Mrs Naib, I'll do all I can.'

'You must be careful,' her husband warned. 'Anil told us you nearly died earlier in the year.'

'Then I was the one being hunted. This time the choice is mine and I've decided I'd rather be the tiger than the deer.'

Anwar was silent. His parents offered Sue tea, anxious to make her feel at home. A phone ringing took away Mr Naib as his wife went to the kitchen and Sue was on her own with Anwar.

'You plan to search for the murderers of my brother?' he asked stiffly, courtesy peeping through.

'Yes. I don't know if I can do any better than the police but for Anil's sake – and my own – I must make the attempt.'

Anwar studied Sue and she waited, knowing the young man had so much anger to discipline. At last his eyes were calm. 'If I can help . . .'

'I'll call on you. I promise.'

The flat was welcoming and Sue kicked off her shoes as she shed her coat and made her way to the answering machine. Before she had time to check her calls there was a knock at the door. A peep through the lens and she was undoing locks and smiling a greeting at Ken.

'Sorry to come when you were longing for bed but Pippa was worried. She's tired so I've made her have an early night.'

As Colin's friend, Ken had helped Sue through the worst days of her bereavement. Attracted to Pippa, he spent increasing time in Islington. Eventually it made sense for him to live with her in the flat up a flight from Sue.

'Come in. I've been at the Naibs'.'

'How are they taking it?'

'It's hard to know. The parents are very dignified and the brother very angry.'

'He has a right to be. Unfortunately, there'll be far too many feeling the same way tonight.'

'I was going to ring the paper for an update on the casualties. Have you any hard news?'

'I talked to Stephen. So far there are seven dead, three of them very young children.'

Sue closed her eyes as despair washed through her. 'Is that from the two bombs?'

'Yes. Dozens are injured. Five are on the critical list.'

'More children?'

''Fraid so. There were a lot of facial injuries. Moorfields is working miracles – so are all the other hospitals.'

'Was it Animal Equality?'

Ken pushed tense fingers through his dark hair. 'No warnings and the explosives in packages of food? Hardly Al Qaeda or the IRA.'

'The size of the bombs? They must have been small to be hidden in freezer chests.'

'Cool cabinets. Stephen explained the detonations were probably at head or upper body height.' Stephen Childs was a senior detective in the Met and had been a good friend to both Colin and Ken. 'The shelves were open and the devastation would be greater.'

Images rampaged across Sue's mind. 'People are quite

irrelevant to the bombers,' she said at last, 'except as a way to get what they want.'

'But what is it they're after? Stephen said their manifesto had been circulated round CID. It was well written but rambling, with no real objectives which could be achieved, none at all. If you try hard enough you can follow warped and distorted reasoning and see why they have a go at labs housing animals – but this?'

'I wonder?'

'What?'

'Ashford, the super, thought the bombers must be getting short of money. Could they be blackmailing the stores?'

'It's possible. One thing,' Keith said as he smiled and showed his tiredness after a long day in the courts, 'the *Journal* won't be allowed to print a word of it – compulsory media conspiracy to deny the group publicity.'

'I don't care, I just want it stopped.' There were already too many homes like the Naibs' where grief sat in state.

'Pippa said you intended to lend a hand?'

'I was supposed to be the victim. Who else should try to get them put away? I'm no lamb to be led to the slaughter – and neither is anyone else in the country.'

'I'd heard you'd come out fighting.' Ken chuckled then became serious. 'One thing they taught us in the police, make sure you're properly protected when you go out there. And then make sure you've got back-up.'

'Is that what Stephen told you to say?'

'More or less.' Ken did not add that Stephen Childs, a ranking CID officer, had asked to be informed if Sue went hunting on her own.

She thought back to her work in the library. 'Today's bombs. Small volume explosives. Semtex?'

'Almost certainly.'

'Like the one meant for me.' She brooded for a while. 'It's difficult to get.'

'But one of the Czech Republic's better known exports – even if it is an illegal trade,' said Ken, the solicitor.

'Semtex was being sold off long before the Warsaw Pact countries split.' Time in the *Journal*'s library had revealed many useful facts. 'Oil-rich states bought plenty of it and they weren't the only ones. Libya was stockpiling and passing it on to favoured groups.'

'You mean Gadaffi? Apart from helping to blow up US planes he's always been very friendly with the IRA because they're anti-English. There are rumours of stashes in farms all over southern Ireland.'

'And I bet any farmer short of cash has sold it on to the highest bidder who brought it to the mainland on innocent-looking yachts. Semtex could have been sailed right into the Port of London.'

'You have been doing your homework.'

'Only browsing through old *Journal* articles. All the information was already in the public domain,' she informed Ken.

'Let it stay there, Sue.'

It was tempting to leave all the work to the police while she stayed hidden, protected. Sue knew that if she let that happen she would have resigned herself to being one of life's victims. A moment of weakness passed. 'I'll do what I have to.'

There was the whisper of wheels next morning. 'Sue?'

She looked up from her work. Sandy's smile was as cheery as ever but his eyes were haggard. 'It brought it all back, didn't it? I tried to sleep last night but I was too scared,' he admitted.

Sue had had little success courting oblivion through the hours of darkness. 'How's Annie?'

'Getting through each day like a Trojan. The girls keep her so busy she tells me there isn't time to think.'

They watched Meg. The features editor was as fresh as always, her fair hair swept away from her face in a French knot. She denied middle age in a crimson shirt and black slacks as she riffled through a bundle of photographs.

'Not much call for us today. Just as well,' Sandy said. 'If I tried to type it would come out a stutter.'

Sue ran a pencil back and forth between her fingers. 'All over London there'll be poor souls trying to cope as we had to here. If it hadn't been for me . . .' The pencil snapped.

'Stop it, Sue! Murderers are responsible for their own crimes, no one asks them to kill. Animal Whatsit had no reason to attack any of us here – and they certainly had no excuse for blowing apart harmless shoppers. They've got to answer for the outrage, not you.'

'And soon' was a silent prayer as pieces of wood and carbon were consigned to a waste bin along with Sue's useless emotions. 'The complete list of casualties will never be known.'

Sandy frowned, was curious. 'What do you mean?'

'Watty's theory.'

A shrewd, burly Scot, Watty had been Sue's friend and Jonah's predecessor in the crime team until murdered while hunting Colin's killer. Sue smiled wistfully as she remembered the strength of the man, his humour.

'He used to say there will be heart attacks and strokes amongst those who merely see the dead and injured, as well as a number collapsing when they're told loved ones have died. A week on, someone who escaped the blast will wonder why they can't stop crying. A few weeks more and there'll be new alcoholics or longer queues at the surgeries for tranquillizers. Three months, six months, doctors will be struggling to treat constant exhaustion with no physical cause.' She sighed. 'Everyone will recover in time, but shock like that can trigger off latent illnesses. It's becoming increasingly well documented.'

'What about here?' Sandy glanced around the newsroom and their colleagues.

'Maybe not so many. We're mostly young, fairly fit and we keep on going.'

'Do you think anyone was deafened in yesterday's explosions?'

'Almost certainly. Unless there was significant physical damage, most hearing will return in time.'

'This melanin business – the more melanin you've got in the ears, the louder noises you can stand, so coloured races can tolerate loud sounds better than white?'

'You do like generalizations.'

'How would you put it?'

'Melanin in ears varies enormously. A white person can have a lot, a black one very little – and vice versa.'

'You're a big help.'

'Tough!'

Sandy wheeled away and an unusual – though not unpleasant – perfume reached Sue.

'How is he?' Kate asked.

'Doing well. Although his leg's healing to order he finds the wheelchair useful – says he tires less quickly and can put in a full day because of it.' They watched Sandy hard at work, dark hair flopping forward as he bent over his keyboard.

'And you?'

Sue looked up. 'Me? Fine.'

Kate's gaze was long and critical. 'Just you keep it that way.'

'I intend to. In fact, since I'm not needed any more today, I'm off to see my parents.'

Kate's expression softened into a warm smile that made her younger, more vulnerable. 'Give them my love.'

Sue promised and, as Kate stalked away, the sound of Jonah's wheezing lungs drew her attention. He leaned on her desk.

'Just had a call from an informant and thought you might be interested. There's been a letter.'

'The bombers?'

Jonah managed the briefest of nods. 'She works in accounts, a shop in – Knightsbridge, shall we say.' A nicotine-stained forefinger tapped his nose. 'No names, no pack drill.'

'Any mention of who sent it?'

'An e-mail and it had this sign across a Z.'

'It is them. What did they want?'

'Used notes, a lot of them – and no big denominations.'

'Ashford was right?'

Jonah's expression became alert, canny. 'Frank Ashford?'

'He's a detective superintendent in Special Branch, that's all I know.'

'That's him. I first knew him when he was in CID and working out of Savile Row nick. Special Branch, you say he is now?'

Sue nodded. 'He did say, once the bombers ran short of cash they'd turn to predictable crime.'

'A pity he couldn't have predicted yesterday's bombs and saved those poor little sods from dying.'

'You know,' Sue said slowly, 'it's strange the shops which were blasted didn't get the letter.'

Jonah regarded her pityingly. 'Yesterday was to show what could happen.'

'All those deaths for a demonstration?' Even as she said it Sue realized the bomb in her car had served the same function. She was suddenly very weary. 'It makes the phrase "wilful murder" seem totally inadequate.'

'Yup.'

'Jonah, how would Passmore and Gibson get hold of Semtex?'

'You mean well-brought-up, middle-class kids, no connections to the criminal world?' His cynicism was a rawness in the air. 'The same way kids like them get any kind of dope they fancy. Demand is always met by supply.'

'In this case, who would supply?'

His eyes were intent, the whites yellowed with age and ill-health. 'Why do you want to know?'

'I'm interested.'

His expression did not change but his eyes became wary. 'You got a death wish?'

'No. Perhaps a need to pull on the scales of justice – even them up a little.'

'Very noble, I'm sure.' Even as he recognized her sincerity he was scornful. 'You're after my hard-earned knowledge! All those years of meeting and paying off chancy little men and women. Still, you never deny me what you know.'

'I just need a lead to anyone supplying Semtex.'

'You think it's that simple? Let me explain.' Jonah pulled up a chair and sat next to Sue. 'It's down to basics. I've got contacts, like the one who phoned me just now about the letter. I can't use the item – not yet, anyway – but I come and tell you because I know you've got an interest. The police work the same way. If they can't make use of what they hear then a kindly soul might pass it on to me, or to Sam. We do the same for them. Information's an invisible network.'

'Like a web. A tug in a far corner soon gets the attention of the right spider?'

'These stupid kids will have been doing the rounds of animal demos, probably talking wild or asking questions. An "interested party" would pass on the message to the supplier of the right commodity and maybe act as a go-between.'

'How about your informants, Jonah? Could they use the same system?'

He pursed his lips and thought about Sue and her motives. 'Perhaps,' he said at last, 'but more carefully. Mine like to stay alive to squeal.'

'What really makes them talk to you and not the police?'

'Cash. I pay more.' Jonah stopped talking to cough and drag air noisily into rackety lungs. 'It's their idea of a job,' he said when he had enough breath. 'They see it as an easy way of making money but it's a risky business. The nearer they get to the big boys and the big money, the greater the chance of an unfortunate accident – and don't you forget it.'

'If I've got the cash ready, can I talk to one of them?'

'*Journal* funds? Sam won't wash it, not in a million years – and there's no use trying it on Gavin, he's as bad.'

Jonah wiped his face. The room was warm but it did not explain the sweat that was pumping from every pore. Sue was worried. The man might not be well but he saw concern in Sue's expression and straightened with tired pride.

'I've got money I'm prepared to spend,' she told him. 'It'd keep the *Journal* in the clear.'

'Then you're a fool. Leave it to Frank Ashford, he'll get to them.'

'But he hasn't, has he? Besides, when they chose to kill me they made it personal.'

Jonah took a long time to answer, wheezing steadily as he tried to make up his mind about Sue's request. She had an innocence he feared, the kind which attracted trouble like a magnet. She had also been Watty's friend and trusted by him.

'I don't like it but I know you. If I don't give you a steer you'll go straight out and start asking questions in all the wrong places.'

Sue grinned. 'You'll just have to save me from myself.'

'Sam'll kill me for this,' he groaned. 'Give me time to set up a meeting.'

'Fine. I'll have a chance to get to the bank. How much will I need to take with me? A thousand?'

Jonah was horrified, his bushy eyebrows climbing in panic. 'Christ, no! Don't go in waving that sort of dosh or we'll be fishing you out of the Thames. Two or three hundred for openers. Settle for as little as possible.' He eyed her wearily. 'Do you really think you should be doing this?'

'Jonah, I may have no success at all but I have to try.' She thought of Anil and his family. 'I just have to.'

It was a weekend off duty. Her mother was calm, cheerful, but the arms which encircled Sue held her tightly. 'Phones are all very well but it's better seeing you,' Mrs Lavin whispered as she released Sue to be hugged by her father.

'Poppet! We're so glad you're safe.'

'Have you seen the Naibs?' Mrs Lavin asked. 'It's so dreadful for them.'

'They're holding up well. It's a large family and they're rallying round.'

Mrs Lavin linked her arm in Sue's while Mr Lavin carried in his daughter's overnight bag. While they were pleased to see Sue, she had to hide her distress at the signs of strain in her parents. Outwardly, they were as they had always been but each had a need to see her constantly and touch her when they could.

Two days went by pleasantly in Dorking and the ritual of Sunday lunch was over all too soon. Sue waved good-bye from her new *Journal* car and drove back to Islington for an early night, preparation for the Monday morning stint in the newsroom.

During the weekend one of the very minor royals had slipped a disc and it was quite hectic for a while as Sue called up stored data and then simplified diagrams and explanations of the various methods of treatment.

'Lasers?' Beth laughed. The sub-editor was short, fair, sturdy and not Scottish, unlike the rugby jersey she wore. A top girls' school product and related to a great deal of money, Beth enjoyed playing the dumb yokel. 'I thought that was for eyes and things?'

'It's a new technique for some prolapsed discs.'

'Ain't science wonderful?' Beth grinned and nodded to the screen. 'Is it finished? Sam wants us to roll earlier tonight for some reason.'

'Perhaps he's printing more copies. What's the front page?'

'Apart from the quasi-royal's spine, some stupid politician's been caught with a bimbo.'

'And that's news?' Sue asked as Beth's chuckle disappeared towards her own desk.

An hour later, Jonah phoned. 'Sue? I've set up a meet for

tonight. Six o'clock in The Bells, Stephen Street. It's just off Tottenham Court Road. Left-hand side going up.'

'Who do I talk to?'

'Benny Rogers. I've given him your description, so he'll make contact with you.'

'Great! Thanks, Jonah. How do I know it's him?'

'You'll smell him. He must be the Avon lady's best customer.'

'Anything I should be wary about?'

'The whole bloody thing,' he snarled. 'Benny's OK as long as he doesn't get grassed up. No trail leading back to him, clear?'

'As crystal. Thanks again, Jonah.'

'I'm regretting it already.'

'Come on, I'm only going to have a drink and a chat with a friend of yours. Where's the harm in that?'

Chapter Four

With a shapeless brown felt hat and his slight figure wrapped in grubby camel hair, Benny Rogers turned insignificance into an art form. The pub was old-fashioned, the wood of its panelling dark-varnished, its settles polished by innumerable backsides. The bar Sue sat in was far from busy but only when Benny stood next to her and bent to speak did she notice him, the mixture of perfumes not as bad as Jonah had predicted.

'Mrs Bennett?' The accent was north London with a slight hesitation here and there.

'Yes. Can I get you something to drink?'

'I'll get it for you.' The note disappeared from her hand and Benny was gone.

He returned quite quickly with a very large whisky and no change. Not the inoffensive type he made himself out to be, Sue decided. 'Is this your local?'

Whisky was disappearing as though down a wide drain. Benny shook his head as he put the empty glass on the table, gazing gloomily at its emptiness. Sue got the message but this time the note she handed over was for five pounds, not ten.

There was a tiny movement in the pale brown sludge of his eyes. 'Anything for you?'

Sue shook her head and Benny eased himself to the bar, waiting patiently for service as he listened to every conversation going.

She was restless by the time he returned. 'So, do you know who's selling the Semtex?'

'Sshh!' There was a feral sharpness about his face, muscles tightening it into the mask of a scavenger, and for a split second Sue saw the real Benny. 'Call it plastic, for Chrissake. It's too easy for someone to be listening.'

'OK. Who's selling it?'

'Price first.'

'A hundred.'

'You must be joking! The risk I'm taking?'

'You? A friend of mine's already dead. That's why I'm here.'

'Your rag can stand more than that.'

'This is personal.'

Benny's face sagged like that of a mechanic discovering the car repair was not an insurance job.

'You knew that already. Jonah Blackburn told you.'

The whisky was finished and the glass waggled hopefully. Another fiver went towards the bar and Sue realized the cost of information was rising fast.

'Three hundred,' Benny suggested.

In Cairo with Colin, Sue had learned to haggle. The Bells did not have the same ambience as a soukh and Benny smelled only slightly better than a gap-toothed urchin in a gellabayah. She fought him down to £150, counting out ten-pound notes. He waited and another joined the pile for whisky.

'Time for a name – or names,' she said firmly.

Benny pursed his lips and looked hard at Sue, his eyes sharp. She could almost hear the calculations going on in his brain. If he diddled her Jonah might dry up as a source of revenue, and the *Journal* paid well. At last he gave her three names and addresses on a scrappy piece of paper. She handed over the money and Benny pocketed it with an enviable sleight of hand.

'Nice doing business with you, Mrs Bennett.' Benny almost smiled. 'If Jonah Blackburn's a friend of yours, get him to give up the fags. He's wheezing like an old ruin – and Gawd he stinks!'

Next morning there were three major stories needing Sue's input but with the latest software available she made good progress. Kate approached but did not stay, the tight line of Sue's mouth a storm warning.

'Well?'

From the laboured breathing Sue knew who questioned her before she looked up.

'Well, what, Jonah? Which of you two decided to stitch me up?'

'For God's sake, Sue, make sense.'

'I will. Last night I forked out a pile of notes, plus a river of Scotch, and was given three names. I've checked them out. The *Journal*'s got a very comprehensive data bank, especially now Julian's added the phonetic program, and I've got printouts of the gentlemen in question.'

Jonah read the sheet Sue handed him. 'So?'

'All three in our records? Strange how every one is either in jail or outside British jurisdiction. My guess is you'd already paid Benny for them months, maybe years ago. All he's done is take my money and hand me useless information.'

'I didn't know he'd do that, honest to God. The little bastard's let me down too and he'll regret that.' Jonah's eyes were almost dropping from the sagging skin holding them in place. 'I told Benny you were in the market for kosher gen.'

'I was. Pity I didn't get it last night.'

'What d'you mean?'

'Where do you meet Benny? Not in The Bells, that's for sure.'

'I can't tell you that!'

'No? Look at the first name you've got there. The Czech one.'

More than ever Jonah resembled an aged beagle, this one dreading a swift kick. 'Prudcky?'

'I remember when he was tried at the Bailey. Wasn't there a screaming wife insisting he'd been set up and she'd sort out the guys who'd sent down her meal ticket? I wonder what she'd do if I found her and mentioned Benny Rogers?'

Jonah was shocked. He stared at Sue and saw she meant every word. 'Benny had nothing to do with that business.'

'His hard luck. Anil's dead, remember? I want the name of the man who sold Semtex to Animal Equality. I won't settle for less.'

'OK, OK.' Jonah looked at his watch. 'It's too early for Benny to be about yet. I'll ring him at ten.'

'Do that – and tell him to be on time. Where do you usually meet him?'

'Vine Street, not far from Fenchurch Street station. Look, Sue, I want to be there too.'

'Why?'

'Because I want to help – and the little scrote needs reminding who's been keeping him in aftershave all these years,' Jonah said and lumbered off.

Across the newsroom was a buzz of interest which normally accompanied a breaking story. A supermodel had been suffering from increasing headaches and her boyfriend, concerned for his financial welfare, had rushed her to a neurologist. As words rolled on Sue's monitor and photographs both candid and posed were dredged from the library, the girl was undergoing surgery. Sue was busy writing up the medical data and supplying essential diagrams as Kate arrived to read the copy on Sue's screen.

'On her brain?' Kate asked. 'Which of the two cells was in trouble?'

'Aneurysm.' Sue placed arrows on her work to indicate surgical procedure. 'Faulty arterial walls can occur anywhere. Hers happen to be at the base of the brain. Normal pressure in the vessel blew the weak spot up like a balloon and it gave the warning signals. She was lucky.'

'Lucky? She might wake up gaga.'

'I doubt it. She's in a good hospital and will soon be back at work – minus the headaches.'

Kate was silent, her expression puzzling Sue.

'Something bothering you?'

A cigarette was ground out on a convenient surface. 'Had she been some poor drudge of a housewife, or a working girl behind a desk, she'd have gone on taking more painkillers until – wham! Yes, Sue, you're right. She was bloody lucky.' Kate seemed unimpressed by another's good fortune.

'You're down in the dumps today. Any reason?'

Kate lit another cigarette and exhaled a steady stream of smoke in a gesture of release. 'I just feel so damned stupid!'

'Why?' Sue was shocked. Kate prided herself on a very tough attitude to life and her own invincibility in particular.

'Every morning I wake up crying. Granted, it doesn't last long but I think I must be doing it in my sleep.'

'Doesn't that tell you something?'

Kate had been the breezy spirit who dragged the inhabitants of the newsroom back into wise-cracking normality after the recent blast. It was not like her to be hesitant, undecided, and Sue wanted to reassure her friend.

'Awake, you're in control.'

'And asleep?'

'You let out your grief.'

Julia had been distraught when Anil was blown apart. It was Kate who had helped and consoled the girl, taking her to her own home and staying with her until an anxious mother had arrived from Edinburgh.

'Not this bloody post-traumatic stress malarkey? Me? It's ridiculous!'

'Of course it isn't. You're human – or are you?' There was mischief in Sue's smile.

Kate's anger at herself dissipated in a rich laugh.

'Who've you dissected now?' Cary wanted to know as he smoothed blond hair streaked with white. He had the air of the leisured classes, perhaps because his shirt was from Jermyn Street, striped and white-collared. As always, Cary was immaculate in the bustle around him. In spite of his Mayfair drawl and veneer of boredom he was a good writer who had a nose for people likely to become newsworthy.

Kate faced him, her posture altering subtly as she prepared for battle. 'I'm thinking of an article on bimbos and you are definitely something of an expert. If Sue was doing it she'd make a list first, wouldn't you, Sue?'

'Leave me out of it.'

'Of course, my dear.' Cary's gallantry was famous. 'A bimbo you are not.'

'I think he means it as a compliment,' Kate said, 'and you'd certainly never be on my list. Now then, blonde bimbos, horizontal bimbos, killer bimbos, breathless bimbos – anything else?'

'Anorexic, lunching, polo?' Cary offered as he and Kate strolled away, capping each other's efforts.

Sue shook her head at them and got back to work.

Jonah drove swiftly through London's rush-hour traffic, swearing at the idiots who crossed lanes in front of him and chanting, 'Come on, come on,' at every red light. The curve into a parking space near Fenchurch Street station was so unthinking Sue guessed it was one he usually occupied.

Benny was not waiting for them and Jonah growled his way to the bar, being served with a rapidity which confirmed his frequent use of the place.

'I've got his whisky. If he doesn't show you'll have to drink it. I've got my ration for the night.' A very large brandy was in front of him.

'I could drive,' Sue suggested, grinning into her spritzer at Jonah's stream of quiet expletives.

The brandy was savoured, swirled, sipped. 'How's that chap who's been sniffing after you?'

Sue raised her eyebrows at the question. 'There're so many,' she said with heavy irony. 'Which one?'

'Tall, dark and handsome – according to office gossip.'

She assumed he meant Miles Beamish. 'Fine, thank you.'

'Serious, is it?'

'No.'

Jonah stared into his glass. 'Where's he working these days?'

The question was innocuous but Sue knew Jonah was fishing for information. Just to answer him truthfully would provide the name of a firm with a possible criminal on its staff.

'Somewhere in Holborn,' she said at last and watched him sigh as he accepted defeat.

'Bloody Benny. Never here when you –'

Sue's nose was aware of him before Benny spoke. She guessed he must have drenched himself with the entire supply of a cheap perfumery counter.

'Good evening, Mrs Bennett. Nice to see you again, Mr Blackburn.'

As she gasped for air Sue saw Jonah light a cigarette with indecent haste, inhaling and exhaling so fast he was a hazy outline in seconds. Benny's face was twisted with his dislike of the smoke and Sue had great difficulty holding back laughter at the sight of two grown men engaged in a war of smells. She also had to fight down her own nausea.

'Benny, who was it?'

'Now, Mrs Bennett –'

'Exactly. Now. The name.'

'It comes expensive, that one. Last night you got what you paid for. They were dealers, weren't they?' A glint of sun on murky waters was the nearest Benny came to a smile.

'Yes, and the Czech bastard's in jail, as well you know.' Jonah dragged on his cigarette.

'His wife's most unhappy about it, Benny,' Sue told him. 'She's still hunting for the informants who got him sent down. I don't give much for their chances if she hears a whisper of even one of them.'

Benny stared at Sue. He no longer saw an attractive girl who might be conned but an implacable woman. Even in the unhealthy fug surrounding them she sensed his fear.

'You wouldn't?'

'Try me, Benny.' Her words were soft, sibilant and Benny shivered.

He turned to Jonah. 'Mr Blackburn, you know I give you good stuff.'

'Because I pay you well. I'll have to stop all that if you've decided to diddle me.'

'I never!' Benny's thoughts were swift, desperate and obvious. 'It's dangerous! Not a good idea for Mrs Bennett to have any truck with the likes of them. I gave her ones couldn't hurt her.'

Sue was tight-lipped. 'You've had my money. I want the man who supplied the Semtex which killed my friend – or I go to Prudcky's wife. Tonight.'

'She means it, Benny.'

The man lifted his hands in a gesture of defeat. 'It'll cost.'

Sue banged her small fist in front of Benny. 'Not a penny more!'

'And you're off the *Journal*'s pension list if you don't come through,' Jonah promised.

Sue noticed dandruff in the dry brownness of Benny's hair as he bent his head and thought.

'OK,' he said at last, 'but he's trouble. It's one thing knowing his name. Tangling with him . . .'

It was Jonah's turn to be impatient. 'Get on with it!'

Benny looked around to make sure no ears were pointed in his direction. 'Sean Beck,' he whispered. 'Got a gaff in Green Lanes, backing on Clissold Park.'

'Is he known to the Bill?' Jonah asked.

'Yeah – much good it does them. They turn him over regular but he's slippery. Never found so much as a sniff.'

'How does he do it?' Sue wanted to know. 'I mean, if

75

I wanted to buy plastic from him, do I just go to his flat and ask?'

Benny became very agitated. 'You got to do something about her,' he ordered Jonah. 'She goes in like that, she'll have us all seen to!'

Sue was not prepared to give up. 'Then tell me, how does it work?'

'There's dealers pass you on.'

'Who? Where?'

'One's Johnny Crosby. Got a garage off the Dalston Road. It's somewhere the fuzz turn over once a month.'

'Supposing I don't want to buy anything, I just wanted to see this Sean Beck. Where can I find him?'

'You could watch his place but he's more often with his girl. Wakeham Street.'

Jonah took an interest. 'Is that where he keeps the goods?'

'Nah. His gran give him the idea. The old girl was real Irish. When the stuff come in on the boats, she tucked it away in her knicker drawer.'

Sue was intrigued. 'Is she still doing it?'

Benny shook his head. 'Popped her clogs six months ago – but she's got friends. All old biddies like she was.'

Sue marvelled at the network of elderly ladies with Irish connections who stowed packages of Semtex away from the sight of the police. It would make a fascinating story . . . but first things first.

'Can you keep an eye on this Sean Beck for me?'

'Me? Nah. I just listen.'

'Then listen to him and anyone he meets. I need to know who they are.'

Benny looked to Jonah for help. 'Is she for real?'

'She's for real.'

A pale chin was stroked as Benny considered. 'What's in it for me?'

Sue opened her handbag and let him see a wad of notes. Benny reached for them but she moved the bag away. 'You had your advance last night. From now on I pay by results – and then only if they're good.'

Jonah's nod was slight but it added emphasis and Benny's gaze returned to Sue's handbag. It was the kind of leather which smelt of money.

'OK. I'll look and I'll listen – but I won't get involved.'

'Fine,' Sue said. 'Information's all I want from you.'

There was a noisy sigh from Jonah. He knew the kind of trash Benny ran with. 'Let's hope it's all you get.'

Sue walked part of the way home, enjoying London's night air. After the miasma around Jonah and Benny, the used and polluted gases she inhaled seemed sparkling and fresh. When she became bored with the empty streets a cruising cab took her back to Islington.

Ken was just parking his car as Sue paid off her driver. 'You're late.' He smiled. 'Been somewhere nice?'

'A meeting.'

'Snap. Bet yours was more fun. Bill was in a mood to talk – endlessly.'

As she led the way upstairs Sue remembered Colin coming home late from such meetings. Bill Farnham was the senior partner in the law firm where Colin had worked with Ken and memories were still hard to deal with.

Ken saw signs of distress in Sue's tiredness. 'Come and have some coffee.'

The thought of Pippa wielding a cafetière was attractive. 'You're on.'

Inside Pippa's domain Sue's fatigue sloughed away. In the soft light of candles two couches covered with sea-green throws promised comfort and her friend's welcome undid knots of nerves. As she slid from her coat Sue felt the burdens of the day go from her.

'Sue! If I didn't know you better, I'd say you'd been in a brothel.' Pippa chuckled at the idea.

'Oh, damn. I thought if I walked for a while the smell would clear.'

'Only from your coat. When you took it off – whew!'

Ken joined them, his office suit replaced by sweater and jeans. Wrinkling his nose he joined in the laughter. 'Where on earth have you been to get like that? I thought you said it was a meeting?'

'Jonah Blackburn and one of his informants.'

'She must be quite a girl,' Pippa decided.

'A man, actually.' Sue described Benny's use of every kind of perfume to breathe pleasant-smelling air when Jonah was intent on fouling the atmosphere with innumerable cigarettes. 'When you're with those two you're in a battle zone. I tried getting rid of the smell but Benny must use better quality stuff than I imagined. It lingers a bit.'

Pippa laughed. 'A bit? I just hope the gathering of minds was worth it.'

'So do I,' Sue said quietly.

She was impatient to get a result from Benny's information, but Sue's yearning to trace Anil's killers was pushed to one side by the constant and varied nature of her job. She had a sneaking suspicion Sam was using his influence to ensure she had no spare time or energy left to spend on what he would see as an unnecessary hunt.

It did mean her days were full and after work her friends did their best to divert her. She could have filled her diary with invitations to gallery openings, barbecues, quiet dinners, black tie functions.

On one such occasion, formally dressed, Sue accompanied Sam to an awards dinner. The huge reception room of the hotel in Park Lane had a generous bar and the excited level of sound suggested it was popular.

'Still helping our editor out of difficulties?' a voice asked, the words clipped to an unpleasant sharpness.

She turned to see the speaker. It was Steve Bynorth, Jan Francis at his side. Sue was determined to keep her smile and her words neutral. 'I help when I can.'

Steve, renowned for his sarcasm, was head of the political team in Brussels. Jan reported from Paris, at home there with her important blonde hair and stylish clothes masking toughness.

'Sam's very lucky,' Jan said. 'Your husband's been dead some time now, hasn't he?'

'Not quite a year.'

'Time enough.' Steve would have moved away after speaking but Sue was not ready to let him go.

'To grieve?' She knew it was not what he meant. 'I don't believe it ever really stops.'

'You're here tonight.' The bluntness from Steve was as a dash of ice.

'Yes, I'm here.' She gazed into pale blue eyes and had the satisfaction of seeing him lower his head to inspect his glass. She had never done anything to harm the man but his spite menaced her and she knew she must fight him. 'I enjoy listening to the speeches for the prizewinners. After working with many of them, it's good to see their efforts recognized.'

Jan's deep bitterness was mirrored in her expression. 'It would be more reassuring if awards went to the people who deserved them.'

Sue was undaunted by the bitchy couple and chuckled. 'You should have met my granny. She had great ideas about getting what is deserved. "Most of the time," she used to say, "we're damned lucky we don't."'

'I wouldn't say that.' Jan's malice was clear in the softness of her words. 'I'm sure you'll deserve everything that's coming to you.'

Sam came to lead Sue to her seat. It was all very formal, each table seating eight. Their companions included another editor with his wife as well as the chairmen of two banks. One, who seated himself next to Sue, was elderly and relaxed. His eyes were bright, his manners charming and his wife a bubbly little lady full of years and wit.

In contrast, the partner of the second banker was a wary-eyed girl in a strapless black dress at least a size too small for her. One for Kate's collection, Sue decided. Predator bimbo. The girl had obviously targeted her prey, probably ousting a wife in the process. Her escort might wear the smugness of a man with a nubile and very young trophy but he also had the drained appearance of a heart attack victim-in-waiting.

With fresh eyes Sue surveyed the diners and saw the patterns they displayed. Courtship could be seen, even when the participants were already mated and there with their partners. Dominance procedures were very much in evidence among women and men but here and there were blank faces. Another for Kate. Bored bimbos.

As the meal progressed Sue learned that her agreeable neighbour's hobby was clocks. Solar time and sidereal time were explained before he enthused on the subject of clepsydrae. Water clocks, Sue gathered, as he talked lovingly of a brass one inlaid with gold and already an antique when it was given by the King of Persia to Charlemagne.

'I'd have given anything to have seen it,' he said, going on to describe the twelve little dials, brass balls falling on a metal drum to strike the hours and, at the twelfth hour, miniature horsemen appearing to close the dials again.

There was a general movement before the speeches began. Cloakrooms were visited and business matters discussed while so many useful people were in together.

'I do hope my husband hasn't been boring you?' the lively little banker's wife wanted to know.

'Not at all. I was absolutely fascinated.'

'I'm glad. It's more of an obsession with him than an interest but it takes us all over the place. You'd be surprised where some of the most valuable timepieces have ended up.'

They chatted generally about pilgrimages made over the years to see obscure clocks and chronometers.

'Colin and I only managed standard holidays, I'm afraid, although we did get to Bali for our honeymoon.'

'Your husband?' The woman was perplexed. 'Forgive me, my dear, I thought . . .'

'Colin died, almost a year ago.'

'I am so sorry. Illness?'

A core of ice was back in Sue. 'An accident, according to the coroner.'

'So sudden! How dreadful – and you so young and pretty. You must remember life does go on.'

'That's something I keep being told, in fact there's a conspiracy to make me get out and about. Friends like Sam take me to dinner, then others make sure I go to concerts and there's a family with young children who drag me to the zoo.'

'With your work as well you must have a busy life.'

'Yes. The days are full.'

A flow of bodies began, dispersing people back to their seats.

'Oh dear, time for the speeches,' the older woman said with a sigh. 'Do you think that waiter could get me a large gin?'

It was the morning after the dinner. 'Anything yet?' Sue asked as soon as she arrived at work.

Jonah shook his head but there was the vestige of a twinkle in his eyes. 'Nope – but I had a call last night at home.'

'Benny?'

'Nope. An informant at Atherton's.'

Sue began to be excited. Atherton's was in Knightsbridge, royal coat of arms above the door. 'There's a lead on the bombers?'

'A lead?' Jonah started to laugh and spluttered it into a bout of coughing. 'A demand for a hundred grand in used and unmarked notes. The cash was assembled and everything went like clockwork – except the bombers got clean away.'

'You're joking!'

'Nope. CID all over the place and the pick-up went as planned, until the money disappeared. My contact said all hell broke loose back in Atherton's head office. After following police advice to the letter they're down a hundred grand.'

'Where was the handover?'

'A platform at King's Cross tube. Circle line, going west.'

Sue reached for a map of the London Underground.

'No need, I've looked. They could have gone in any direction. Probably kept changing at every station to make sure they weren't being followed.'

'Two of them?'

'At least, but there's no guarantee the brains of the outfit were anywhere near King's Cross.'

'Could that be the end of it?'

'For a hundred K? I doubt it,' Jonah said. 'It'll be like a game to them now, a game with a life of its own. Getting cash so easy – they'll be back for more.'

It was what Sue dreaded. Andy Passmore was hungry for attention and animals had long gone from the equation in which they had only ever been a transitory influence. Money had become the major factor. Money to buy more Semtex, more deaths, and it had all begun with Sue's car and Anil.

'When will it stop?' she whispered.

Jonah had reported too many casualties. 'When d'you think?'

Sue did not have to wait long to hear more of Animal Equality. This time when the letter was sent, its recipient was an importer of leather goods. Ari Spiridakis was not a man to part with £200,000 without a fight but his attempt to delay payment resulted in another explosion.

In the Saturday afternoon bustle of Oxford Street a burger bar disintegrated. It was one of a major chain and the casualty list of dead and injured read like a school register. TV news had film of the building, its windows blasted into passing humanity. Stunned witnesses could barely speak.

Men and women of the emergency services carried out their work without fuss. Occasionally, one would cover their face and Sue guessed it was to shield eyes from carnage and let tears flow.

'So many children,' Pippa said as she sat with Sue through yet another news bulletin. A group of seven-year-old boys had packed a corner of the restaurant.

Sue was devastated. 'It must have been because of the hamburgers they were chosen. They couldn't have known about the party, could they?'

'It can't go on – it mustn't,' Pippa said, her eyes full of tears. 'The police have to get to them quickly.'

'They're doing everything possible. Anybody who can help is being called in – even me.'

'You? Why?'

'To see if I can spot Gibson or Passmore. A car's due to collect me at eight. Relevant security tapes, I was told.'

Sue was driven through a quiet London and assembled with others who had encountered Passmore and Gibson. In the group were researchers and lecturers, laboratory workers and animal activists as well as teachers, a doctor, a landlord, all escorted in from the Midlands, the West Country, East Anglia.

It was a strange Sunday. From the many cameras in Oxford Street had come miles of film to be viewed until eyes ached. Sandwiches and coffee broke the monotony but Sue never saw Gibson's springing walk in the crowds, nor in the orderly queues of people waiting for food.

The burger bar film was being shown again and a senior police officer pointed out the waste bin into which customers dutifully emptied the debris of their meal.

'Just to remind you,' he said, 'this is the site of the explosion.'

Jerky figures came and went.

'Wait!' In Sue's tired mind there had been a faint click.

'You've seen Gibson?' There was eagerness for a clue, however small.

'No. It's the old lady. There's something . . .'

A technician ran the film back until Sue said, 'There!'

The room full of people watched an elderly woman tip the contents of her tray on top of other remains. As she turned to stack the tray she saw the boys partying and nodded to them, smiling.

'What is it?' a woman detective asked Sue.

'Something about her tray. Can we see her collect it?'

The film was searched and the appropriate section of the queue found. 'She's being served – now,' a voice said in the dimness.

'Coffee and an apple pie.' It was the man next to Sue who identified the purchases.

'That's it!' the policewoman exclaimed. 'When she emptied the tray, she had a large bag on it.'

'Perhaps it was her own rubbish,' someone called out but the image, enhanced by computer, showed the burger chain's logo on the heavy bag sliding into the bin. Magnification blurred the features of the figure stooped with age but there was no mistaking the way she smiled at the children before she turned to walk out of the camera's range.

The sequence was shown again and again. The idea that primed Semtex could be planted by an old woman was discounted by many.

'She's not old,' Sue said.

A detective inspector was interested. 'What makes you say so?'

'From the front she appears ancient but watch her walk – especially from the back. It's the way a young woman walks, not one doubled up with arthritis.'

That was when the activity in the room became intense. In groups around TV screens the films were run and rerun for any other sign of the female in disguise. Gradually, it was revealed that she had been recorded on several occasions by the street cameras, an apparently frail pensioner going quietly about her business.

Computer experts worked as fast as was humanly possible and produced printouts of the face from every angle, all enhanced from the jerky blurs seen on the original films. Those who knew her recognized her at once. Andrea Passmore was the woman in the crowded street who had gone into the burger bar to kill all she could.

'Dear God!' a woman whispered. She had been a teacher in Passmore's school. 'Andrea knew about the children and didn't care. She just didn't care!'

A tea trolley arrived and was surrounded but no one had much stomach for the food carried round by attentive constables. Sue made her way to the teacher, still shocked by Passmore's actions. The middle-aged woman was shivering, fingers clasping her teacup to get some comfort from the warm china.

'What was she like?' Sue asked.

'Andrea? Intelligent but not a happy child. She was quite a pretty girl when I first knew her – except for her expression. There was no reason I could see for her to be so miserable but she derived enormous satisfaction from belittling any child who appeared cheerful. It meant no friends, of course. Normal children migrate towards smiles and laughter.'

'In class, was she difficult to teach?'

'She shouldn't have been – Andrea was very bright. As a young girl she read a lot and could have done well at A level had she made the effort. It was impossible in the end. She was one of those students who already know all there is to know – and despised every teacher she ever encountered. It saved her working hard.' The woman looked hopefully at Sue. 'Perhaps it's this man she's entangled with who's the really evil one.'

Sue shook her head. 'From all I've heard he's the weaker of the two.'

'Then what's his part in all this?'

In Sue's memory her car exploded yet again. Leading

from Oxford Street to Soho were many narrow side streets packed with small cafés.

'He was probably sitting somewhere, ready to detonate the bomb.'

'It's like waiting for the other shoe to drop,' Sue said when she met Jonah on Monday morning.

'Oh, I think Spiridakis will pay up now,' he said, nodding his head like a wise mandarin.

Jonah had been contacted by a helpful informant. A new letter had been received by the leather importer, the grammar and spelling impeccable, the cash demand doubled.

'I've also had a whisper from the Yard,' Jonah added when he had made sure no one could overhear. 'Any interference with the pay-off and another bit of London goes up. Spiridakis was told the bomb was already in place.'

'Can the police let the handover go ahead?'

'Home Office rulings about terrorists and blackmail? They can't play. No, and it's not the top brass in the Met who'll agree to let the money go. After all, it's their boys and girls who help pick up the human bits which get scattered.'

Sue thought of Ashford's toughness. 'But they can't be seen letting the bombers get away with it?'

'No? It's as good a way of tracking them down as any I know – follow the money.'

'But Passmore's clever. Her disguise on Saturday was very convincing.'

'Yeah? Ten minutes in Oxfam, I bet that's all it took to get an old woman's clothes in good condition.'

'And she gets what she wants? All she has to do now is threaten death for us little people and she can buy whatever it is makes her happy. Death?'

Jonah sighed and Sue realized the man was ill, exhausted. He sensed her watching and lifted his chin, stretching the wattles of his neck.

'Too right, she's got us all by the short and curlies. It's worrying me what she's going to ask for next.'

Sue thought of a network of information spreading through London. 'What's scaring me is what we know.'

'Make sense, girl,' Jonah demanded.

'The power she has, death at the press of Gibson's finger. We can see it – who else will?'

'You and that bloody web again!'

'Well, we can see she's collecting untraceable cash in large amounts.'

Jonah stroked his chin, his eyes focused on the far distance. 'And if it's there for the taking . . .'

'Who'll come running?'

Chapter Five

At the request of the police no mention of blackmail reached the pages of any newspaper. This did not prevent rumours flying through a city shattered by bombs, the latest atrocity reminding the elderly of V2 rockets slamming into indiscriminate targets.

The number of shoppers in Oxford Street dropped sharply and those who walked its pavements did so with an air of defiance. Towns and cities across the mainland increased their own security, anticipating that increased vigilance in the capital would make terrorists look elsewhere for new targets.

Days passed and interviews with bereaved and recovering victims moved from the front pages. There were plenty of other stories to fill the columns, newer tragedies to draw sympathy, and daily life resumed a wary normality.

Sue's resolve had not lessened, neither had her workload. Four days after the blast she had her head bent to the task of shaping two hundred words on harbour porpoises, Britain's smallest dolphins.

'Forget that!'

She looked up at Kate. 'What on earth –'

'Just get your bag and come.'

'Why? What's happened?'

'Don't argue!'

Kate picked up Sue's coat, almost running with it towards the stairs. The sense of urgency was infectious and Sue followed her out of the building. In the car park, which was still being rebuilt, Kate pointed Sue to the back of her car.

'Get down so no one sees you leave.'

Crouched in the capacious well of the stylish motor, Sue was bumped uncomfortably as Kate drove in her usual cavalier manner, away from the *Journal* and Wapping.

'You can get up now, it's safe.'

'Safe from what, for heaven's sake?' Sue was irritable, aching muscles complaining as she straightened up and leaned over the back of the passenger seat. 'Will you please explain what all that was about? Was it the bombers?'

'You'd be a bloody sight safer!' Kate said as she swung the car sharply. 'Sam's got a whisper of tomorrow's main feature in *Nova*.'

'So?'

'It's you.'

'Kate! You can't be serious?'

'Deadly. Sam's to be sent up for having a girlfriend who's two-timing him. They've got photos.'

Kate weaved her way through the traffic at Marble Arch, aiming for her flat in the Bayswater Road. Behind her Sue sat silent, stunned by what she had just heard and trying to make sense of the situation. Sam had been a good friend, nothing more. There could be no incriminating photos.

'It's ridiculous!'

'A stitch-up, certainly, 'Kate agreed, 'and who would it benefit – that's what I keep asking myself. You'd better get down again in case they've staked me out. It's unlikely but I trust *Nova* hacks like I trust out-of-control rottweilers.'

They arrived without incident at the stately old house, now divided into prestigious apartments. Sue released her pent-up breath only when they were safe inside the flat with its view across Hyde Park. The decor was in pastel shades of sea green with touches of pink which reminded Sue of flamingos. A laptop was ready for instant use on an antique desk and beside it a compact unit held a printer and fax machine. Books almost covered one wall to the high ceiling.

Her hostess headed for the gin bottle and waved it enquiringly at Sue who shook her head, deciding her brain was in enough of a spin without sending it into orbit. Kate poured herself a large measure, adding the merest dash of tonic.

'Why, Kate?'

It took a long drink before Kate was ready to reply. 'There are probably a dozen theories. Take your pick.'

'Is it the bombers? They're the only ones who've had me on a list – as far as I know.'

'They wouldn't have enough clout to get action out of Corcoran, *Nova*'s laughable excuse for an editor.' Kate lay back in her chair and examined the ceiling. 'Pistachio nuts. Do you know what I hate most about them?'

'The colour?'

'No, I like that and I like eating them. It's the ones you can't open. There's the nut, begging to be devoured and you can't get at it. Either you have to break a nail or get something to prise the shell apart.'

'Am I supposed to be the nut?'

'Actually, I think Sam is. You're saving someone breaking a nail. In this case, breaking their cover.'

'Who'd go to all that trouble?'

'Ultimately, someone who wants Sam's job and thinks public humiliation will get rid of him.'

'Sam would never be affected by that sort of thing.'

'I agree – but what of the *Journal*'s financial backers? Money men tend to be the most sensitive little flowers when gossip starts flying.'

It was Sue's thoughts that flew this way and that, defying logic and refusing to make sense.

'Don't forget, Sam was in the right place when Jepson keeled over,' Kate reminded her. 'He got the chance to show what he could do as editor and the banks gave him the green light.'

Sue recalled the time a few months ago, when tensions around the executive offices were almost igniting. 'Jealousy rearing its ugly head?'

'In spades, my dear.'

Kate refilled her glass and Sue wondered yet again how her friend could keep functioning so well on almost neat alcohol.

'It can't be anyone on the *Journal*. There's nobody could do the job half as well as Sam.'

'I know that,' Kate said, wagging her glass at Sue, 'and you know that. It doesn't mean some pea-brained idiots agree with us. Perhaps there's an individual who'd settle for the prestige and the pay and let a deputy like Gavin do the work.'

'As Sam did for Jepson?'

'Spot on. Cary and I have been having a little chat now and again on that very subject.'

'Cary wants to be editor?'

'No way! He doesn't approve of working too hard and it really would confine him to the straight and narrow. I grant you he was anti-Sam at first but apparently the *Journal*'s status has gone up since our Mr Haddleston took over and Cary's getting a very nice class of party invite these days. He's got a good nose, you know.'

'It's all the breeding he boasts,' Sue snapped. She was angry, hungry, and a little more than curious. 'I want to see what's been written about me.'

'Oh no you don't!'

'It can't be that bad.'

'Usual *Nova* style?'

Sue groaned. *Nova*'s teams were downwind of the gutter press and revelled in their reputation.

'I ought to ring my parents.'

'Sam's got that in hand – and by now Miles Beamish has been contacted. He's the other man in your sordid little life.'

'I can't believe it!' Sue stood, and began pacing the floor. 'For pity's sake, since Colin died I've never even kissed anyone – let alone slept with them!'

'*Nova*'s readers won't care. All they'll see is a girl who's

91

got looks and brains and is being held up to be reviled. It's what that particular scandal sheet does best.'

'Can't I get an injunction?'

'Too late. The article's gone to press.'

'Can I sue?'

'Corcoran would be delighted. No, all you can hope for is a major royal marching stark naked down the Mall as we speak, or a plane crashing on a block of flats in Notting Hill. If neither of those things happen, it's you for the pillory.'

Sue stood in the centre of the elegant room, drooping with the disgust and humiliation she feared was about to engulf her. 'Who hates me so much?' she asked Kate in a whisper.

'No one who really knows you,' Kate said softly and smiled. 'Now, food.' A pile of leaflets was tossed at Sue. 'Choose your takeaway. It's an evening in for you and me.'

As they waited for the nearest Cantonese restaurant to deliver, Kate listed the possible candidates for Sam's job. 'John Corcoran would like it himself but he carries the stench of the gutters. No, Jocelyn Wharmby's most likely. After all, the *Mercury* specializes in exposures and he'd have had the contacts to set you up.'

'And give the story to another rag?'

'Why not? That way he'd be seen as having clean hands.'

'What about someone on the *Journal* playing dirty?'

'Ah, there you have quite a queue. Jan Francis for starters – the stuck-up cow!'

Sue was in a mood to be diverted. 'She certainly hates my guts, so does Steve Bynorth.'

'A grade A front runner in nastiness, if ever there was one – and you'd better add Wasim Khan to the list. He's got the track record to take on the responsibility and he's been badly bitten by the ambition bug.'

Sue reflected on the arrogant leader of the financial team. 'Does he hate all women?'

'Only those competing with him.'

It was a possible explanation for the rudeness she had experienced from that quarter.

'Of the up-and-coming ones there's Andrew Carroll and Sandy –'

'No! Sandy would never do that to me – neither would Andrew. It's not in them.'

'You're right,' Kate agreed. Her eyes were steady over the rim of her gin glass. 'Mind you, there'd be no problem if you looked like the back end of a bus.'

'Someone's jealous of me?'

'You and Sam. Never leave jealousy out of the human equation. It's the most dangerous characteristic we have.'

Sue slumped into a chair, lying back and closing her eyes. 'Why now, Kate?'

'After the *Journal* bomb, you're vulnerable. Whoever wants Sam out of the picture knows it.'

Later, Kate rang the *Journal*'s night desk and asked for the *Nova* article to be faxed. She held the pages as they arrived, glancing at them before passing each one to Sue.

It was quite a spread. The main photo was of Sam smiling at Sue. They were sitting together at the awards and sharing a private moment. An adjacent shot was of Miles taking Sue's arm to steer her across the road, both of them laughing as they left the Festival Hall. There was even an illustration of the house in Islington, Sue's flat marked with an arrow.

Weakness hit her legs like a blow and she subsided into the nearest chair to read the accompanying words. One long sneer belittled the struggle and all the hard work which had forged her career. According to *Nova*'s spleen, Sue was an attractive but calculating halfwit and Sam had given her a high profile job of which she was incapable.

It was spelled out for the readers of the rag just how Sue earned an excessively high pay packet, but that was not libel enough. The concerts to which Miles escorted her were simply camouflage, excuses to return to Sue's flat for nights of lust. Nothing had been left to the imagination of *Nova*'s public and they were encouraged to ridicule Sam for being publicly cuckolded.

The smell of brandy stung Sue's nose. Kate's idea of first aid was liquid and immediate, it was also very welcome. Sue grasped the glass and sipped.

'That's better,' Kate said. 'Your colour's coming back.'

'Is there nothing I can do?'

'Sam's seen to everything.'

Sue talked to her parents and, although they were aghast, their love and support flowed freely. 'Sam's persuaded Mum and Dad to go to Aunt Hettie's for a few days.'

'Good – and I know he was getting Miles to move to a hotel. If none of you can be found and Sam carries on as usual, looking cheerful and unconcerned, the dust'll soon settle.' Kate grinned. 'I mean, can you imagine politicians keeping their pants zipped longer than a couple of days and staying off the front pages?'

Standing under the shower for an age and scouring herself again and again reminded Sue of the bomb. Being caught in the blast of someone's hatred destroyed and dirtied as unmercifully as Semtex.

Kate had hot coffee ready. 'Do you feel any better for that?'

'I should do . . .'

'But there's no way you can ever get clean again?'

Sue sniffed back tears.

'Listen, darling. Because of all the articles I've done on the subject, I've talked to many women who've been raped.' Kate was concerned, gentle. 'They felt just like you do now.'

Wet hair was rubbed vigorously as Sue considered the idea.

'You have to make the same decision they did. Someone has used you, violated you. Are you going to let them think they've defeated you?'

Sue was tired of fighting. 'First the bombers, now this.

Do I have to spend my entire life deciding not to be a victim?'

'Why not? Everyone else has to.'

The spurt of fury was short-lived, exhaustion replacing rancour. 'You're right. It's the law of the jungle and ours is no different. Predator or prey.'

It was quiet in the high-ceilinged, graceful room. The smell of Kate's cigarette mingled with her perfume and the sharpness of gin. 'Sam and Miles . . .' she said slowly. 'Have you ever done anything which could give credence to the *Nova* smear?'

Sue sat up, her eyes flashing. 'No!'

'Good – and hang on to that anger. You've no reason to feel guilty. The only filth in the situation is in the minds of the *Nova* sewer rats and their readers – for want of a better word. Remember always, there's no way they can pull you down to their level – unless you let them.'

'That's easy to say. If only I could do something positive! At least with Animal Equality I could try to find them.'

'All you can do is to keep out of sight for a while.'

'And let that lying drivel stand?'

'Leave it to Sam – he's the real target. By now he'll have the *Journal* lawyers longing for their beds, Jonah's runners hunting down whoever took the pictures and passed them on. I'm guessing a few favours'll be called in before morning.'

'How long will it go on for?'

'As long as it takes. Our esteemed editor will definitely fight dirty if he has to. My bet is that by this time tomorrow he's well on the way to getting enough on Corcoran for an apology and a sizeable compensation.'

Sue had met John Corcoran only on one occasion. Once was enough. Expensive tailoring failed to hide the thug in him, and his obsession with financial success was a major irritant.

'Making them part with cash is the only way to smack Corcoran and his buddies where it hurts most,' Kate said. 'I just hope it brings tears to their eyes.'

'But I don't want money,' Sue protested.

'Then start thinking of a charity it can benefit.'

The next few days passed in a blur.

Sue was furious, frustrated, as she worked from Kate's home, her search for Passmore, Gibson, their supplier, put on hold for the duration. At least her assignments were absorbing, the variety of topics she had to deal with driving away some of the helplessness she endured.

Checking her answerphone in Islington kept Sue in contact with her family and friends, but whenever she made a call herself 141 was dialled in first to prevent anyone tracing her.

Pippa had arrived on the second day of incarceration with a suitcase of Sue's clothes.

'I never realized this cloak and dagger stuff was such fun.' She sat with Sue on the window seat and enjoyed the vista of Hyde Park's trees marching into the distance. 'I made sure I wasn't followed and changed taxis twice on the way.'

'I'm so sorry I dragged you away from your work. I know you were on a deadline.'

Pippa illustrated a successful series of children's animal stories. 'Forget it,' she told Sue firmly. 'This is much more exciting.'

Sue could not sit still. She walked round the sitting room moving books, papers, ornaments, as she tidied an already immaculate room. 'Did you read the article?'

'Of course! Every word. You were in the pictures but who was being written about I haven't the faintest idea. It certainly wasn't you.'

Pippa's common sense and good humour thawed cold corners of Sue's mind but the unpleasant question persisted. 'If I only knew why . . .'

'You will. Wait long enough and all will be revealed – my mother was great on that theory.'

'I can't be so patient.'

'Then learn!' Pippa moved from the narrow window seat and settled into the corner of a chesterfield. 'I gather you're working from here?'

Sue nodded. 'Anything unexpected in the office, Paula's covering.'

'She's back?'

'Very tanned and as confident as ever.'

'Nice she got taken away on a cruise by Mummy and Daddy to help her recover from the blast.' It was unusual for Pippa to be sarcastic.

'Why not? She did what she could at the time and now she's taking more responsibility and is fresh enough to cope. Beth'll keep her in line.'

'And who's keeping you in line?' Pippa wanted to know. 'All day on your own and brooding.'

'You are.'

Sue studied her friend. There was something different about her. Maybe it was the light from the huge window and the reflected colours from the cushions. There was an aura of health about her. Pippa's skin was always creamy but it had gained luminosity.

'You're pregnant!'

'I wondered if you'd guess before I told you.'

'When?'

'Another six months.'

Guilt swept through Sue. 'You carried my case here.'

'No, I did not. I had three very nice cab drivers. Besides, I'm as strong as an ox.'

'Ken – how's he taking it?'

'He's over the moon and insisting we get married.'

Sue knew how much Pippa valued her independence. 'Will you?'

'Maybe.' There was a wicked grin for Sue. 'Until then I'm enjoying being persuaded.'

When Sue returned to the *Journal* offices there were few

glances or whispers. Everyone was busy, most greeting her normally with a 'Hi, Sue. You OK?'

Paula was at Sue's desk, relief bringing a smile to her face when she looked up. 'Thank heaven you're here. I was just going to ring you.'

A busy fifteen minutes later Sue spotted Jonah heading for an exit and hurried after him. 'Benny?'

Jonah wiped his face free of sweat. 'He hasn't phoned me.'

'It's more than a week, Jonah. He should have dug up something by now.'

'He probably has and is deciding where he's likely to get the best price.'

'You get hold of Benny and remind him I've not only got Mrs Prudcky's number, I've also got an itchy dialling finger.'

'The *Nova* splash has made you edgy,' he decided. 'Don't let the bastards get to you.'

'Jonah, I need at least one name from Benny.'

'Sure you do,' he agreed, wheezing badly.

She had long ago guessed Jonah was enduring emphysema but it seemed worse. It worried her to see a bluish tinge to his skin, his lips almost purple.

'The little toad should be up by now,' he muttered.

Jonah rummaged in an inside pocket and produced a well-worn leather notebook. Scooping up the nearest phone he dialled and waited, shaking his head at Sue to leave him in peace. It was a brief call, Jonah grunting as he replaced the handset and scribbled in his book. He raised his head and Sue could see he was satisfied by what he had been told.

'Beck's met with a couple of faces but Benny says to keep off.'

'Why?'

'They're Irish and being shadowed. Benny says it's by Special Branch who're "sticking out like sore bloody thumbs", to quote his lordship.'

'He'll keep on looking?'

'Until I tell him to stop.'

When it was safe to return to her flat Pippa and Ken were waiting to help her unpack. Their happiness was infectious but she shooed them away and busied herself, filling the washing machine and taking sheets from the airing cupboard.

She used polish and dusters as though removing every trace of John Corcoran and *Nova*'s existence. A mirror was receiving particularly furious attention when a thought stopped her. Corcoran had been used too. Sue stared at the shining expanse, struggling to see in it the face of her enemy, but no one appeared.

When the flat smelled fresh again, Sue packed an overnight bag then drove to Dorking and the home she had always known.

'I'm so sorry,' she whispered, her arms tight around her mother.

Mrs Lavin held Sue's face between her hands. 'What on earth for? You don't think we believed the lies in that dreadful paper?'

'No, but it can't have been easy.' Her parents were still in their church clothes. 'Did anyone have a go this morning?'

Mr Lavin hugged his daughter. 'Mrs Stroat tried but Mrs Willoughby set about her.'

'For once I was very glad of that loud voice of hers,' Mrs Lavin admitted.

Sue's father chuckled. 'Poppet, you should have been there. It boomed round the churchyard as the vicar was shaking hands. "Anyone with so little intellect as to read *Nova* is hardly in a position to criticize individuals libelled in its pages,"' he quoted. 'She was in full flood, glaring at Mrs Stroat and her cronies. She even insisted on walking home with us.'

Worries and fears fell away as Sue went into the house.

She followed her mother to the kitchen, the familiar room warm and fragrant with Sunday smells.

Her father grinned at her. 'If you've been staying with Kate Jeffries I'd better offer you a tumbler of neat gin.'

'I've let her drink it all but I'd love fruit juice, Dad. I think I need it after all the time I've spent indoors lately.'

'Mrs Willoughby's sure you've upset someone very nasty. "Definitely the type of person who can't stand the truth – and that girl of yours would never dream of writing anything but the unvarnished sort. It must be her scientific training,"' Mr Lavin said, mimicking Mrs Willoughby's distinctive vowels.

'I doubt it. Honesty was something demanded of me long before I went into a lab.' Sue smiled at her parents. 'You'll just have to take the blame.'

Mr Lavin cleared his throat and searched for a change of topic. 'I thought your editor came over well in the interview he did for Sky news last night. He mentioned *Nova* paying a lump sum to a charity of your choice – a million, I understood. How on earth did he manage to make the other side cough up so much and so quickly?'

'I wasn't told all the details,' Sue told him. 'Apart from the lawyers, I know Julian was working on it – he's the computer whizz-kid – and Sam called Miles in to help.'

Her mother was puzzled. 'A rather strange situation, darling? I know you don't have a – a special friend, but Miles and Sam do rather regard each other as competition.'

'It's not how I see it.'

'I suppose,' Mr Lavin began thoughtfully, 'if the two men were seen to be at each other's throats, someone would have leaked the fact to *Nova* and the story would still be running.'

'I'm glad they could be so civilized in the circumstances.' Mrs Lavin sipped her pre-lunch sherry. 'It must have been hard for you, being shut away for almost a whole week.'

'It wasn't so bad. Kate kept me up to date every evening.

Miles vetted what Julian found and the whole staff saw Sam and Miles collaborating happily.'

'Computer data and a fraud investigator? Sounds like the *Nova* finances are a bit questionable,' Mr Lavin decided. 'If the *Journal* got hold of that sort of information, pressure could easily be exerted.'

Mrs Lavin was horrified. 'But that's blackmail!'

'Of course it is, my dear, and if it clears Sue I'm all in favour. You have to paddle in sewers if you want to get at rats.'

'Can we change the subject?' his wife pleaded. 'I'll see to the vegetables while you two lay the table – and I'll need some mint from the garden.'

Sue sniffed. 'Lamb. It smells great.'

'Your mother's delighted to have a chance to feed you, Poppet. She's been so worried for you.'

It hurt Sue to see the signs of recent strain showing in her parents. 'When people decide to use you, they never care what effect it will have – or the repercussions.'

She went out into the freshness and sanity of the garden, walking around and visiting plants she had watched grow. It was very reassuring and after Sue had gathered the mint, she washed and chopped it with sugar. The strong smell of the herb helped snap an idea into life. 'Perhaps they do want you to suffer,' she murmured to herself.

It was time for a meeting, Sandy being ready to raise the topic of sound pollution. Sue picked up a notebook, turning back with a groan as her phone rang.

'Mrs Bennett? Anwar Naib.'

'It is good of you to call, Anwar. How are your parents?'

'Well, thank you.' The young voice was hesitant. 'I wanted to know if you had made any progress?'

'I've someone watching a suspect but Special Branch is interested in him as well. I guess he knows it and is leading a blameless life – for the moment.'

'This man was involved in Anwar's death?'

'If he was, it was only indirectly.'

'Mrs Bennett, if I can help at all, you will call me? I need to feel I am doing something, however small.'

On the way to Sam's office Sue thought of the Naibs and their deep need for answers. When she arrived at the meeting the room was unexpectedly full, discussion already in progress. Sue sat beside Sandy as Wasim Khan hectored everyone in sight and took any opportunity to embarrass Sue. Ethan Jones listened calmly, as did Gavin. Clive Bauman offered advice on the legalities and Sam missed nothing. Before he closed the meeting Sam authorized a back-up campaign, led by Sandy, to gather evidence on noise nuisance and the legislation needed to control it.

Sue stretched aching muscles in her neck as she made her way back to her desk and checked fresh news items. Little was her particular concern until one small item caught her eye. A rustler in Wales had liberated a sheep for his oven. Unfortunately for the thief the sheep had just been dipped. The animal would be toxic and police warnings were being broadcast to prevent the man and his family suffering any ill-effects from the free meal. She sat staring into space as she recalled data. Organo-phosphates. Scrapie. Suicides amongst sheep farmers. She let odd facts seethe and merge, deciding she must investigate research already in hand.

Even as she asked Karin to find which of the pesticides had been used in the present dip, Sue found her thoughts slipping away to the Naibs. Would any of them be able to lead a normal life again? Seeing Anil's killers caught and dealt with was the only thing which would allow them a new beginning.

It rankled, bit deep, that the scum attacking Sam had made her lose a whole week of hunting Animal Equality's supplier. She was determined there would be no more delay but Jonah was missing from the office and there was no way she could contact Benny.

'Back to basics,' Sue told herself as she headed for the library and began her search.

Sean Beck had featured twice in the *Journal*'s pages. He had been picked up with three members of the IRA and all four of them charged with conspiracy to cause explosions. That time the charges against Beck had been dropped. Two years later he had been tried for possession of explosives and escaped conviction. A jury considered the evidence too circumstantial and police experts had been unable to link the tiny amount of Semtex found to Beck.

Sue selected the best photo of the man and folded a copy in her bag. It was time for action but Jonah was still missing. She tried to remember the streets Benny had mentioned, pulling out her *A–Z* and riffling through its pages. Annoyed with herself for failing to write down the information when it was fresh, she closed her eyes, recreated the situation and let memories float up. Clissold Avenue, she thought, or was it Clissold Street? Then there was Wakeham . . . Street? The ring of her phone was a diversion.

'Sue? Sergeant Webley's here and needs your help. My office.'

Sam had been abrupt and Sue ran, fearing what she might hear from the sergeant.

'We'd like you to be at Heathrow and have a good look at some passengers as they arrive.'

Sue stared at the sergeant, calm, controlled, elegant in a grey trouser suit with a long jacket. 'An identity parade?'

'In a way.'

'Who am I looking for?'

'Dennis Gibson.'

Sue wanted to help but she hesitated. 'Wouldn't it be wiser to have someone he worked with? They'd know him.'

There was a minimal inclination of the head. 'Perhaps. At the moment we're trying to involve as few people as possible.'

'And I'm already involved.'

Sergeant Webley's posture was excellent and her slight bow of acknowledgement graceful.

103

'Is there any danger of Gibson seeing her?' Sam wanted to know.

'None at all, sir. We just want Mrs Bennett to watch a monitor and tell us when she sees the target.'

It sounded so simple.

The drive to Heathrow was uneventful and there was little conversation. At the airport Sue was ushered into a room away from the public. Superintendent Ashford was there, persuading her to sit, drink coffee, wait.

'Where's Gibson travelling from?' Sue wanted to know.

'Vienna.'

While she waited, Sue chased street names in her mind. She was planning to use the street map facility in the *Journal*'s computer files when Sergeant Webley's radio crackled.

'Coming through now, sir,' the girl told Ashford as she stationed Sue in front of a screen.

'If you see Gibson, point to him, that's all you have to do,' the superintendent said. He turned to his sergeant who had been using her radio. 'All in position?'

'Yes, sir.'

The first passenger came into view, a young man festooned with a rucksack and cameras. Next, a young couple looking as though they were returning from a honeymoon which had gone well.

'He'll probably come in a crowd,' Ashford warned as the flow of luggage-laden passengers increased.

Sue watched carefully, searching for the unique walk which marked Gibson. The flood of passengers became a trickle, stopped. 'I'm sorry. He wasn't there.'

Superintendent Ashford was not pleased. 'He must have been. Is the suspect still in view?' he asked Sergeant Webley.

'Yes, sir. White and Sillitoe are with him, Andrews and Bourne in reserve.'

A recording of the arrival was played for Sue but she

shook her head. Not one of the passengers had Gibson's way of moving, although one or two were like him in appearance. Ashford curbed his impatience and ordered the film slowed, his suspect isolated for Sue to examine.

'This is the man who used Gibson's passport in Vienna,' he told her.

The build was right, so were the features to some extent, but this was a confident man she watched. The one she had seen in a lab coat was a nervous type, his shoulders hunched together with tension on an ordinary working day. She was sure of her own facts.

'Whatever his passport says, that man is not Dennis Gibson.'

Chapter Six

It was a silent return to Wapping, Sue alone in the back of an unmarked police car. At the entrance to the *Journal* the driver thanked her politely for her assistance in a way which made her feel she had just failed a set of exams. It was a relief for Sue to slump at her desk and wonder if she could face the office coffee.

A burst of laughter across the room caught her attention. News just in appeared to have caused merriment and Sue called up the relevant page on her own monitor, smiling as she read. A labour official in the Philippines had declared that 'a slice of papaya a day keeps sexual urges at bay'.

Jonah wheezed as he walked past. He was definitely worsening but he arrived promptly each morning and his copy was as clear and concise as it had ever been. Sue was diverted by the ringing of her phone.

'He didn't see you?' Sam asked. 'Gibson?'

'I didn't see him.'

'Wasn't he on the flight?'

'Not the Dennis Gibson I saw in Norwich. I think some-one who looked very like him had used his passport – at least, that's the impression I got.'

'Where was he flying in from?'

'Vienna.'

'Ah, then I bet there's now money in a Sparbuch account.'

'What on earth does that mean?'

'It's possible to open a savings account in Austria in a matter of minutes – no questions asked. It's a marvellous way to hide cash and a money-launderer's dream. There's pressure building to get the Austrian government to change the system but at the last count there were 26 million of these savings books for a population of 9 million Austrians. Probably every crook in Europe banks there.'

'It seems too simple. What's the catch?'

'Dealings have to be done in person.'

Sue heard another voice as someone entered Sam's office so she said goodbye and returned to her train of thought. Walking to Jonah, she pulled a chair to sit next to him and saw that his skin was grey, shining.

'I haven't heard from Benny, if that's what you're after.'

'Not Benny, Atherton's. Any more information about the money they paid out?'

'The chairman's threatened to sue the Commissioner personally. No one's saying how the money escaped surveillance so I gather there must have been a complete cock-up. The bombers got away with that and the Spiridakis cash.'

'Apparently to Vienna.'

Jonah's chuckle turned into a bad spell of coughing he tried hard to control. 'Our CID would be better staking out the bloody banks over there, then they'd really know who had cash they shouldn't,' he said when he could breathe more easily.

'Jonah, when Benny talked about Sean Beck what streets did he mention?'

'For God's sake, Sue, you're not going to look for him?'

'Of course not.' She hoped she would be forgiven for a small lie.

Jonah was not reassured, eyeing Sue suspiciously. 'Green Lanes,' he said at last. 'I don't know the number – nor for his bit of skirt. She's in Wakeham Street.'

'That's terrific! How do you do it?'

'Practice, my girl. You're a scientist and remember the names of animals and chemicals. With me it's faces and streets. Now then, you got dragged off by the Bill. What for?'

'To see if I could identify someone landing at Heathrow.'

'And could you?'

Sue shook her head and Jonah nodded.

'They'd flown in from Vienna and you didn't spot 'em,' he guessed. 'That means one of two things. Either you were wrong and that's unlikely, or Passmore and Gibson have brought in a third party.' Puzzlement etched extra lines on his face. 'I'd have gone bail they'd never go down that road.'

Back at her own desk Sue's thoughts echoed Jonah's. The unholy pair had waged an elitist war yet they used a Gibson look-alike. Why? Before she could solve that riddle Miles was calling, reminding her of a concert. He teased Sue gently and blood warmed her cheeks, making her feel a schoolgirl again.

Heartened by the exchange she set to and dealt with the list of work waiting for her attention. Next morning the *Journal*'s readers would be entertained by the new use for papaya but, however much they laughed, the facts must be accurate. With Karin's help, Sue contacted laboratories, adding to her stored data on the exotic fruit. The cartoon for the next day was on the same topic and Sue allowed herself to flavour her prose with humour, an element usually missing from accounts of cancer treatments or animals pursued to their deaths for imaginary aphrodisiacs.

'Any more for the list, Sue?' Cary asked, pausing as he strolled by.

She looked up, puzzled.

'Bimbos.'

The only reading matter to hand as Sue waited at Heathrow had been a copy of *Nova*, two TV presenters snarling insults at each other across the front page. 'Bitchy?'

'Got it.'

For some reason an image of rhinos charging, panting for their freedom, filled her mind. 'Endangered?'

Cary walked on, satisfied.

'How can you?'

Sue looked up, surprised by the venom directed at her. Karin had spots of colour high on each cheek, fury sparkling in her eyes. 'How can I what?'

'Talk about other women like that. Bimbos! That's all Cary Mitchell and his kind understand. I thought you'd be different – and Kate.'

'Karin, I had to work very hard to get my job here and I expect it was the same for you. What we do gives us a certain status, a reasonable standard of living. If any female thinks she can callously get from a man, with sex, what I've had to earn, she won't find me rooting for her.'

'You didn't say that when *Nova* front-paged you,' Karin sniped. 'You didn't like being called a bimbo.'

'I objected to the lies, Karin, as well as the smears and innuendos – so would anyone who's been libelled. Only the truth is acceptable as far as I'm concerned, whether it's what I write or what I am – even what's printed about me. If you can't take that then see Gavin and ask to be moved to another department – or another paper.'

Sue ignored her own flaming cheeks and a white-faced Karin to return to the innocuous papaya.

An evening with Miles promised escape. Always good company, he was undemanding yet attentive. Sue was grateful for his friendship, even as she acknowledged his need for a deeper relationship.

The concert to which he had escorted her had been different, attention deflected from the music by the flamboyance of the Russian pianist. It had been so extreme the applause at the end of his playing was an almost unnecessary fillip to his self-esteem.

It would take the virtuoso some time to descend from the state of euphoria he had worked so hard to achieve, but Sue and Miles had forgotten him as they sat in a quiet corner of what had been an old warehouse near Waterloo station. The solid floors scattered with sawdust hinted at a bygone age and the food they were served tasted fresh from a garden.

'Have you decided yet which charity the money will go to?' Miles asked as they finished their first course.

'Yes. There's a research lab producing a new family of cancer drugs. The first one was very effective and the latest seems even more promising. I'd rather they had the means of developing it themselves than have to sell out to a big pharmaceutical company which would cream millions off their hard work.'

'Good. Corcoran's money will never have been so well spent.'

'How did you get him to empty his pockets and apologize for the story?'

Sue had been curious ever since she had first learned her good name had been restored. Sam would not be drawn, although Kate worked hard on him and Kate's tongue could open clams.

Miles's left eyebrow climbed as he smiled enigmatically. 'Julian's unique with a computer – at least I hope he is. No file is safe when he's around.'

'Hacking? You're not going to tell me the end justifies the means, are you?'

'Not at all. Julian merely allowed us to check financial records which are more or less in the public domain.'

'That sounds fishy. More or less?'

'They're supposed to be generally available but Corcoran hides them. He was anxious the authorities didn't do the same as us and find them.'

'Very anxious if he allowed Sam to crawl all over him in public and contributed to charity as well.'

Miles grinned cheerfully. 'Couldn't have happened to a nicer chap.'

'Shouldn't you have passed your discoveries on to the police?'

'No.'

'Who should you have told?'

The grin widened. 'Customs and Excise. We recommended he open his books to them before they asked awkward questions about VAT. It's up to Corcoran now – his decision.'

'But your suggestion is on file somewhere?'

'Dated and verified.'

A dish of pasta, creamy and bubbling with cheese, was placed in front of Sue, the bowl of salad alongside it crisp, inviting.

'Who was behind it all, Miles?'

'You'll know in time.'

'Was it someone who hated me?'

'No way. They were after Sam. You were just a tool to be used. Handy.'

'And vulnerable?'

''Fraid so. They're the "kick you when you're down" variety.'

'Was it because I'm to blame for the deaths at the *Journal*?'

'Of course not,' he said a little too quickly. 'Did you specifically ask for a bomb in your car? It was pure chance you weren't blown up. Like everyone else who knows you, I thank God for it.'

She gazed at the bright colours on her plate but they were blurred. 'It would be great to believe the nightmare's over.'

'Side effects?'

'You could call it that. Hate mail.'

Miles groaned and reached for her hand. 'You didn't read any?'

'Some. All unsigned, of course.'

'Haddleston was to see your post was filtered.'

'He did. These arrived at the flat, pushed through the letter box.'

'Damn Corcoran! He needs stringing up!'

'What about the person who gave him the so-called story?'

'Leave it – and eat your pasta.'

Sue did, and the balance of flavours tempted her to

111

enjoy her meal. As they waited for coffee she noticed Miles was abstracted, drawing rectangles on the wood of the table with the end of his spoon.

'How's James? He's certainly too young to know about the *Nova* mess.'

'Yes, he is.'

'Something's wrong? You've been spending the weekends with him as you normally do?'

'That's just it. He's listless and each time I see him there's a fresh bruise.'

'Not his mother?'

'Never – but Anne has this boyfriend.'

'And you think he's hitting James?'

'It certainly looks that way.'

'Oh Miles, I'm so sorry.' It was Sue's turn to reach for a hand and pass on comfort. 'Have you said anything to your wife?'

'I'm due to pick James up on Friday evening. If there's any sign . . .'

'How is he in himself? James? Is he scared of the boyfriend?'

'No, that's why I've not tackled Anne sooner. James quite likes him, I think. They play football, go for pizzas, play video games – just as I would.'

'Could he get the bruises playing football?'

'If he does, it's pretty rough stuff.'

Sue reassured as best she could and Miles was in a more relaxed frame of mind when he stopped the car outside Sue's flat.

'You stay here,' she told him. 'There could be a freelance snapper about, hoping to sell to a *Journal* competitor.' Sue was about to open the car door when Miles kissed her, quickly but not lightly. She began to respond instinctively then hesitated and pulled away.

It was too soon.

An envelope protruded from the letter box and Sue pulled

it free. As she read her name, written in a neat, character-less script, her spirits nose-dived. Only when in her flat and safe behind the front door did she read the letter. In her tiredness she had a mental image of a pathetic nonentity venting venom at her as would a trapped snake.

Tears blurred the words, and she shredded the paper with angry fingers. Sue longed for an open fire so she could watch the evil blacken and disappear up the chimney like an expelled demon. She had to settle for the rubbish bin in the kitchen, consigning malignity to the detritus of her life.

Max Franklin, the *Journal*'s tame sociologist, was fair and thinly handsome in designer leather and Gucci loafers. He was trawling for back-up information from Sue and Jonah on reasons for juvenile crime.

'High serotonin levels in the brain equal aggression, I know that, Sue, but vitamins?'

Jonah had read the report and was not in a good mood. 'Home Office seeing banged-up hoodlums get their ABC pills? Don't the silly buggers realize the young gentlemen will be off like a shot to the human rights crows in Brussels to demand large sums for chemical assault?'

'I checked with Clive first,' Max told him. 'It's legal – ensuring a healthy diet.'

A quiet stream of expletives was Jonah's way of coming to terms with a new idea.

'Would you say some form of malnutrition could excuse the criminal?' Max asked them.

It was Sue's turn to be indignant. 'No, never! Look what happens with alcohol. Judges go easy because an idiot robs or kills when he's out of his skull and the next thing everyone's offering, "Sorry, me lud, I was drunk at the time."'

Jonah blew his nose, trumpeting endorsement. 'A very useful line of defence, very useful – being too pissed to know what you were doing.'

'Especially when they all chose, of their own free will, to drink themselves stupid in the beginning,' Sue added bitterly. 'There's no difference between an angry person taking a knife to someone or a drunkard getting in a car to drive over any victim in their way.'

Max would have gone on debating the issue all morning but Jonah thought of pressing matters and Sue went back to her desk to shape words around a photograph of a capybara, the world's largest rodent. It had escaped from a research unit and was free to roam. The size of a large dog, it might terrify but the animal was vegetarian and would probably die when nights and stream water became too cold for it.

The image of Andy Passmore's tight little face rose and persisted. Would she enjoy the story of an animal that had found its freedom? Passmore was a clever girl who had been well cared for as a child, no malnutrition to blame. Self-control, too, enough to plan indiscriminate slaughter.

Clever?

'Of course! She sent the look-alike to Vienna to see if he'd be arrested. If he was, the police were on to her and Gibson.'

Cigarette smoke wreathed in her vicinity. 'Talking to yourself, darling? I'd better send for the men in white coats.'

'No. Just thinking aloud.'

'Anything useful?'

Sue shook her head and Kate went on her way, leaving Sue to wonder what evil was in Passmore's dreams. The need to find the girl who could answer so many questions burnt in Sue with a strong, persistent flame.

Sue sat in her car in Wakeham Street, Sean Beck's photo propped against the steering wheel. The phone book had not revealed Beck's address in Green Lanes, neither had the electoral register. She had spent a fruitless evening there, watching for him, before deciding the next attempt must include his girlfriend, hence the sojourn in Wakeham Street.

There was a rapping on the glass. A man in his forties, sweat shirt and jeans speckled with paint, peered in at Sue. He seemed nice, harmless, and she rolled down her window.

'You OK?' he asked

'Yes, thank you. I'm waiting for someone.'

He tutted and shook his head. 'Not a good place to do it.'

'I'm not giving him much longer, then I'm off.'

There was a new shrewdness in dark eyes. 'You the police?'

'No,' Sue assured him. 'Nothing like that.'

He nodded. 'I get you. Hubby trouble. You be careful.'

After he had gone she left the window open a little to clear the thin layer of steam obscuring her view of the street. It could be a good cover story, watching for a cheating husband, but would a mistress live in Wakeham Street? Who could tell what was hidden behind the closed doors and curtains?

An hour passed, another. Sue was convinced she was wasting her time yet she could not bring herself to start the engine. Beck was her only link with Passmore and the bombs. Instinct, blind hope, faith, kept her there until muscles cramped and she went home.

The routine of work helped Sue through the next day until she was free to drive again to Wakeham Street. There was a café with a good view of the houses and she sat by its window with cooling coffee.

'Anything else?'

Sue looked up at dry blonde hair hanging round a thin, tired face. The girl could not be much more than fifteen but her T-shirt bulged hugely and her eyes had the deadness of lost hope.

'Another coffee, please.'

115

'Nothing to eat?' A list of things with chips was reeled off in a sad monotone.

Sue took pity on the pregnant child and asked for bacon and egg. It might be a long evening and would save the gesture of a meal when she arrived home.

The food came quite quickly and was surprisingly good, the girl smiling as Sue ate. Sipping fresh coffee, Sue wondered about her waitress. She was far too young to be fully developed physically and her baby was effectively a parasite, feeding off its mother to her detriment. Sue doubted there had been a boost of folic acid before conception, probably no regular vitamins or check-ups since.

A movement in the street drew Sue's attention. A large, sleek car had drawn up fifty yards away. From it stepped a man not yet in his middle years. He flicked glances around him as he locked the car's doors, and there was no doubt it was Sean Beck. To the details of his picture could be added the way he swung round, pivoting like a boxer, before he strode across the road. Not tall, he was quick, well muscled and walked with his head held forward.

Sue noted the number of the building at which he stopped. Beck ignored the bell, used a key and was inside at speed, the door shut. She finished her meal and went back to her own car, ready to follow Beck.

It was not a long wait. Beck reappeared with a tall young woman, dusky-skinned and with dark hair rippling past her shoulders. She was wrapped in a fun-fur coat which had never seen a real leopard, and when the coat flapped open Sue could see a tiny skirt and slim legs. The couple were laughing as they passed Sue, so intent on each other there was never any likelihood of them noticing a lone female. She let them reach the corner of the street before hurrying after them on foot.

Their destination was a tandoori restaurant, Le Raj, but Sue hesitated to go in. Apart from the fact that she had already eaten, a woman on her own might be too noticeable amongst the dining couples. She decided to go home, the rest of Beck's evening clearly mapped out in her imagination.

The next night followed the same routine, although Beck arrived in Wakeham Street an hour earlier. She waited to see if he came out again and, after a very long delay, Beck and the girl started walking in the opposite direction from Le Raj. Sue was glad to move, stretching stiff muscles as she used her new skill of shadowing all the way to the bright lights and spicy aromas of the New Kashmir's dining room. Definitely a man who likes curries, Sue decided as she walked back to her car and drove home to a salad.

Evening surveillance revealed a pattern. If Beck arrived in Wakeham Street late, he spent little time in the flat before seeking his supper. Early, and there was a long delay until Beck and the girl walked slowly, entwined and oblivious to passers-by.

Sue compiled a list of their favoured eating places. It included every curry house within walking distance. On the one evening the couple stayed at home, a Chinese takeaway was delivered.

Beck's social life might have been recorded but Benny Rogers had not produced even one of the dealer's business contacts. Sue demanded an explanation from Jonah.

'Bloody little scrote's two-timing, you mark my words.'

He was still smoking heavily and the emphysema was gaining ground. She wondered how much longer Jonah could go on with his punishing schedule of crime scenes, police stations and courts.

'Will extra cash help?' she asked. 'I can manage more if that's what it takes.'

'Still feeling guilty for young Anil? You shouldn't.'

'Why not? If I can help catch the bombers, maybe then I can ask why me?'

'Sue, don't expect an answer from nutters that'll make any sense – even if you do find 'em.'

'If?'

'Just a hunch.'

He turned to Beth who wanted a cut of fifty words in his front page copy. Sue left them to the usual argument and sat at her desk, ignoring her monitor as she swivelled this way and that, chasing an idea. It was still obsessing her as she drove home.

Shoes kicked off and the kettle switched on, Sue was ready to flop into a chair when the doorbell rang. Without her shoes she had to stand on tiptoe to identify her caller.

'Pippa! Come in. Cuppa?'

Settled by the flames of the gas fire the two women cradled their mugs.

'Ken OK?'

'He's fine. Busy – you know how it is.'

Sue knew only too well because Colin had worked with Ken. They had shared the same chores which must be dealt with in the evening if clients were to be satisfied. 'And you?'

'Better after lunch.' Pippa stroked a belly hardly swollen. She looked up at Sue. 'I should ask you what you've been up to?'

Sue's surprise had Pippa chuckling.

'Being your neighbour has its downside, you know,' she told Sue. 'I've been getting calls from Sam trying to find if you're with Miles, then Miles rings to ask if you're working late or out at an official dinner. Have you ditched Tweedledum and Tweedledee for yet another admirer?'

At first Sue was annoyed, then her sense of humour focused the situation into perspective. 'I'm sorry they've been pestering you. It was just something I wanted to do and I knew they'd both be against it.'

'Then you are going after the animal people yourself.

118

Oh Sue, you know what Stephen said – and Ken. It's dangerous.'

'I've been nowhere near the bombers,' she protested. 'There was supposed to be one at Heathrow that day when I was tucked in a side room with half the Met and Special Branch.'

Pippa was not convinced. 'I know you. You've some kind of lead you want to follow and you won't let go – or let anyone help you.'

'That's just it. I think I have to get help – of a kind.'

'Anwar?' Sue had made contact with Anil's brother at work in a large firm of accountants.

'Mrs Bennett.' The voice was deeper than she remembered. 'Do you have a problem?'

'I'm not sure. Could we meet after work today? Somewhere near you?'

'Of course,' he agreed, suggesting the place and the time.

Shortly after five thirty Sue was waiting outside a narrow-fronted restaurant in Red Lion Street, not far from Anwar's office in High Holborn. He arrived promptly, looking older in City clothes.

She was ushered into a restaurant almost empty at that hour, then led towards the back and up a flight of stairs to a small dining room. A waiter brought tea and tiny cakes. Anwar poured an aromatic brew, added slices of lemon, offered sugar.

Sue sipped, startled by the fragrance and the subtle bite of the liquid. 'This is delicious.'

Anwar smiled, something she had not yet witnessed, and his resemblance to Anil was uncanny. 'It gives pleasure as well as a clear head. Now, your problem. Is it to do with Anil's murderers? My father talks to Superintendent Ashford regularly but there is no progress.'

'I believe the superintendent wants those who caused the explosions as badly as do you or I.'

'Then why are the vermin not in custody?' There was an

imperious tilt to Anwar's head and, for a moment, Sue could see his father as a young man.

'Your vermin are two insignificant people in London.' She outlined for him her own struggle to find Passmore and Gibson, the Heathrow incident, the frustration she felt all around her.

'This man you have been following, he's one of them?'

'I don't think so, merely the most likely supplier of the Semtex.'

'Which blew my brother apart,' Anwar said softly. 'He should answer with his own death.'

'First, let him lead us to the others.'

'You say you've tried that without success?'

'Not entirely. Part of Beck's life I feel I know quite well. It's his business contacts I have to find.'

'The man you paid has been no help?'

'Not enough. It's very likely he's running with the hare and the hounds.'

'A double agent. Unpleasant – but he could give you information if he chose?'

'Benny would never give anybody anything, that's why . . .'

'You thought of me?'

Sue was unsure if she should involve him. Studying the very young man she saw grief and bitterness cross-hatched in his face and knew he needed action, as she did.

'Anil often talked of your father. He told me once he was the accountant for many Indian restaurants in London. Beck could be one of their best customers.'

Anwar was intrigued but wary as Sue told him of the evenings she had watched Beck and his woman.

'You might be able to help me find an angle on Beck's behaviour. Something which might never occur to the police – or to me.'

'You say the man eats only curry?'

Sue nodded. 'I've a list of the ones he's visited in the evenings but I've no idea where he goes for lunch, or who he meets.'

120

'Mm. Interesting. Tell me, have you been in any of these places when he talks to waiters?'

'No, although I did see him ordering on one occasion. I was outside.'

'How did he do it? Give his order?'

Sue closed her eyes as she conjured up the moment. It had been clear, the evening light holding well. Beck and his companion had been easily seen, the candle on their table burning brightly. 'He held the menu and read from it, slowly, as if reading was not easy.'

'Did he look at the waiter?'

'No. Not at any time.'

'Good. It means we are invisible to him.' Anwar grinned and was suddenly young and mischievous. 'I have friends who would be prepared to help.' He rang a bell and the soft-footed waiter appeared, deferential until Anwar invited the boy to sit with them. 'Sube is the son of the owner – a friend of my father's.'

Sube turned liquid eyes to Sue. 'I was at school with Anwar. He was older and protected me.'

Anwar leaned towards Sue. 'Mrs Bennett –'

'Please, Sue.'

'Very well, Sue. I would like to watch with you this evening. We could eat in the same place as this man Beck and I will be able to identify him.'

'After that?'

'I don't know. It may be possible to have him followed.'

Sue was concerned for the boy. 'Promise me you'll take no chances.'

'Believe me, Sue, I'm in no danger, nor are any of our friends. Our skins make us invisible to men like him – but he will learn respect,' Anwar said with a soft sibilance which chilled.

'There must be no violence.'

'Don't worry. When I first knew Anil was dead I could have taken his murderers by the throat and ended their miserable existences. Since then I've had time to think. Killing them quickly would be a blessing for such people.

121

Rotting in a stinking prison would be a much better fate – for them and for this Beck person.'

'He's managed to escape the police so far. It won't be easy getting him convicted.'

Anwar had matured and it was a man's smile that reassured her. 'The law of this land is very comprehensive. I'm sure Beck's committed many crimes the police do not yet know about.'

Sandy's voice was raised, his arguments reaching most of the newsroom. 'Sue will back me!'

She looked towards the verbal scuffle, wondering what Steve Bynorth was doing slumming it amongst the lower classes of the *Journal*.

'The infamous Ms Bennett? What's her opinion worth these days?'

Bynorth's sneer had a few interested listeners prepared to relax in their chairs and enjoy the skirmish. It also brought out Sue's defenders.

'Steve! How nice of you to visit us poor mortals and drop your pearls of wisdom.'

Kate was welcoming in a way which made Sue shudder. She knew Kate in this mood. Only blood flowing from the enemy would satisfy.

'I thought you'd become so much the Eurocrat you despised us Britishers.'

'Not at all,' he said smoothly, 'but one does get anxious now and again about the mad cow situation. One hardly knows where it will crop up next.' He glanced around the newsroom. 'Here's as likely as anywhere, I would think.'

Kate's chin was up. 'Do you? Think, I mean? I know we all have to be careful and use words of one syllable for you now you root in the troughs of Brussels and have forgotten you're English.'

'Go to Paris, Kate,' Bynorth advised. 'A little culture wouldn't come amiss. I could recommend a stylist who might be able to do something with your hair.'

Hardly pausing for breath Kate swept her gaze across the increasing forehead of her adversary. 'How kind – especially as I see you've almost lost yours.'

Sue relaxed. Cary was in the States picking up gossip at a race meeting and Kate had been spoiling for a good row.

'Sue, give us a minute, will you?'

Jonah did not waste oxygen on unnecessary words. She followed him out of the door, to the quietness of the corridor leading to Sam's office.

'I've had a couple of calls this morning. There's the beginnings of a story. It's the animal people.'

'Animal Equality?'

'That's them. They're at it again but this time it's big – and I mean big.'

'More bombs,' she whispered.

'A letter, sent by e-mail. It quoted the blast here as well as the frozen food ones which made Atherton's cough up – and the burger bar. It added a reminder of their skill at planting explosives.'

'Who're they targeting this time?'

'The full list? I've no idea. From my sources I know of at least four firms which've been contacted. There could well be more.'

'Oh God, no! It's a mail shot.'

'And then some,' Jonah groaned. 'A quarter of a million each – or else.'

Chapter Seven

As far as the public was concerned, life went on as normal. Headlines in all the media centred on another Al Qaeda scare and the affected flights to the US and Middle East. Of terror at home, in the capital, there was not the slightest hint, Animal Equality never mentioned, the news blackout on that subject imposed by the police. In the *Journal* offices it was forty-eight hours before a clear picture emerged. Jonah had stayed at his desk making every possible contact while Sam had the City experts checking any firm which might have been targeted. It proved to be a long list.

Jonah growled as the story grew, snippet by snippet. On the first day he had beckoned Sue to him and handed her a fax from an informant, a copy of an e-mail. It was addressed to the chairman of a huge meat packing firm and had been sent to his home.

We deplore the criminal ways in which animals are treated in the death camps run by you. Animals have the same right to live as you do and we are dedicated to freeing them from the pain you inflict on them. You must be despised and shunned by everyone and we will continue to fight for this with every means in our power.

Time you bastards paid. Five (5) minutes before end trading Friday have £250,000 ready to move on computer.

NO POLICE. Remember Oxford Street and the Journal.

The words 'Animal Equality' and the equals sign across the diagonal of a Z ended the letter.

Sue read it again and again and was puzzled. 'Has Sam seen this?'

'Nope. Take it to him, will you? I can't leave the phone.'

Sam looked up from his work, a smile starting in his eyes when he saw Sue. He took the paper she offered and read swiftly. 'They don't hang about, do they? A quarter of a million? Only a few companies have to run scared and they're laughing.'

'There's something . . .' Sue was thoughtful.

'About the letter? I'd guess two fists involved.'

Sam tapped the last couple of paragraphs. 'When they get to the cash the tone changes. Less rhetoric.'

'That part doesn't feel like Passmore. Perhaps it's the mystery man from Vienna.'

'Unlikely. He's an out-of-work actor who looks vaguely like Gibson. Ashford's having him watched round the clock.'

'So, he's not been picked up. That follows.'

'What does?'

'I wondered if he'd been set up by the terrible two to see if the police were on their trail. If the decoy was arrested they'd know they'd been identified and go to ground.'

'That's Ashford's reasoning.'

She pointed to the fax. 'At least the original e-mails should be traceable.'

'They were, within minutes. No luck. All from a cyber café in Willesden. Too small for CCTV and usually inhabited by geeks, so I'm told. Ashford's got people on chasing them up but he doesn't hold out much hope. It may have been a first visit by a gormless teen who'd been asked to do it for a laugh.'

'Ashford's confiding in you?'

'Quid pro quo. He expects us to pass on all we hear.' Sam's face darkened. 'We do have a vested interest in getting them behind bars. Three very good reasons, for

125

starters – and Peacock's wife lost her baby. It was their first.'

Sue felt tears rise and tried not to sniff. Sam saw her distress and became brisk, cheerful.

'Don't forget I'm picking you up early tonight. Celia's putting on a special meal to celebrate your return to normality.'

Celia had been married to Sam's brother until an IRA bullet found its mark. When she began a new family Sam was included as an honorary uncle.

'You're sure the children will be safe?'

He smiled. 'Sure.'

As she made her way back to her desk Sue pondered the bombers' promises. They could still have enough Semtex to cause chaos. How many people were enjoying life today, not knowing they were condemned to be slaughtered when the Friday deadline passed? It was a massive change of tactics, and if only one firm being blackmailed paid up there would be enough funds for unlimited explosives.

It irritated Sue that she could do nothing useful, and she dialled the Holborn office. 'Anwar. Any news?'

'We are making progress,' he told her and she could hear excitement in his voice although he tried to sound very adult. 'Several of Anil's friends have joined us and we should have a list for you soon.'

'That's terrific! There's been no danger?'

'My dear Sue, I told you. As far as our quarry is concerned we do not even exist. Should any of us be spotted there is no way we could be identified – we all look the same to Beck and his friends.' Anwar's loathing of the man travelled through the line. 'It will be most enjoyable when we can expose his activities but I am finding it very hard to wait. It will be such a joy when Beck realizes the least of his fellow men, as he would consider us, put him behind bars.'

'Please be careful.'

'Don't worry. We look and listen. We make notes and my

cousin, Sunitra, sits at her computer. She gets much of the information we need.'

'Hacking's illegal!'

Across London, Anwar tutted. 'Sunitra is not hacking. She tests the security systems of installations for their insurers. Whatever information she obtains is reported by the insurance companies to the firms under investigation – along with a suggested program to remedy the problem. It is all very civilized and Sunitra earns very good fees.' There was a pause then, 'It is for Anil she passes on information and then only to me. I use what we need, the rest is destroyed.'

When the line went dead Sue was left wondering if she would stand in the dock herself and be accused of innumerable crimes, not the least of them conspiracy.

It would be worth it.

'How's Pippa?' Sam asked. He was driving to Blackheath as fast as the traffic would allow.

'She's fine – trying to make up her mind to marry Ken.'

'If she's decided to keep the baby it's no longer her decision.'

'No?'

'The child's future is at stake. It gets a say in what happens.'

'It's Pippa's future, too.'

'And Ken's,' Sam reminded her. 'At least he's already come out in favour of a commitment to family.' He had to spend time and energy coping with a rogue driver determined to force his way into an orderly queue at traffic lights.

'Pippa's always been so independent,' Sue murmured when they were at last on the move again and Sam was more calm. 'It'll take time for her to adjust.'

'She gets the statutory nine months any woman does. What's important is the aftermath. A baby needs two parents – and she'd do well to remember it.'

'I thought you liked Pippa?'

'I do. I think she's a terrific girl but the feminist attitude to independence is no help when it means you're on your own all night, every night, with a screaming baby.'

Traffic snarled around them and Sam muttered under his breath at idiot drivers as he manoeuvred his way through. Sue's thoughts were elsewhere, hearing Pippa . . .

'Come on, Sue,' her friend had protested. 'You can't keep two men like Miles and Sam dangling indefinitely. They understand about Colin – we all do. A year and a day it used to be.'

Sue had put up her hand to ward off more. 'I know – but grieving doesn't stop because days turn into weeks and then months.'

Pippa had knelt by Sue, holding her as tears flowed. 'Colin will always be part of you and neither of your would-be men would have it otherwise. Has one an edge on the other?'

Sue's lips had formed a 'no' but it had been a hesitant one.

'Tell me.'

'I like being with both of them – as friends. With Miles I feel comfortable. It's as though he knows how I think and he makes the time we spend together so enjoyable. I look forward to seeing him.'

'And Sam?'

It had been difficult to breathe. 'Sometimes he frightens me, Pippa.'

'Sam? He would never hurt you! He might put you on a pedestal and keep the rest of us at bay with whips –'

'Not that sort of fear. It's not physical. I know he loves me and I know it's total. That's what's scary.'

It had been warm in Pippa's flat and Sue was tired, her eyelids heavy with sleep.

'No,' her friend had said softly. 'What you fear is loving anyone as you did Colin – only to be hurt again.'

A blaring horn dragged Sue back to the present. Another

driver had objected to Sam's cornering but the culprit was unrepentant.

'It's amazing how many firms have been approached – and that's only the ones we know about.'

Sue realized he was talking about the blackmail. 'There can't surely be that many businesses dealing with animals?'

'No? Big holding companies like to diversify – they need to if they're to survive and grow. Quite a few have food production units in their portfolios. Take Gillingham's, for example.'

'The hotel chain?'

'That's their public face. They also have a furniture factory as well as an abattoir and packing plant, poultry units and a cannery.'

'I bet foot and mouth hit them, and BSE before that, not to mention salmonella.'

'Swings and roundabouts. With BSE, for example, they made a mint killing off elderly cattle as well as selling extra chickens and turkeys. They're used to coping with those sorts of crises.'

'You're saying Gillingham's got a demand?'

Sam nodded as he waited for lights to change. 'So did Beta Construction.'

'Why them? Do they build cattle pens?'

'It's not official yet but they're taking over Watson's, the butchery chain.'

'And Passmore knew that?'

'It'd seem so, yet it's very specialized knowledge.'

It was quiet in the powerful car. Sue was frowning. 'No pharmaceuticals?'

'Very few, so far.' He glanced at Sue. 'Something bothering you?'

'I've taken on board everything I could about Andy Passmore. I've tried to get under her skin, think like her. There's no doubt she's been the planner in all this, it's her forte. I know she thinks big, breathtakingly so, but all this financial stuff is so detailed that when I'm trying to think of it like she does, I'm overwhelmed.'

'Perhaps it's Gibson's style?'

Sue shook her head. 'The big chemical firms and their labs, that's where his grudges would lie – and his knowledge. He'd know which of them used animals in research and I'd have expected those to be targeted first.'

'Makes sense. Perhaps their early attempts to get cash for the cause were so successful they decided to punish a wide range of firms by hitting balance sheets.'

'Will they pay? Those who've had the e-mails?'

'I expect a few already have.'

'A quarter of a million? Just like that?'

'Even if they're not insured for such a crime they can probably get the money offset against tax. Then it's not so much and remaining capital is safe.'

Sue's brow furrowed. 'Against tax? That means . . .'

'In practice, every taxpayer in the country forks out. That much less for hospitals and schools.'

She was silenced by the scale of the crime.

'As for the *Journal*, we've a massive outlay in staff time and resources on a story which can't be printed.' Sam's determined jaw jutted upwards. 'When it can I'll make sure it's a fitting epitaph for young Anil, as well as Barber and Peacock.'

They were nearly at Blackheath. 'The children will be safe?' she asked again.

'Yes. I cleared it with Ashford. He thinks our young terrorists are too busy making money to bother with the minor detail of a nosy journalist.'

At the door in Blackheath Celia was small and serene. Sue was hugged and, 'We've missed you' whispered in her ear.

Peter was older, a slight stoop reducing his height a little, extra grey in his hair and beard. He took both of Sue's hands in his. 'Welcome back,' was all he managed before Rosalind and Phoebe were hanging from Sue's arms

130

like two blonde limpets while Adam, a dignified school-boy, stiffly butted her shoulder.

In the basement kitchen which looked out on a garden given over to grass and children, Celia stirred a casserole. Sue could smell fresh herbs and lemon blending with vegetables and chicken. Wide-eyed, Phoebe was listening to a tall tale from Sam, Rosalind arranged cutlery with all the care she could muster and Adam helped his father with the wine, carrying Sue's with such studied nonchalance she found it hard not to smile.

There was the aura of a party and the children were unwilling to leave the table for their beds. Only when Sam promised to inspect the latest additions to Adam's dino-saur collection and Sue allowed herself to be dragged away by Phoebe, did the procession upstairs begin. Rosa-lind snuggled under her duvet but Phoebe climbed on Sue's lap with the book she had chosen.

It was difficult for adult eyes to stay open. The story of Flopsy Bunny had been used so often to persuade Sue to sleep she could almost hear her father's voice and had to fight hard to stay awake. The familiar words were read aloud and Rosalind succumbed quickly but Phoebe was intent on the pictures as Sue turned the pages.

At last the little girl's head was heavy and Sue lifted her. Phoebe stirred, nestling into Sue's neck. There was an ache, a longing, then Phoebe was covered, the two sleeping girls kissed, while from downstairs the smell of fresh coffee tempted.

'Thank you for that.' Peter smiled as he handed Sue her cup.

'My pleasure. How on earth do you manage to get your children to behave so normally?'

'He is a child psychiatrist,' Sam reminded her.

'Exactly.' She grinned at Peter. 'You and your colleagues are supposed to be the cause of all problems in homes and schools.'

Peter was rueful. 'We deserve it – some of us. The rest believe that from day one the parents must be in control.

131

If it is so, the baby senses it and rebellions are brief, normal contests of strength. As long as the parents win each time, and with as little fuss as possible, the child grows up to feel secure.'

Sam was not so sure. 'Pity it doesn't work for gymslip mums.'

'You had quite a spread on that recently,' Celia said. 'Poor little souls. At thirteen their hormones are in turmoil, just at the time they're trying to move from the fantasy world of childhood.'

Peter reminded them of the dolls available to some schools which worked so well girls were only allocated one if parents signed an agreement. 'The electronic marvel is programmed to start crying and screaming at unpredict-able times, the noise lasting minutes, maybe hours, and there's no way of altering it. At the end of the contract the girl's shattered – as is the whole family.'

'Why just girls? Shouldn't boys have the dolls too?' Sue asked.

'Perhaps they should do,' Celia agreed, 'especially if they're indulging in under-age sex. It would be a massive reminder of the consequences of their actions.'

Sue mentally stored the information and Sam grinned at her. 'More data for Sandy?'

'Is that the journalist who was badly injured?' Peter wanted to know. 'How is he now?'

'Fine,' said Sam. 'We try to make sure there's no undue strain.'

'Has he had counselling?'

'Not as far as I know.' Sam looked at Sue and raised an eyebrow.

'No, he hasn't. Not many took advantage of the offer.'

'What about you?' Celia asked.

Sue hesitated. 'Talking won't help me. I need to know if I did anything which made them choose to kill me and destroy the *Journal*. No counsellor can give me that.'

Peter did not argue and the ensuing conversation was easy, unforced. As the evening passed Sue relaxed, tension gradually wiped away as silently as mist dispersing at sunrise.

There were hugs for Sue when Sam held open the car door for her. 'Come again,' Celia said. 'I like to cook for people who appreciate my efforts.'

Peter echoed his wife's plea. 'Any time, Sue. You know that,' he said with a gentle smile and Sue wondered if the invitation was for a meal or to talk.

It was late and Sue was dozing against the soft leather. Sam glanced at her when he could, a smile flickering at the sight of her beside him. Traffic was sparse at that time of night and the return to Islington was swift.

'You're home,' Sam told Sue with quiet regret.

She struggled awake, thanked him for the evening and brushed an unthinking kiss across his cheek. She was out of the car and across the pavement in moments. He watched her turn at the door and wave, then she was safely inside, not knowing what it had cost him to let her go.

Since Karin's outburst on the subject of bimbos she had been very careful to tread warily around Sue. Everything asked of her was carried out promptly and her copy was increasingly good. In addition she watched Kate. As she did, Sue was intrigued to see Karin's appearance gradually improve. The once dull hair gleamed, its colour became lighter and new pastel shirts tinted and warmed her skin.

It was obvious the girl must have a reason for her attitude, but Karin was intelligent and her hang-ups she must sort out for herself, Sue decided. There were far more important matters pressing for attention. Jonah would have to be pushed hard to let her see Benny Rogers but in the busy newsroom there was no time for wandering thoughts.

'I suppose you're deep into this jellyfish business?' Kate was wrapped in an emerald green pashmina and the newest Givenchy.

'Me? No. I've persuaded Meg to let Paula have a go on her own.'

'You're risking her on a sizeable spread?'

'It's time and it's hardly a major scoop. Every paper will be on to it after tomorrow.'

'Jellyfish?' Kate flourished her cigarette and a graceful swirl of smoke emphasized contempt.

'Don't despise them. They can be breathtakingly beautiful. They can also be totally deadly.'

For someone with such a high gin intake, Kate's eyes were clear and lustrous. 'To humans?'

'Even in a relatively harmless variety the sting's a powerful irritant. A few of those and you're in agony. A young child on a beach can be at risk in seconds.'

The phone on Sue's desk rang and Kate walked away as she answered it.

'Sue? Anwar Naib. Can you meet me this evening?' He sounded as if he was trying to curb enthusiasm and a frisson of excitement grew in her.

'Of course. Where and when?'

'Same time and place?'

She assured him she would be there and was intrigued when he told her gleefully, 'I don't think you'll be disappointed.'

Sue was impatient and left work early to get to Holborn. Punctual to the second she was spotted, the door opened and a beaming Sube led her to the upstairs room. Talking ceased as she entered and Sue was startled to find herself the focus of innumerable eyes.

'Anil had many good friends,' Anwar said softly. One by one he introduced them as they stood round the table. 'Deepak, Karim, Vidya, Chatan, Nirmal, Gauri.'

There was no way Sue could remember all the names but she gave a nod of acknowledgement to each of them. Only one had remained seated, a very beautiful girl with chiselled bones and a flawless skin.

'Mira,' Anwar said with pride.

There was a rustle as everyone settled and gazed at Sue with the same eager intent as Anwar. He was obviously the unofficial chairman of the evening.

'We have a list for you,' he told her and from a large envelope took several sheets of paper which he handed to her.

A quick glance revealed tightly packed names, addresses, restaurants used, banking details, company membership, holiday homes. A few of the men so carefully detailed even had a startling collection of mistresses.

'How did you —'

Sue was silenced by a smiling Anwar with a finger to his lips. His companions chuckled, pleased with the results of their diligence and persistence.

'How, is not important. As Beck was tracked he led us to so many other little groups. Each of those had its own ramifications. For example, here is Beck with two men and their wives.'

A photograph, the definition good, was handed to Sue. Beck's companions looked solid, respectable, the women rather dull. She was passed another shot. The men were the same but they seemed to be at a rather boisterous party.

'Who are they?'

'Accountants. They like to enjoy themselves away from home. Beck supplies the women.'

A pile of prints was in front of Sue, Beck in each one and the names of his contacts carefully itemized on the back. Some were indoor scenes while others had been taken outside with a zoom lens, the focusing sharp, clear.

'There's a reference number tying each of the prints to the list,' Anwar explained. 'I hope this will all be of use to you?'

'It's incredible! I can't believe you could all have done this so quickly.'

'It's not usual for us to be asked to help in this way but it was for Anil. Beck was easily followed. As he met people

135

during the day we used whatever method was appropriate to identify them. It took a little time but we were not hampered by police methods – although we did not break the law. Mira made sure of that.'

Mira inclined her head regally. She was formally dressed in a black suit with a white high-collared shirt. The clothes were tailored, expensive, reminding Sue of barristers.

There had been so much effort made to help her. 'I can't begin to thank you enough.'

'All we ask is that Anil's killers – and Beck – are punished. What you, or the police, do with the rest of the material is irrelevant, although I would suggest you draw Superintendent Ashford's attention to the men starred on the third page.'

Sue turned to the sheet he had specified. There were four asterisks, each followed by a name and a very senior police ranking. 'How did you get all this information?'

'From their bar bills. They used credit cards to pay and Sunitra had little trouble matching up account numbers and identity. After that we made sure there was a photo to show them enjoying life with Beck – just to add emphasis.'

'Something disturbs you?' Mira asked. 'You have my word no law on the statute books has been broken – not even slightly bent.'

'It's not that.' Sue looked at Anwar. 'You mentioned Ashford. I'd prefer to get this into police hands discreetly. Our agreement is separate from *Journal* business and I'd like to keep it that way.'

Some of the young men were restless, made uneasy by Sue's reaction. Like them, Anwar needed reassurance. He pointed to the papers and photos.

'All this will go to the police and Beck will be arrested?'

'You have my word. There's a chief inspector I know and can trust. He can make sure no hint of these lists reaches anyone who might try to escape due processes.'

'Ah! I take your point. The corrupt officers might be warned. You will deal with your chief inspector and we will go on watching. Any more information which could be of use, we'll see it reaches you.'

There were murmurs and nods of agreement from all those around the table.

'None of us will stop until Anil's murderers have been dealt with to our satisfaction.'

Anwar's words were quiet, light, but Sue shivered.

Back at the *Journal* it took time for photocopies to be made of all the lists and photographs gathered by Anwar and his friends. A technician came to help but Sue thanked her with a smile and insisted it was no bother. As she waited for finished material to roll Sue sat at a nearby desk and added the data compiled by Sunitra to a disk of her own research into Passmore and Gibson. It was time-consuming and boring, the men and women on the lists merely ciphers until they could be matched against the photographs.

Before she left her desk Sue checked a number and dialled. There were the usual delays and connections until a familiar voice was in her ear.

'Stephen, I've got some information which might be useful but it's a bit sensitive. I'd like to hand it over to you personally and make sure there're no accidents.'

'Me? Shouldn't it go to Ashford?'

'I'm hoping it will eventually. I'd be glad, once you've had a look at it, if you can get it to him without it being seen by anyone else.'

'You're saying there's something iffy in it?'

'Yes. Maybe there's no connecting those particular items to the bombers but my sources picked up more than I bargained for.'

'Right. Go home and stay put. I'll get there as soon as I can.'

Sue tidied her desk and made her way back to the flat, feeling more hopeful than for some time.

She had made sandwiches and was brewing coffee before

the doorbell rang. The monitor showed Stephen moving from one foot to the other in the cold night air.

'Come on up,' she called and released the front door lock.

'I'm glad to see you're still following safety measures.' It had been Stephen who had helped her install them when she had been haunted and stalked by Colin's murderer.

'Habit.'

Tall and muscular, Stephen had fine-boned features. He had taken off his raincoat and was smoothing short, light brown hair when Sue returned from the kitchen with a full coffee pot. She filled a large mug and persuaded him to take a sandwich.

'Well? The information?'

Sue handed him one of the large envelopes she had brought home with her, settling herself where she could easily watch his expression. He scanned the data on the first page then stared at Sue.

'How did you come by this?'

'Legally.'

'Is it *Journal* material?'

She shook her head. 'No, it's private.'

'Sue, I warned you to leave the hunt for Anil's killers to the professionals.'

'I wish I could but they were the ones made it personal.'

'I doubt it was. More likely they saw your name on an article and it gave them an excuse to use you.'

'I wish I could believe it.'

The depth of longing in her voice surprised him. 'Try,' he said gently, then turned his attention to the sheets of names.

Sue had a notebook and pencil to hand, ready to record data which attracted Stephen's attention. His professionalism ensured a mask over any emotion but Sue had also been well trained. In her case it was to detect and interpret the slightest change in the behaviour of an animal. To a casual observer Stephen was going through the list and giving no hint of interest or surprise. But Sue noted the position on each page to which his eyes returned a second, even a third time.

'The asterisks are important,' she said quietly as he began to read the third sheet.

'Important? They're dynamite! I can see now why you wanted to make sure all this went directly to Ashford.'

'I can trust Sergeant Webley and Inspector Eden. I wasn't sure who Ashford might send.'

'You're right to be cautious. Even Special Branch has the odd little bird which might sing to some guv'nor they've served under in the past.'

'The photographs are pretty conclusive.'

Stephen reached into the envelope and took out the thick pile of prints held together by an elastic band. Sue had numbered them on the back and made sure they were in numerical order. She kept a careful account as Stephen examined each one. Some were scrutinized longer than others and Sue made unobtrusive notes of the ones on which he lingered.

'The negatives?' he asked.

'My sources have them.'

'And you're not saying.' He smiled. 'I'll make a guess. Most have been taken in restaurants, Indian restaurants to be exact. The boy who borrowed your car was popular and his father important. If you're working with his friends I'll say no more – providing I have your word no law's been broken?'

'Better than my word, that of a QC in the making.'

When Stephen realized no more information was coming his way he got up to go. 'I'd better get these notes to Ashford. He'll go ballistic when he sees who you've unearthed.'

After he left, Sue locked the door and matched her notes against the copy of the lists and the photos she had made. Closing her eyes she recalled Stephen's exact movements, stopping when he did and circling the name. The photographs were counted and the ones identified in her own notes put on one side. Comparing lists and prints gave her an indication which of Beck's contacts were already known to the police.

'The trouble is,' she told the coffee mugs as she began to tidy up, 'I'm still no nearer Passmore and Gibson.'

Sue spent what was left of the evening checking and cross-checking data until her eyes began to swim with the strain. At one point the phone got her to her feet. It was Miles, anxious to know how she was, yet having to postpone tomorrow's dinner meeting so he could visit James.

'Any improvement?'

'Not really. Anne insists there's no problem between James and her so-called friend but I don't know. I want to see for myself – if you don't mind?'

'Of course not. Go and get it sorted out. I hope James is himself again soon.'

The flat was quiet and Sue could make no more progress until she could get amongst the *Journal*'s records of past articles as well as the database Julian had organized for Jonah's department. As she finally made the decision to go to bed the phone rang again.

'Sue?' The awkward breathing told her who it was.

'Jonah, I've just been thinking about you.'

'I won't be in tomorrow. Some bloody test the sawbones thinks is a good idea.'

'If you're doing as you're told at long last, I'm –'

'It's Benny. He wants a meet. You'll have to go on your own. Seven, tomorrow. Same place as last time.'

'I'll be there,' Sue promised.

Chapter Eight

A senior cleric was in disgrace. The original layout of the next front page had been scrapped and every member of the religious team produced copy to order. In the library Beryl worked hardest of all finding data on past decisions, practices, indiscretions.

'Makes a change from political low-life, I suppose,' Cary said.

He and Kate had silently agreed to suspend their pleasurable war and tear the clergy to pieces.

'Perhaps they should wear their underpants back to front?' she suggested. 'Others do.'

'It wouldn't make a blind bit of difference. If the urge is there, nothing stops it.'

'The voice of experience, darling?'

'If I'd bedded every woman you'd ever credited me with I'd no longer be able to crawl, let alone walk in here fresh as a daisy.'

Paula stalked towards them, her chin high, proud.

'Loved your jellyfish piece,' Kate threw at her. 'You must be improving.'

'Take no notice of her,' Cary advised the girl. 'Kate's in a bad mood because her rich bitch interview's been postponed.'

'How lovely for the bitch.' In spite of flaming cheeks Paula smiled sweetly before swinging out of range.

Behind her Kate stabbed the air with an empty holder. 'That girl's coming on. Before you know it she'll be

poached to do a column in one of the minor Sundays.'
There was reluctant respect in her voice.

Cary watched Kate screw another cigarette into place.
'Let's hope she's not the only one to go.'

'Of course! The board meeting's today? Here or in
town?'

'With the spartan hospitality Sam provides? It might
remind our masters how hard he works – and that would
never do.'

Kate was unusually serious. 'What are his chances of
hanging on?'

'My source on the board thought it a close call. Someone's been burning the midnight oil to persuade the members our recent blast was due to a weakness of
Haddleston's because his girlfriend works here.'

'How bloody ridiculous! Sue's acknowledged the best in
her field – and anyway, she was picked by Jepson.'

'Ah, but our late and unlamented editor had an eye for
the ladies,' Cary reminded Kate.

'Never Sue. Not Jepson. He knew he'd not get to first
base with her – let alone a home run.' Few on the staff had
liked Sam's predecessor, certainly not Kate. 'Anyway, that
fat slug only ever wanted to bed females with no brains.
With them he felt masculine and attractive.'

'But he could make money for the City boys. In the end
what matters? Now then, time for lunch? The new chef
they've got in the pub is doing duck quite well.'

Behind stacked reference books Sue had been an unwilling listener, unnoticed as she sat with head bent over copy
which needed a severe editing.

She was worried. Sam had not talked to her, or to
anyone, of the coming battle for his job. When Jepson's
stroke had left the editor's chair empty Sam, as deputy,
had taken over. Good returns had given him the promise
of a longer contract, nothing more.

There was a new tightness about the running of the
paper, a sense of purpose which had been lacking during
Jepson's tenure. The man had progressed from whim to

142

whim and his staff lacked certainty, loyalty. Sam had changed all that, forging a hard-working team of professionals as he raised the standard as well as the advertising revenue of the *Journal*.

Many would have been prepared to help Sam but he had confided in no one, believing today's boardroom arena one in which he must fight alone. With a sigh, Sue returned to the shapeless copy until Beth appeared.

'Your piece on the marvel that is the earthworm,' she said. 'Due to high-powered priest losing his trousers as well as his frock, it has to be cut to fifty words or postponed. Which do you want?'

'Postponed. The earthworms are introduced into a derelict area and not long afterwards it's possible to plant groves of alder and willow. The trees help reduce carbon dioxide, they take contaminants from the soil and can be cropped for cash. The idea is brilliantly simple and ought to be given a chance.'

'OK. I'll try for space tomorrow.'

Space, Sue thought as Beth ambled on her way. It was always at a premium, news and articles fitted in between adverts which paid overheads and created profits.

She worked steadily and when everyone sought their lunches, Sue picked up the folder from Anwar and went to the library. There, in her small office, the elderly librarian was enjoying a home-made salad, as a mug of soup steamed gently at her elbow.

'Do you need any help?'

'Thanks, Beryl, I know what I'm looking for.'

It was peaceful in the low-ceilinged room. Sue searched through archives, matching names from the list she had compiled after watching Stephen. Most were in past copies of the *Journal* and Sue noted the microfilm references before settling herself at a small screen, calling up data and making print-outs. By the time she sat back and rubbed her eyes there was a sizeable stack of paper. Sorting took a little time and she clipped together any copy on the same individual.

Beck certainly had friends at court, the reports on him all from cases dealt with at the crown variety. Sue matched photos to paragraphs and chuckled.

'Anything wrong, Sue?'

'No, I'm fine, thanks, Beryl. Shan't be much longer.'

'Take as long as you want. I've had my rush for the day.'

'Another tomorrow?'

'I expect so. There'll be a flood of calls about yet more clerics of all denominations who enjoy the odd sinful wallow. They're only men, after all.'

That was what had roused Sue's imp of mischief. All the references and cross-references she had worked on were of men. A case for suing Beck? He was definitely sexually biased when it came to working colleagues, women valuable only as light relief in bed.

She flicked through her collection of photographs. A few of the women Beck used were coloured but all the men were white. He was certainly no equal opportunity employer. The thought sent another mental hare running and Sue held each photo at arm's length, studying the body language. In nearly all of the shots Beck had his head and shoulders thrown back, his chin at an angle which declared him the dominant male. It was particularly noticeable when he stood with women or senior policemen.

A few times his stance was that of a subservient. Shoulders in, head tilted to hide his chin, eyes on the man he acknowledged his superior. Sue looked for the other man's name on the back of the prints.

Ray Fletcher.

Sue called up references on a handy monitor and ended up with a small dossier of *Journal* reports on Fletcher's trials, most with the byline of Watson Skinner. Jonah's predecessor had been a first-class crime reporter and he had obviously felt Fletcher warranted close attention. Most of the court cases ended with Fletcher walking free, many dismissed for lack of evidence. The one time he had been convicted there was an appeal and a blurred shot of a jubilant Fletcher in the Strand, fist raised in triumph.

'Watty, what did you know about him?' Sue whispered but Watty was a dusting of ash on a Scottish moor. All that was left were his words and she reread the accounts of Fletcher, trying to hear Watty's voice and catch his innuendoes.

A vague internal rumbling reminded Sue to look at her watch and she was surprised how long she had spent on her research. Normally, lunch hour long gone, she would have waited to eat until she reached home but she was to meet Benny Rogers after work and there was no way she could face him with an empty stomach.

'He's done it!' Kate called to Sue. 'Sam's fought off the bastards. Cary's friend just phoned it through.'

Sue was pleased for Sam. 'So, everything's as it should be. I wonder who it was playing dirty behind the scenes?'

'Didn't Sam tell you?'

'No. I got the impression he had a pretty good idea – but you know Sam.'

'He wouldn't tell and he wouldn't use it to roll in the mud with the other fella.' Kate grinned. 'I wouldn't be in that chap's shoes now. Sam hated you being used the way you were. He'll get even now – and how!'

Kate marched off to celebrate and Sue returned to her earthworm story. As a follow-up she prepared an account of a quick and simple way to reverse the threat of global warming, carbon dioxide taken from the atmosphere and liquefied. It was then pumped deep under the sea to be stored in rocks.

With engineers active in the North Sea and earthworms eating themselves fat in Scotland the world would be in better shape, she decided as she packed away her disks and headed for Vine Street and Benny Rogers.

Waiting alone in the pub, Sue had been well scrutinized by

the customers when Benny appeared. Expecting Jonah he had come ready-scented but he was as thirsty as ever and drank Sue's cash in a steady stream of Scotch.

'Where's Mr Blackburn?' he asked respectfully enough.

Sue explained the hospital tests.

'Will they make him give up those bloody fags? It's the only way the poor bugger's going to get any better.' He surveyed their neighbours, many hazy behind veils of smoke. 'Why don't someone tell the silly sods?'

She turned to the matter in hand. 'You've got some names for me?'

Sludge stirred in Benny's eyes as he made sure no one was watching them. A slip of paper was passed to Sue and she read the names of two men. One already featured in Anwar's lists.

'Do these two work together?'

Benny nodded. 'Usually.'

'Except when they're inside?'

'Screws don't like them carrying on normal business then – stands to reason,' Benny said with a sniff.

'And these are possibles for supplying outsiders?'

Benny was thirsty, restless, until a banknote had changed hands and a large Scotch was being relished.

'Beck, he only deals with professionals.'

'How does it work?'

'Normally, it's guys like Johnny Crosby pass on a shopping list. Sometimes a whisper gets to Beck. He farms it out to the two I just gave you and they do the actual dealing.'

'That way Beck gets the sale, there's no real connection to him personally and he can keep out of trouble?'

'Got it in one.'

'Only Semtex?'

'Nah. Other stuff the Micks don't want.'

'Guns?'

'Shh!' Benny was scared. 'You talk too loud. Anything spare he can sell – Beck's in the market.'

His gaze focused on an empty glass and Sue was an

146

extra fiver poorer as she made her way towards Fenchurch Street and her car. Most evening traffic had left the City and the roads were clear enough for comfortable driving.

Sue was not sure when she became aware of a car keeping a steady distance behind her. She tried an unexpected left and it followed. Another left and it was still with her. By now she was driving west along London Wall. When she reached the London Museum and the Rotunda she turned left again into St Martin's le Grand but a glance in her rear view mirror made it obvious the car was clinging like a limpet.

A junction loomed and Sue made a quick decision to drive along Newgate Street and then Holborn Viaduct. A stop at lights gave her time to think. All that made sense was that she must lead her pursuers amongst buildings, people, vehicles, and away from her home in Islington.

'Pippa and Ken,' she murmured to herself.

Minutes later snarled traffic held her and she dialled their number on her mobile phone, tucking it into its holder on the dashboard. Pippa answered the call but when she heard of Sue's predicament, Ken was involved.

'Where are you?' he asked.

High Holborn was passing quickly. 'Just turning into St Giles.'

'Get into Oxford Street and head for Marble Arch.'

'I'm not going through Hyde Park!' Instinct made her dread tree-lined darkness.

Oxford Street was busy and there were many stops. 'I seem to be stuck near John Lewis for some reason.'

'Have you a good view of the car behind you?'

'Are you kidding?'

Ken's laugh was faint but welcome. 'Any chance of the number?'

Sue peered this way and that. Using all her mirrors she had time to cobble together the registration number before the driver of the black cab in front of Sue released his brakes and they were on the move. Sue passed on the

147

information and, at Ken's request, she added her own car's identity number.

'I'm handing you to Pippa while I ring Stephen from your flat. My mobile needs recharging.'

As Sue thanked heaven for the spare key left in their charge, Pippa's voice diffused calm.

'Hi, Sue, and here's me thinking you were out enjoying yourself.'

'Pippa, I'm nearly at Marble Arch!'

'That's great. Ken said to tell you to do the round-the houses-bit and head up the Edgware Road.'

'Why?'

'Because halfway along there's a turn to Harrow Road South. Take that until you get to the roundabout under the Westway flyover.'

Sue followed the instructions and Ken came back on line. 'I've just passed Sussex Gardens,' Sue told him.

'Not long now. Take the first left after Praed Street.'

As Sue manoeuvred she heard Ken say he had talked to Stephen. 'He's calling Ashford and hoping to set up a welcoming committee.'

'I'm at the roundabout!'

'When you're on it, follow the signs for Harrow Road North. Tell me when you've done that.'

Sue was intent on the road ahead and, with other drivers, she negotiated for a position in the lanes. 'OK. What next?'

'Left at Paddington Green.'

Enlightenment dawned. She was near the most secure police station in London. 'Yes, please!'

Once she left the major road the looming station was a relief.

'Drive up to the main entrance but don't get out of the car,' Ken advised. 'And keep down.'

As she braked, Sue saw her stalkers whoosh past. There was also time to see an unmarked police car slide silently and fast from the side of the station.

The policeman was young, keen and wore a flak jacket.

He opened the car door and helped Sue out. Behind him there were minimal movements, bodies leaving protective cover. Like her escort, they were armed.

'What about my car?'

Courteously, she was asked for the keys. Sue collected her handbag and made her way into the station on shaky legs.

Many questions and several cups of tea later, Sergeant Webley arrived.

'Who were they?' Sue asked.

'At the moment your guess is probably better than mine.'

Once more Sue had to give her account of leaving the pub where she had met with a contact and finding herself with a tail.

'Your informant?'

'You know I can't say.'

Benny was on Jonah's payroll. If anyone uncovered Benny it must be Jonah. Tiredness made Sue giggle. Benny uncovered?

'Thought of something?'

'Nothing relevant,' Sue said.

The questioning went on. Ashford arrived, Inspector Eden close behind him. Sergeant Webley vacated her chair for the superintendent and stood behind him in the shadows.

'Who was it?' Sue asked him.

'We don't know. It certainly wasn't Passmore and Gibson, of that we're absolutely sure. The driving was very skilled indeed after they left here. I'd say it was a crew used to evading police cars.'

'Any clue from the car?'

'I doubt it. Stolen, of course, and taken from a side street so no useful security cameras. I don't expect there to be prints when we do find it dumped. Those boys were professionals.'

'Why on earth would they want to follow me?'

Ashford's gaze was steady, uncompromising. 'That's what I keep asking myself, Mrs Bennett. When I first heard you were being hunted I had to keep in mind it might be paparazzi trying for revealing photographs.'

'What made you change your mind?'

'A stolen car? I usually find when someone is dedicated to bending the law in one way, they're very careful not to break it in another. That way, if they're caught, the book doesn't get thrown at them.'

Inspector Eden handed him a large brown envelope. Before he opened it Ashford looked at Sue with narrowed eyes. 'Even before you sent us the lists you acquired we were aware of your interest in Beck.'

Sue remembered the watchers Benny had mentioned, sticking out like sore thumbs.

Ashford used a muscular finger to smooth the seal on the envelope. 'After the first bomb I understood your need to fight back. As long as it didn't interfere with our investigations, all well and good, but we've been busy too. After all, our resources for finding people are better than those the *Journal* is likely to afford.'

Sue was annoyed. 'Any costs are my own.'

'So that was why you went after the supplier. He'd be based in London and easier to track than the animal rights folk.' He pulled photographs from the envelope. 'Take a look at these, will you?'

She looked at each one carefully. 'They look like rent-a-mob.'

The harsh planes of Ashford's face relaxed a little. 'Not far off the mark. Anyone familiar?'

After going through the pile again Sue singled out a print. Inspector Eden took it from her, read the name on the back and nodded with satisfaction.

'When and where did you see him?' he asked.

'I'm not sure. Possibly a port somewhere. How did you get on to him?'

'We've been tying up the intelligence from local forces as well as the specialist units. He cropped up a few times.'

The very young man had all the outward signs of aggression. He was thin, in camouflage gear and heavy boots laced to his knees. A black beret was drawn low over his forehead and a stubble of beard hid a weak chin. In Eden's photo the subject had an air of bravado but Sue's memory of him held pity for weakness, the acid of hate etching age into a boy's face.

She closed her eyes as exhaustion washed through her. 'Felixstowe. Calves. That boy was screaming abuse at lorry drivers. I don't remember him getting physically involved.'

The inspector was cynical. 'Too much danger of being arrested.'

'He's in your sights if you caught him on camera,' Sue said and Eden left it to his senior office to reveal any more.

'We are interested in him as a known associate of Beck's – in a small way. It's possible he was the link between Animal Equality and Beck.'

Sue realized Ashford gave out information as willingly as a politician kept a promise. 'Does he know where they are? Passmore and Gibson?'

The superintendent shook his head. 'We can't ask him yet. He's under observation and we want to see where he runs.'

Sergeant Webley was curious. 'I thought you worked in the newsroom. Do you cover many demonstrations?'

'I do, except when I go to labs to talk to researchers, or to symposia, conventions, that sort of thing.'

'The demonstrations,' Ashford reminded her.

'It was Jepson's idea – the previous editor. When I started at the *Journal* he sent me out to all of them.'

The sergeant's face was classic planes and shadows. 'Was that before or after he propositioned you?'

'After.'

It hung in the air that uncomfortable assignments were the punishment for rejecting a powerful man.

'What was your brief at the time?' Inspector Eden wanted to know.

'To find out if there was a scientific basis for the protests.'

'And was there?'

'Sometimes. All too often the emotion on show was based on vague or inaccurate data. A half truth and a twist – the most dangerous kind of gossip.'

'But if you were at all the demos –' Eden began.

Sue sensed the reason for the question. 'I might have registered with someone else? Your rent-a-mob element?'

'It's possible,' Ashford said. 'It could explain the links to you personally.'

'Does it explain tonight's drivers?'

'Ah, a different kettle of fish, I grant you.' Ashford saw Sue's tiredness and took pity on her. 'It's time you were in bed. We'll continue this again.'

'I'm due to go and see my parents in the morning.'

'No problem. Sergeant Webley will go with you when you leave here and stay with you at all times.'

Sue's temper flared. 'I can look after myself!'

'I've no doubt you can but we must identify – and quickly – anyone with you in their sights. It could give us the lead we need so badly. Whoever's behind all this, Mrs Bennett, already owes me for too many deaths.'

'There's one snag to you wearing my clothes.'

The sergeant had always kept herself discreetly in the background but now Sue had a chance to see the person behind the rank. Sue's guard was tall, lissom, super-fit. The girl glanced down at the sweater and jeans she had borrowed for the weekend. 'What's that?'

'You look a darn sight better in them than I do.'

Laughter went out with them into the Surrey countryside. Sue was unencumbered but her companion kept a leather bag hanging from her belt.

'Have a good walk,' Mr Lavin encouraged from the garden. He was pleased to see colour back in his daughter's cheeks and stood watching the girls stride away from the house towards the open space alongside the railway.

It was a weekend of fresh air and talking. The girls were on first name terms and could have been two close friends enjoying each other's company. Sue hoped her parents had not noticed Leonie always walking ahead of her into a new situation, body poised and eyes flashing from side to side, missing nothing as she kept a hand on the bag at her belt.

Mrs Lavin cooked superb meals and they all played Scrabble when not working or gardening. Church on Sunday morning was a ritual so familiar to Sue it was a comfort, her prayers for Anil and the others killed in the bombings.

While the vicar was as intent as ever on his ministry, his wife's attention was on more secular matters. Mrs Stroat was disturbed to see Leonie part of the congregation she must meet and to whom she must be gracious. Once again Mrs Willoughby, staunch in a felt hat, good tweeds and gleaming shoes, took command of the situation. She loudly told the vicar's wife how good it was to see Sue amongst them again and happy to bring her friend to the service.

As they walked back to the house Mrs Willoughby monopolized Leonie but it did not prevent the sergeant's awareness of anything that moved near Sue. The elderly friend was persuaded to join the family for lunch and it was a happy occasion, wit seasoning conversation.

Mrs Lavin had just suggested a move to the fire in the sitting room when Leonie's mobile phone rang. She excused herself and the table was cleared by the time she returned.

'Everything all right?' Mrs Lavin asked.

'Fine, thank you. It was my boss.'

'Does it mean you have to go back?'

'No, not yet. In fact, I'm going to insist on washing up. Sue can make coffee for you all while I get lost in the sink.'

The girl's unconscious air of authority had them all following orders. Sue saw her parents and their guest settled by the fire before she shut the kitchen door behind her.

'What's happened?'

Leonie turned from the piled plates. 'Two more bombs. Mid-morning.'

Sue was appalled. 'Anyone killed?'

'No one. The two went off at the same time. One was in an abattoir in North Wales, the other in an egg-processing plant in Norfolk.'

'What's the connection?'

'The installations belong to two firms refusing to cough up. Homes, families, cars, of the chairmen have been under a twenty-four-hour guard. The factory units must have been all that could be reached.'

'Animal Equality – they still mean business.'

Leonie stacked vegetable dishes. 'Is it still the same "they"?'

'What makes you think it might not be?'

'Passmore and her buddy went for spectacular explosions in very public places. If they'd been behind today's bombs it would have been very hard for a news blackout to be effective. As it is, the poultry blast is due to a build-up of methane gas and the abattoir was a failure in a gas supply. Officially.'

Sue tried to think like Andy Passmore and then decided Leonie was right. 'What do we do?'

'I finish the washing up and you take in the coffee. Come on!' she said as she grinned at Sue. 'You haven't even switched on the kettle yet.'

The drive back to Islington was uneventful. It was only as Sue reached the front door and inserted her key that she heard her name called.

'Get inside – now!' Leonie shouted, pushing Sue until she was inside the house.

'It's OK, Sergeant Webley.'

Sue knew the voice and peered round the door. Sam

154

stood with his hands high, palms towards Leonie and the short-barrelled gun she held aimed steadily at his heart.

'That's my boss,' Sue said, weak with relief.

'I can see it is now.' Leonie put away her revolver. 'What are you doing here, Mr Haddleston?'

'Waiting for Sue. I heard about the explosions and guessed what they were.'

Sue was curious. 'How long have you been here?'

'An hour, maybe more.'

Leonie was not happy. 'Can we all please get upstairs?'

When they were in the flat and the door locked behind them, Sam held Sue's shoulders and searched her face for signs of distress. 'I thought you might be with Miles. I even tried his number but there was no reply. It was only this evening I thought of your parents. Your father told me you and your friend had just left. Somehow, I assumed it was Miles.'

'He's with James. The results of some blood tests are due in the morning.'

'What's wrong?'

'They're waiting to find out.' Sue did not mention the dread which possessed her when Miles first told her of the visit to a specialist. Extreme tiredness, nosebleeds, unexplained bruises. Combined, the symptoms had an all too familiar ring.

Sam's eyes followed Sue as she moved about her home. 'When did you first hear about the bombs?' he asked Leonie.

'When I was about to start the washing up. This time, thank God, no one was hurt.'

Sue was frowning as she came in from the kitchen. 'That's what's so odd. Andy Passmore would sooner kill people than animals.'

'Not her day then,' Sam said. 'Lambs waiting for slaughter were blown sky high. A local stringer e-mailed.'

'That's strange,' Sue said. 'It's not her way and I always thought she was the one making the decisions and giving the orders.'

Sue returned to the kitchen and began warming milk for hot chocolate. Sam followed to help, leaning against the counter as he watched her.

'Thank you for your letter.'

'I was delighted you got the job on a permanent basis. You deserve it.'

'I've got a good team behind me but I have you to thank as much as anyone.'

'Me?' Sue was startled. 'I thought I was the one who had fouled everything up for you.'

He smiled. 'No. All through the meeting one of the finance men backed me to the hilt. When your name was mentioned he came out as your champion – said he'd had the pleasure of talking to you and insisted there was no way you were a scarlet woman. If you were pilloried in the press it was as part of a campaign to get rid of me and he demanded the board had better make sure the instigator never sat in the editor's chair or, "We'll rue the day, gentlemen,"' Sam quoted.

Sue was mystified. 'Who was he?'

'Sir John Preston.'

She shook her head, still puzzled, then her expression cleared as she remembered. 'The clock man!'

'That's him.'

'He's such a sweetie – and his wife.'

'I've to take you to dinner when it can be arranged.' Sam became serious. 'Perhaps we'd better wait until Animal Equality's behind bars.'

'We can all breathe then,' Leonie said.

Sam had forgotten the sergeant was there. 'If you're to be with Sue all the time there must be a reason for you being in the office every day. I'll have to find you a job. Is Paula doing OK?' he asked Sue.

'Still a bit over-adjectival,' Sue admitted, 'but Beth has her measure.'

'In that case I'll promote Paula and find her an assignment to keep her out of the way.'

'Her French is excellent so what about Brussels?'

'Not yet, Sue, but it's a sound idea. I'll send her to Jan Francis in Paris. They'll do each other good.' Sam's ears almost pointed with the mischief he intended. 'That leaves space in the science team. Can you cope?' he asked Leonie.

'A level chemistry and physics?'

Sam was amazed. 'And you went into the police?'

'They need those subjects too.'

'Of course, I'm sorry – but it's a pity you didn't read for a degree.'

'I did,' she said quietly. 'Law. I thought it might come in useful sometime.'

In the next few days it was as though the terrorists and their accomplices had forgotten Sue. She was able to get on with her job, no scares to upset her routine. Leonie was a good companion in Islington and in Wapping she fitted in well. It was explained she had been seconded from a communications firm to gain experience.

Jonah reappeared at his desk, daring anyone to comment on his absence. His colour was a little better, his breathing fractionally quieter, his temper as short as ever.

'Any whispers from your eyes and ears in the food firms?' Sue asked him

'Not a lot. A few more have paid up since the abattoir business.'

'Didn't the police advise them not to?'

'Police? When capital and income are at stake, who bothers about the law?' Jonah coughed and it took time for his breathing to calm down. 'Nah, they only involved the Bill because it was part of the insurance deal. After that, it's what costs less. A quarter of a million is chicken feed to most of 'em – and safer than having your back yard go up in smoke. Mind you, I've heard a whisper one of the chief execs has been shouting his mouth off. He's refusing to pay and he's trying to encourage others to do the same. Silly sod hopes to save himself some cash.'

One aspect of the whole affair had puzzled Sue. 'The actual payment, how does it work?'

'I got young Julian to explain it to me. Money ready to be shifted by computer. Via e-mail comes a code and orders for immediate transfer. By the time the money's been sent and its destination investigated the cash's already gone – split to a number of untraceable accounts.'

'Surely the e-mails can be traced?'

'Not if you've gone into a stranger's house and used the laptop he's left there so handy. A few minutes and you're out again, no one the wiser – until Special Branch come calling on some poor sod who'd gone out for a curry.'

'What's the original destination?'

'Cayman Islands.'

'So there's no hope of getting the money back?'

'Snowball in hell.'

Sue was thoughtful. 'Is there no way of getting a line on who's doing it?'

'Not by the usual methods. My guess is Ploddie's got his eye on some likely characters, or else has a stalking horse out to grass and being watched.'

Ashford's bait went back to her desk wondering if she should have a sandwich for lunch or a bale of hay.

'A call for you,' Leonie said and nodded towards the waiting phone.

'Sue? Anwar Naib. I have more information for you. Can we meet?'

'It's become difficult. Could you fax it to me?'

'As long as you immediately remove and destroy the data at the top of the sheets.'

'Of course.' Anwar's working address and fax number would be too awkward to explain to Ashford.

Sue waited by the fax machine, neatly scissoring away the top inch of each sheet and watching the narrow strips glide through a shredder.

'Useful?' Leonie appeared at Sue's shoulder as the last scrap disappeared.

'More for your boss. No new names as far as I can see,

only extra addresses to be added to the list of properties owned by Beck's associates. I'd guess they're second homes, holiday cottages, that sort of thing.' She photocopied the sheets and handed the originals to Leonie. 'Can you see he gets them? They have to be given to him personally.'

'No problem. He's coming to your flat tonight for an update and if it's OK with you, my sister will call sometime with extra clothes.'

'No problem. By the way, Sandy's discovered you're a lawyer —'

'Hardly!'

'Well, good enough. He wants to talk over the legal implications of noise pollution with you.'

'As long as I can still keep you in sight, I'd be delighted.'

By the time the two girls were ready to go home it was late and darkness had settled over London. Sue was driving, busy threading her way between home-going cars and cabs. Leonie was quiet and Sue realized the other girl was watching the mirror to her left.

'What is it?'

'A car.' Leonie was abrupt, intent on her observations.

'Trouble?'

'Possibly. Can you keep the car steady?'

Sue did as she was asked and Leonie unfastened her seat belt, swivelling to get the best view of their pursuers. She reached into her handbag and Sue was afraid, expecting to see a gun. Instead a camera appeared, a nightsight in place.

'Talk about coming prepared,' Sue joked through stiff lips.

'When I say stop, do it immediately.'

Sue drove slowly as the traffic inched forward.

'Stop!'

The camera whirred, Leonie out of her seat as she matched up driver, passenger and number plate.

'Call Ashford on your mobile!'

Sue did so as Leonie dealt with the camera and extracted the film. It was Inspector Eden who answered. He learned where the girls were and asked Sue to turn at the next junction and go back to Wapping.

'Why?' she asked him.

'Just do it!' Leonie ordered.

It was a strange journey back to the *Journal*. 'Why don't you use the digital system? You could have sent the film straight there?'

'No way! It could be viewed by eyes other than the super's. Too risky.'

By the time Sue edged the car under the barrier of the car park her shoulder muscles ached with tension. As she pulled up the brake Leonie opened her door and was out of the car. In seconds a police motor cycle was zooming towards them.

'Sergeant Webley?' the rider called as he halted the powerful machine.

Leonie showed him her credentials and after checking his identity details, she handed over the film. 'You know where it's to go?'

The young PC nodded and was off in a burst of sound.

'Now what?' Sue asked

'Inspector Eden will be here soon. Then it's Islington and bed.'

'Just like that?'

'This time it's in one of our cars and with me driving.'

This was no criticism of Sue's skill at the wheel. She was marked prey but who was it watching and waiting for the ghost of an opportunity? She had thought Ashford over-cautious when he enforced her protection. Tonight had proved him right. Someone wanted her.

Badly.

Chapter Nine

'You're not to use her!'

Sam was furious but Inspector Eden was immovable. 'That was not our intention, sir.'

'No? Then why was Sergeant Webley taking photographs?'

'We need to identify who's trying to get to Mrs Bennett.'

'And you put her life in danger to do so?'

The inspector was a young man, normally pleasant and now surprisingly stern. 'May I remind you, sir, who it was that selected Mrs Bennett in the first place? The terrorists have been making all the moves. They set off explosions with no prior warnings and sometimes with great loss of life. Finding them is an A1 priority and Mrs Bennett is at no greater risk than any of our officers.'

'You admit she was in danger tonight?'

Eden's pause was momentary. 'Until we know who was following her, we can't be sure.'

Sue was aching for her bed and sleep. 'It's very confusing. All this began with two lone members of an animal group and their style of attack was very distinctive. Then there was the man at Heathrow who had Gibson's passport. Where is it? Has it gone back to Gibson – and what about the savings book from the Vienna bank?' She knew she was making little sense but they would not go away and leave her alone.

'Mrs Bennett, there's no need to go into all this.'

'But there is. I have to talk to Andrea Passmore, Inspector. If I have to upset the whole of the Metropolitan police
force, then so be it.'

'We won't get upset, Mrs Bennett, but we will not tolerate you trying to question one of our officers to get details
which should be confidential.' He glared at the sergeant.

'Leonie? I haven't!' It was Sue's turn to be furious. 'How
dare you suggest it! Any facts I have I've found out
through normal channels.'

'Normal?'

'You must understand, Inspector,' Sam intervened, 'a lot
of information comes our way. If it's useful we pay quite
well so individuals ring in, talk to me or to any reporter
whose name they've taken from our pages. For instance, a
phone call this morning told me Andrew Sedgely was
taken from outside his home and is being held until his
firm releases the blackmail money. I believe the amount
demanded in his case has gone up to half a million.'

'If he's the one who's been shouting the odds against the
bombers, it means cash has definitely become the most
important issue,' Sue said.

Inspector Eden stared at Sue, then at Sam. 'Who told
you?' he asked him.

'That's my business. Your only concern is the news
blackout. Because of it not a squeak about Sedgely will
reach our readers – not yet.'

'Was your information from someone in the Met?' The
inspector glowered at each of them in turn.

'It certainly wasn't me, sir,' Leonie assured him. 'I've
been with Mrs Bennett all day and this is the first I've
heard of Sedgely going missing.'

'The money transfers. Have they all been electronic?'
Sue asked.

Inspector Eden was stiff with anger but he needed help.
'Yes. Always the last five minutes of trading.'

Sue's thoughts raced. 'What's happening now is completely at odds with what they've done in the past. For a
start, I doubt they could set up such detailed financial

162

arrangements. Is everything still being carried out in the name of Animal Equality?'

Eden nodded. 'The words and the logo.'

'It looks like they've had a takeover bid they couldn't refuse,' Leonie said slowly.

Sue agreed. 'Yes, it does – and at least the random killings have stopped.'

By ten the next morning Sue had already dealt with a mutinous Karin. The recent smoothing of rough edges had gone and she had been her former, belligerent self.

'I'm next in line,' the girl had protested. 'Just because a token black female is thrust on us you don't have to wet-nurse her and push everyone else aside.'

Sue had almost laughed. Tempted to reveal the truth, she wondered how Karin would respond to the idea that it was Leonie doing the nannying. Not because she was black but because she was fit, trained and a crack shot. Instead of exposing a secret she had given Karin a calm, level stare which had the girl flushing.

'Go and see Meg, she's expecting you. I've given you the puffball story. She might let you go to a half page.' A giant specimen of the fungus had been found in deepest Sussex. 'See if you can interview the owner and find out if they have any secrets for growing one of that size. I'd guess most papers will use a child next to it for human interest. Go for a shot of a cat instead.'

Karin had stumped off to Meg and returned only slightly mollified. Demands for data on puffballs from Sue had a negative result.

'If you do your own reading up it'll make for a much better story.'

'I'm not a botanist!'

'Tough.'

Sue had bent to her own work when the hum of the newsroom was disrupted by shocked exclamations. Sue lifted her head and saw Jonah scribbling fast. Even from a distance Sue could see the gleam of sweat on his forehead. She raced across the room.

'What's happened?'

He waved her to silence as he listened and made notes. Hardly had his phone reached its cradle before the ringing began again.

'That's the third,' he said. 'No warnings, nothing – God damn them!'

'More bombs?'

As Sue spoke, Leonie was beside her. 'Casualties?'

'Chemists' shops this time of the morning? What do you think?'

'Where?' Leonie asked urgently.

'Ealing, Stoke Newington, Harlesden.'

Leonie needed to know more. 'Were the three shops part of a chain?'

Jonah shook his head. 'Not from the names.'

'And that means no network of security cameras to give us any clues.'

'Us? I thought so. You're a busy.'

'That fact is to be kept quiet, understand?'

'You keeping an eye on Sue?' Jonah asked. 'Good luck. I wouldn't want the job,' he said with great feeling.

He reached for his jacket and a notebook and hurried towards the door. Reporters from every paper would be scouring the scenes of devastation for any angle they could find while their editors cleared the front pages for the most dramatic shots and headlines. Sam and Gavin were no exception, space stretched to accommodate follow-up stories from eyewitnesses and victims still alive and able to talk.

The science team had to keep on working as usual, preparing for the day normality returned. Leonie was good on phone enquiries and Sue gave her a list of hospital contacts, asking her to find out if any were unhappy with the use of paracetamol. Even after a few calls Leonie was horrified by what she had been told.

'Take a dozen aspirin in a cry for help and you could

wake up with a bleeding gut. When that's healed you're OK.'

'Paracetamol's a different matter,' Sue agreed.

'Are you kidding? Thirty thousand admissions to hospitals each year. It's a miracle only a hundred or so die. Not enough of their own glutathione, apparently.'

Sue smiled at her enthusiasm. 'You're enjoying this.'

'It's an eye-opener.'

'I suppose you spend most of your time thinking dangerous drugs arrive as white powders in the holds of ships from exotic locations, or the boot of someone's car after a holiday.'

'It's what we usually have to chase.'

Sue stretched complaining muscles. 'Do you want to ring Ashford and see if his account of the explosions tallies with ours?'

'Eventually. He'll be busy.'

With everyone else in her Special Branch unit extended to the limit, Leonie felt sidelined yet the superintendent was sure there was a link to Sue. There would be another attempt at abduction and, in in the course of it, a desperately needed lead could materialize. It was important Sue did not know that, or the danger which threatened her.

'The super will be flat out at the moment. There was already a big push on to mop up anyone who's ever smelt an explosive. One or two areas are a little sensitive.'

'Al Qaeda? IRA?'

Leonie shrugged her shoulders. 'A few locations and individuals of all factions are kept under close observation. Going in and taking them now could ruin a potentially successful operation. If they're nothing to do with the case in hand, they're best left alone.'

'But not pulling them in leaves supplies in the market place, supplies for whoever's running Animal Equality now.'

'That's doubtful. It's only Sean Beck and his like who exist as traders that are the present danger.'

Across the room Meg peered at a VDU, nodding her

head at some items, shaking her head at others. The sound of a big story reverberated, the pace of work was fierce.

'Anyone who sees other human beings as of less value than themselves is a potential terrorist,' Sue said. 'They become actual terrorists when they start wiping out innocent people to get what they want.'

'That's a bit sweeping, isn't it?'

'No, it's reality. The criminals you hunt down, isn't that how they see you and me?'

'Lesser creatures?' Leonie laughed. 'As a black female it's what I'm supposed to accept I am.'

'But you don't, do you? Accept it, I mean?'

'Of course not!' The girl's amusement was whole, rounded. 'I learned from my father to look at the person trying to belittle me and realize that every time it's done it's because the other person feels so insignificant, so unintelligent. He taught me to pity them – and my mother taught me never to trust such people.'

'Very wise.'

Leonie turned to her keyboard and tapped in the code for the latest news. 'One of the casualties taken to St Anne's Hospital has died,' she read out. 'That would be from the Stoke Newington blast.'

'Does that make it six dead?'

'And twenty-three injured.'

'All three bombs going off at the same time? Either it's very good planning . . .'

'Or three teams did the planting and detonating. There's no way two individuals could have coped.'

'Was the latest exercise to make the companies holding out pay up?'

Leonie was bitter. 'Six deaths this time? Maybe more to come? Whoever they are, these bastards are after a really big pay-off and they just don't care.'

Work had to go on and Sue scanned news coming in for useful material. Doubts were being raised about immunizations before the Iraq war. She looked for mention of organo-phosphates.

'Why?' Leonie wanted to know.

'One of my hobby horses. They're a pretty deadly brew.'

'They're meant to be.'

'Yes, originally as nerve gases for war and now as pesticides, especially in sheep dip and agricultural sprays.' Sue found and slotted in a disk, searched for the file she wanted and watched Leonie read.

'How many farmers did it affect?' she asked quietly.

'Who knows? It was government-recommended but no one had taken into account what happens to the human body if the dip or the spray gets on to the skin and bypasses the liver which could detoxify it – and these are chemicals originally designed to wreck the nervous system. Granted the modern ones are supposed to be dilute enough merely to kill off insects that way but if it gets into mammals? Usual political approach is to ignore it then it can't have happened.'

'But that's criminal negligence!'

'Of course it is. It could also explain scrapie in sheep and BSE in cattle – not to mention unexplained and incurable nervous degeneration in humans.'

'What can you do about it?'

'Keep nagging – and wash my fruit and vegetables.'

Sue was writing up the army vaccination story, linking in the data on pesticides used in the area, when Ted Keneally marched to her desk. He was ex-army and it showed.

'Sue, this immunization business. They've not learned from the last action in the Gulf.'

Leonie hid a smile as Sue finished typing and pressed the print key. 'Is this what you wanted?'

Ted read fast. 'You're a bloody mind-reader!'

'Leonie helped.'

'Can I sort this out with Meg?' he asked Sue.

'Be my guest.'

'I'd like to do a commentary on senior staff, medical and otherwise, risking the lives of other ranks.'

'Lesser men and women?' Leonie enquired gently.

'That's how they see 'em – always have done. My old captain's doing a bum job in an office but when we meet he still sees only my first pip. I'm still Keneally, never Ted.'

After he had gone Leonie went on a coffee hunt.

'I wonder,' Sue mused as she accepted her mug and cradled the warmth between her fingers.

'If you don't tell me, I won't know.'

'Children. In spite of all the shampoo adverts there's a massive increase in headlice and fleas. Are treatments exposing them to organo-phosphates? And then there's when their pets get new flea collars.'

'So, the choice is lice and fleas or exhaustion and depression. Life's a bitch,' Leonie decided.

Sue had been grateful for an interlude which took her mind off the new blasts. For all of them in the newsroom it meant dark memories of terror and pain as they relived the explosion in the car park. All of them had endured the aftermath and she knew as work went on around her there were silent prayers ranging from the well-learned formal pleas to the heartfelt and irreligious.

The phone rang. 'Sue?'

'Anwar?'

'I'm sorry. I had to talk to you.'

'Is something wrong?'

'All those killed this morning.'

Desolation was in his voice and Sue understood. 'Yes, it brings it all back and strips away the protective skin you thought you'd grown. Everyone expects you to carry on as usual when all the time you want to scream with anger.'

'Is it still the same ones doing the killing?'

'I don't know, Anwar. Since the last bomb in Oxford Street the rest have a different feel – I can't explain.'

'I know what you mean. There were too many bombs all at once this morning.'

'Exactly.'

'I am sorry our research could not prevent today's deaths.'

It was not only Anwar who was angry. An unknown competitor for Sam's job had deprived Sue of more than a week of her own hunt. It might have given a lead to the killers. She forced herself to be calm, normal.

'Unfortunately, the police have to have hard evidence to take killers off the streets,' she told Anwar. 'Murderers have rights apparently.'

'So do victims! How many more must be sacrificed like Anil?'

'Oh Anwar, I wish I knew.'

Leonie had been watching. 'Someone believes we should be moving faster?' she asked when Sue had finished her phone call.

'The brother of the boy murdered in my place.'

There was the gentleness of pity. 'Today's been hard on both of you.'

'You could say that. Whenever I hear they've taken another life I want it to be the last.'

'And the police get the blame if it's not.' Leonie shook her head. 'The most galling thing about our job is working hard to get a conviction, only to get the case thrown out because some idiot hasn't dotted an i or crossed a t. You know the guy in the dock is as guilty as hell, so does he – and he's probably paid or intimidated to get a cooked-up defence. That's bad enough but when he walks free, it's the arrogance! Courts allowing such scum to feel superior – it should be made a criminal offence.'

'Hang the lawyers?'

'Don't tempt me!'

'This must be hard on your social life,' Leonie said as Sue sat upright.

They had followed the usual procedure for leaving the *Journal*. Leonie drove, Sue crouched below window level until the sergeant's radio informed her their back-up had encountered no pursuit. Each night their arrival in Islington was varied and Sue's Special Branch protectors were in place when she reached her home. It galled her she could do nothing positive, simply wait it out as bait.

Sue settled back against the cushioning, happy to be taken home by a skilled driver. 'My social life? What about yours?'

'I'm working.' Traffic lights held them but Leonie shot away as soon as she could. 'I expected to be escorting you to a round of wild parties – or at least long evenings in a wine bar.'

'Not my scene. Do you find my life that dull?'

'Dull? That's the last word I'd have used! But no dates?'

'I have friends who drag me out occasionally.'

'There's your editor, I know about him. I thought there was someone called Miles on the list I was given. Doesn't he figure any more?'

'Possibly.' Sue looked at passing shops and saw nothing as she heard Miles's voice again, apologizing for not seeing her . . .

'How's James?' she had asked.

'I've said I'll go with him and Anne in the morning. He has to see a specialist at Great Ormond Street.'

'The results of the blood tests.'

'GP wouldn't commit herself. All she did say was the white blood count was very high and she wanted a second opinion.'

Sue had been silent, determined not to scream 'No!' The pattern had already been too clear and she had pictured the happy little boy who was James subjected to chemotherapy in the attempt to reverse his body's cancer.

'You can't get better than Great Ormond Street,' she had managed at last.

'Sue, you know these things. What are his chances? If he does have leukaemia?'

'The treatment of the childhood form is very skilled these days. Prognosis can be very hopeful indeed. Very,' she had added in an attempt to comfort.

'I must be with him.'

'Of course. He needs you.'

Leonie's radio crackled, dragging Sue back to the present and a voice reporting in code. 'All clear,' Leonie agreed and parked neatly in front of the vehicle in which her two colleagues waited. Sue sat for a moment, hiding a sigh before she left the safety of the car. Her thoughts were with James. Miles was distraught but no one would ever know. For the boy's sake he would smile. The son would know his father was the same as always and was there.

That was all that mattered.

The evening routine was comforting, the meal from the freezer appetizing and filling.

'Something worrying you?' Leonie asked later as they cleared the supper dishes.

'Nothing specific.' James would have the best of care and his chances of growing up to live a normal life were good.

'It can't be easy for you,' Leonie said, 'waiting for Animal Equality to bite the dust.'

'You've helped.'

Leonie was startled, her eyes huge. 'Me? How?'

'The way you've fitted in – especially at the paper. Even Karin's behaving since you had a word with her and I bet you never let on why you've been seconded to the *Journal*.'

'Anyone like Karin who has so much submerged aggression is easy to handle. They just need to let it out and get their energy channelled in a more satisfying direction.'

'So, what's her secret?'

'A very attractive older sister who's the apple of Daddy's eye.'

'And that's why Karin's slogged so hard to do well?'

'Probably – but it won't work. If a parent's prejudiced, nothing changes.'

'You sound like an expert.'

'Not my own family. I'm the middle one of three and my parents were scrupulous about fairness, even if it didn't seem so most of the time. We all knew they tried and that makes a difference. My uncle now, he has a favourite – his eldest son. The trouble that's caused!'

'You should meet Peter, he's a child psychiatrist. You'd get on well.'

Leonie grinned. 'To help with my retarded development?'

Sue flung a tea towel at her and it was in a gust of chuckles they made their way to the warmth of the sitting room. The doorbell brought Leonie to her feet and reaching for the gun in her bag.

Sue looked through the peephole. 'It's Pippa.'

Only when she was in the flat and the door shut behind her did Pippa relax.

'You're looking remarkably well,' Sue informed the newcomer.

'I've come to invite you to a wedding next week. We've managed to get a cancellation so it will be very simple, at Chelsea Register Office and lunch afterwards at our favourite restaurant in Mallord Street. Both of you,' she said, smiling at Leonie.

Sue's hug conveyed more than words. 'I'm so happy for you,' she whispered.

A bottle of wine was opened, toasts drunk and the evening promised to become quite merry.

'Will you be my matron of honour?' Pippa asked Sue.

'Of course I will – and honour is exactly the right word.'

'Great! Ken will be so pleased but it does leave me with a problem. Who do I invite as your partner? Sam or Miles?'

Sue inspected her fingernails before she met Pippa's gaze. 'Miles is with James for the foreseeable future.' She explained about Great Ormond Street.

Pippa's eyes were enormous and protective hands cov-

172

ered the barely noticeable swelling at her waist. 'Will he be all right?'

'I should imagine his chances are excellent.'

'It happened to one of my cousins,' Leonie told them.

'Did they . . .' Pippa began.

'Ten years on he's the most objectionable teenager ever. All that energy!'

'And in ten years treatments have improved even further,' Sue added, watching Pippa's fears subside until only a vestige of unease was left.

'It's Sam then? For your partner?'

'He may be busy.'

Leonie's laugh was a merry sound. 'I've a feeling our illustrious editor will make time for the occasion.'

'What about you, Leonie? Who can I invite as your escort?'

'Me? No one. You'll have enough with your friends and family.'

Pippa talked lightly of her father housebound by a stroke and a church blessing later, in her home village. When she went back upstairs Leonie switched on the TV news. The blasts had been given full coverage as had the hospitals treating the injured.

Eyewitnesses told their stories. One man in Ealing, myriad cuts on his face, had survived the explosion to talk of his shock and disgust. In Stoke Newington a woman had cradled a dying child, blood still marking her clothes and neck. Sue could see little through her tears. Was all this waste of life so bank accounts could be plundered at will?

Leonie was intent on the screen, not watching the raw emotions reaching out to viewers. She was looking at what could be seen of the three crime scenes.

'You'd be in the middle of that if it wasn't for me.'

Leonie shook her head. 'My job's to make sure you're not another casualty. If I stop that happening I've earned my pay this week. At least it puts what's happening in Westminster in perspective.'

'Yesterday it was MPs, their sex lives and lies – now this.'

The two women made the best of their quiet prison. Leonie diverted Sue with snippets of gossip from past cases. They watched a documentary on animals in the African bush, more than a thousand miles from their own worries. A film was tried and discarded.

'How about an early night?' Leonie suggested. 'My turn to make the cocoa.'

In spite of the nightly ritual, sleep eluded Sue. She tossed and turned, her pillows hot and duvet tangled. Nowhere was there an escape from the idea that she might have been responsible, even in part, for the most recent of London's massacres.

Animal Equality might now only be the front for an even greedier group but her death was to have been the first, setting the pattern for terror. Knowing why she had been selected could help unravel the knot of blackmail and murder which was strangling the capital.

'Where's Jonah?' Kate's query was loud and demanding.

'Haven't you heard?' Meg might have been working all hours but her hair and make-up were immaculate, her shirt crisp, her manner still brusque. 'He collapsed last night. The silly fool had to go to Harlesden in person. Why he couldn't have left it to stringers I'll never understand.'

'Where is he now?' Sue wanted to know. Without Jonah she had no link to Benny, no way of finding who it was had bought her name.

'Willesden General. I don't know what ward and it's no use trying to visit – family only. Sam was there first thing and wasn't allowed in.'

The editor had been in and out of the newsroom all morning. He looked tired but his grasp on every aspect of the paper was as firm as ever.

'Miss Webley, are you beginning to get the hang of what we do here?'

'Thank you, yes.'

'Your duties are not too onerous?'

The sergeant made a supreme effort and stopped a grin in its tracks. 'Not so far. Sue looks after me well.'

'Glad to hear it.' Sam turned to Sue, anxious when he saw dark smudges under her eye and guessed the reason. 'Tomorrow morning I'd like a meeting with you and Ted. Bring your data on these organo-phosphates, as well as the immunization programme. Time we appraised the state of play and see if it's military or ministry cock-ups. Ask Maimie for a time.'

Sue made a note of the request and when she looked up again Sam had gone.

'Very attentive to his staff's needs, your Mr Haddleston.' Leonie swivelled in her chair. 'What's our job today, boss?'

'Nothing that'll go to press for a day or two but we'd better have it ready.' Sue called Karin to join them. 'How are you on history and geography?'

Since the success of the puffball spread Karin had mellowed but was still wary. 'What's it for?'

'There's a suggested plan to build a canal right across the north of England.'

Leonie's eyebrows rose. 'Hadrian had the same idea only he used a wall. What's the problem?'

Sue outlined the ecological disturbances which were inevitable.

'But human politics come first?'

Karin was surprised at Leonie's question. 'Don't they always?'

Beth ambled over to listen to the discussion and as Sue tapped her teeth with a pencil, Leonie leaned forward.

'Why not concentrate on the animals and plants – how important they are. Mention the politics and let Joe Public make up its own mind.'

'You're the expert, I suppose,' Karin sniped.

'Science, no. Man in the street, yes. Definitely.'

They worked without a break and it startled Sue to see

175

the windows facing the roadway were dark. 'I'm sorry I've kept you so long,' she said to Karin.

'That's OK.'

There was about the girl an air of contentment Sue had not seen before. 'Come and have a drink with us.'

Karin hesitated, then her chin rose. 'Thanks. I'd like that.'

There was a burst of laughter nearby and Kate advanced, a Kate with eyes blazing with triumph. 'There you are, Sue. All debts paid!'

She took the paper Kate thrust at her. It was the next day's copy of *Nova*. 'What am I looking for?'

'Front page.'

Patiently, Sue inspected the sheet. It was mostly pictures, few words. A royal emerging from a party showing legs more Hollywood than Windsor. A shot of a façade of a high-class brothel in Mayfair was next to a plea for a liver donor desperately needed by a four-year-old child.

'I don't get it.'

'For God's sake, Sue! Look!'

Kate's red-tipped finger tapped the house in Mayfair. 'Who's coming out, having had a marvellous time indoors?'

Sue studied the photograph more carefully, then frowned. Usually, such an illustration would have the house in focus but here the client was sharply defined. 'I don't believe it!'

'You'd better.' Kate smiled wickedly. 'Steve Bynorth's come out rather well, hasn't he? I understand the evenings are carrying the same happy snap but *Nova* goes nationwide.'

'So he uses prostitutes. He's hardly the first journo in history to do that.'

'I rang a contact. This particular establishment has strong links with one in Brussels and our Steve's well known in both. The *Nova* hacks have stacks of interviews with prossies, all describing Steve's preferences. He likes 'em young, Sue. Very, very young. There are hints he's

176

linked in with the Brussels paedo crowd.' Kate pointed to the paper. 'The write-up inside even hints at it.'

Sue stared at Kate and the older woman smiled. 'You still haven't got it, have you?'

'Got what, for Pete's sake?'

'It was Steve behind the *Nova* story crucifying you to get to Sam. Steve used lies but Sam saw to it the truth was used instead. Then and now.'

'Steve?' Sue whispered. She had sensed hate emanating from him. As she realized what he had done, anger flared and burned steadily. It was Steve who had tried to rob her of her good name – but worse, he had stolen so much time, time she could have spent finding Beck and, through him, Andy Passmore. How many lives had that delay cost?

Sue went through the motion of taking Karin to the wine bar, surprised by how many raised a glass with a 'Good on yer, Sue.' No one had said a word to her in the past weeks but many seemed to have been aware of Steve Bynorth's weakness for under-age girls and guessed his was the false smear campaign against Sam. In the world of newsprint, justice was being seen to be done.

Sam's call reached Sue when she and Leonie returned to the flat. 'When did you know it was him?' she asked.

'As soon as I was tipped off about the original *Nova* spread.' Sam sounded tired, relieved. He chuckled. 'You're not the only one who reads body language, you know. The bastard's always been patronizing but when he had a nasty gleam in his eye and strutted, super-smug, I knew he had something planned for me. I'll never forgive him for involving you.'

Sue almost felt sorry for Bynorth.

'I've tried to get hold of Miles to tell him,' Sam said.

She explained about James's blood count and Great Ormond Street.

'Poor little devil. Is there anything we can do?'

'Nothing really. The doctors will have it well in hand and Miles is staying with James so he has maximum support through it all.'

'You mean Miles is back with his wife?' Sam could not keep hope from his voice.

'James needs both of his parents and that's what he'll have.'

'For how long?'

Now Sue was tired. 'As long as it takes.'

The newsroom was gradually filling early next day. Leonie had gone to fetch coffee and Sue had only just taken off her coat when her phone rang.

'Sue!' Anwar's voice was high-pitched with excitement. 'Sean Beck's been arrested!'

'How do you know?'

'Deepak heard from his uncle, the one who has a shop near the girlfriend's flat. As he opened up this morning, he saw Beck taken away in handcuffs!'

Chapter Ten

Sue sat through an editorial discussion, her mind on Anwar's call. He had been triumphant as he told her Sean Beck was not the only one in custody. From all over that part of London eyes and ears in a network of newsagents, corner shops, curry houses, had reported the sudden arrival of police at addresses which had been under observation. The time had been the same, 6 a.m., the search of premises extremely thorough. In each case the haul of guns, ammunition and explosives had been taken away in large plastic bags, human items quickly dressed and arrested. The same treatment had been afforded harmless-looking grannies.

Sue hoped the policemen on Anwar's list had also been rounded up. For them would be reserved a special grimness. Once, in the labyrinths of the Old Bailey, Sue had encountered a group of officers waiting to give evidence against a former colleague. The bitterness was silent and fury had a life of its own. Men and women had been betrayed and they would see the traitor suffer the maximum penalty.

When Sue returned to her desk Leonie's manner was as cool as ever but she had about her an air of suppressed excitement. 'Good meeting?'

'Interesting. Tell me, did they arrest all those policemen this morning?' Sue asked demurely.

'How did you . . .'

Sue tapped the side of her nose. 'I have my sources.'

'Off the record, every one of them's in the bag. How did you know about the operation?'

'The same way the list was drawn up, shall we say?'

'I'd like to know who. So would Super Ashford.'

'Maybe after I get to talk to Passmore and Gibson I might give him a hint.'

'Are you trying blackmail?'

Sue smiled but her thoughts were with the dead Anil. 'No,' she said softly, 'just balancing the books.'

Grateful for the assignments which kept her fully occupied, Sue did not have time to dwell on any frustrations she might have.

'I feel like a drink,' Kate said when work eased and the main stories were ready for the presses.

In spite of the pressures of the day Sue had a sense of celebration. 'Why not?'

As was her habit she checked the breaking news. Another royal aide had bitten the dust. A Tory MP was accused of making too much money, a Labour one of betraying his roots with a champagne lifestyle. Sue shook her head, it was all so predictable, then words rolled on the screen and she leaned forward, intrigued. Animal activists in Canada claimed to have poisoned turkeys in a supermarket chain, their way of protesting against the cruel rearing and slaughtering of the birds.

Kate was a fast reader. 'More pathetic inadequates waiting to be noticed.'

Sue was not so sure. 'It could have begun with a genuine concern. It's one reason the number of vegetarians keeps growing – even in France.'

Kate's laugh rang with cynicism. 'I'd like to see that lot in Canada taking on French farmers. Those gentlemen get a touch primitive when their pockets are affected.'

Sue was still reading the report from Canada. 'This group seems to have been well organized.'

'How organized does one have to be to put the wind up

the money men?' Kate wanted to know. 'A black cat running away from them's usually quite sufficient.'

'Which is why the claim of damage does as much harm as actual poison,' Sue reminded her.

Karin had been an interested listener. 'How?'

'Would you buy a turkey from one of those shops?' Sue asked.

'Not likely!'

'Exactly.' Sue switched off her monitor. 'And next time, some inspired clever clogs will realize they don't even have to lift a finger to make supermarket bosses pay up, just to keep them quiet.'

Karin was not totally convinced but Kate was restless, ready to lead the way to the wine bar. 'Everyone, but everyone, darling, has their price.'

'That's not true!' Leonie said.

'Don't forget, it may not be money. Take Sue, for instance. You'd get nowhere with cash but if someone she cared about was in danger she'd go to the stake for them.'

'So would most people.' Leonie had no doubts.

Kate smiled at her, a weary gesture. 'Would they?'

The women headed for the lift, Karin detouring and saying she would join them later. The other three stood in the privacy of the steel-lined cubicle and waited for it to reach the ground floor.

'You'd go to the stake,' Kate said softly to Leonie, 'which is why you're so good at your job.' She turned to Sue. 'It must be nice to have a full-time minder.'

Leonie had guessed from day one that Kate had not been fooled by her presence. 'Do you need a minder?'

Kate surveyed the tall, slim girl, her skin and features beautiful, effortlessly elegant in a simple tan trouser suit and pale orange sweater. 'I couldn't do with you, darling. Who'd give me a second glance? No. Make mine male and brimming with hormones.'

'Testosterone,' Sue reminded her.

Kate sighed wistfully. 'If you say so,' she said and led the way out of the building.

By the time they found seats in the wine bar Kate was ready to fall into the nearest gin and tonic as long as it was large. Karin joined them and Sue noticed the girl had refreshed her make-up and brushed her hair into a more becoming looseness.

A pleasant half-hour passed. Sue and Leonie were content to sit and watch as Kate's eyes roamed the room, descending on any likely-looking male. Karin was more at ease than Sue had ever seen her.

Leonie's mobile ringing took her away to a quiet corner. 'Nothing urgent,' she assured them when she returned. 'my father checking on me. He may call this evening.'

Her words had been casual but a slight tilt of her head delivered a message and Sue prepared to leave.

'Finish your drinks first,' Kate insisted.

Karin was uneasy at being left with the older woman. 'Do you both have to go?'

''Fraid so,' Sue said. 'Leonie's driving.'

The time spent in the wine bar had allowed traffic to clear. Leonie's skill ensured a smooth ride and Sue lay back, eyes closed, almost asleep. The journey followed its usual pattern and Sue noted the Special Branch men still on duty. 'Will Ashford keep them on now?'

Leonie concentrated on parking the car. 'Have to wait and see.'

A penny dropped. 'It's Ashford who's coming tonight!'

'Yes. He wants to see you. I had to get you home by eight.'

'Thank heaven for microwaves,' Sue said. 'I'm starving.'

Supper had been eaten and the dishes stacked when the doorbell rang. On the monitor Sue saw Ashford, Inspector Eden at his shoulder. She pressed the door switch, wondering why both men had come. Leaving Leonie to open the door of the flat, Sue thumped cushions in the sitting room, puzzled by the urgency in the conversation going on in the hall.

'Mrs Bennett.' The superintendent was affable but brisk.

The doorbell rang again and it was Leonie who checked. 'Your boss this time,' she grinned at Sue.

Ashford was annoyed at the interruption. 'Better let him in,' he said reluctantly.

As soon as he came in, Sam thrust his way to Sue's side and stood, one shoulder forward in an attitude of defiance. 'Are you OK?' he asked her.

Sue nodded. 'Superintendent Ashford and Inspector Eden have just arrived. They haven't yet told me why they're here. Perhaps if we all sit down, they will.'

Her suggestion was followed. 'Well?' she asked the senior detective.

Ashford glared at Sam. 'You understand what goes on here is strictly off the record?'

'As long as Mrs Bennett is safe,' Sam bargained.

It was clear to all in the room that Sam's presence and attitude annoyed the superintendent. 'It's our objective, too,' He turned to Sue. 'Sergeant Webley informs me you already knew about this morning's raid. How?'

'Mrs Bennett claims confidentiality.' Sam's belligerence was coming to the fore and Sue put a hand on his arm.

'All I will say is that I heard the news from an informant.'

'And this – informant – knew of all the early morning raids?'

'Most of them, I think.'

'Then your informant must be in our ranks,' Ashford decided. He was making a point of not looking at Leonie. 'You won't give me your source?'

'Privileged information – and not from the police,' was all Sue would say.

'This still doesn't explain why you're here.' Sam was in a mood to argue. 'Have you come to tell us Mrs Bennett is off the hook?'

'I wish I could, Mr Haddleston. Maybe Animal Equality is no longer interested in her but someone is.'

'What's happened?' Sue asked him.

Ashford waited for his inspector to explain. 'This morning's operation was not strictly our pigeon. We were only informed after the event – a matter of courtesy since it was gen, by way of you of course, which led to the arrests.'

'Sean Beck is in custody?'

'Yes – and he'll stay there. Enough links to Semtex were found to keep him inside for a reasonable stretch.'

'Has he admitted supplying Animal Equality with explosives?'

'I don't know, Mrs Bennett. My guess is that at this moment he's admitting nothing. It'll take hours of questioning to get him to that stage.'

The words 'if ever' were in everyone's minds.

'What about the last two names I passed on?' Sue asked. 'I think one was Field, the other –'

'McCarthy,' Eden said. 'Richard, usually known as Daft Dick – but not to his face.'

'I understood they might be the middle men for Beck, carrying money in and Semtex out?'

'Gone to ground,' Ashford growled. 'By the time we had the information, they'd vanished.'

'Along with any lead to Passmore and Gibson.' Sue decided to tackle Benny Rogers again as soon as she could.

'Don't give up hope, Mrs Bennett, I haven't,' Ashford said. 'Now, did you have contact with any of the people on the list compiled by your informant?'

'No, none at all.' Sue was puzzled. 'I did follow Beck myself on a few occasions but I never talked to him and I'm sure he never saw me.'

Sam was horrified. 'The risks you took!'

'Not at all. I always kept my distance.'

'What was he doing when you had him under observation?' Ashford wanted to know.

'Eating, mostly.'

Sue explained about the watch she had kept in Ealing and then in Fulham, trailing Beck and his girlfriend to restaurants. Eden wanted to know what sort of restaurants.

'Ethnic.'

Leonie was intrigued. 'What sort of ethnic?'

'I think he's partial to curry,' Sue said with an attempt at a grin.

Ashford relaxed in his chair. Sue's answers and her reluctance to talk had given him the clues he needed. 'You're quite sure Beck never saw you?'

'Yes. Quite sure.'

'Why is that so important?' Sam asked.

'Mrs Bennett's name was found on a pad in Beck's home.' Ashford faced Sue. 'He may never have seen you but he knew you existed.' The superintendent did not tell her what else had been scrawled alongside her name.

As Sam argued with the two policemen Sue's thoughts were a maelstrom. How had Beck known about her? Only Benny could have sold her out. It would explain the car trailing her after she had left the meeting with him in the Vine Street pub. That was when she had been identified.

Deciding the double-dealing little bag of stench would answer a few questions next time they met, Sue became aware of the import of Sam's attack on Ashford.

'The list you were given, I knew nothing of it. Believe me, if I'd had any idea do you think I'd have let her go on with it? Add to that I'd never have allowed *Journal* resources to be used to put Mrs Bennett in jeopardy.'

'I wasn't in any danger,' Sue insisted, 'and I paid for the original information myself. After that, any observations were carried out in my own time.'

'You mean, when I thought you were with Miles –'

'Miles has spent every possible moment with his son, so how could I have been with him?' Sue turned to Ashford. 'The lists and photographs, they were purely personal and had nothing to do with the *Journal*.'

'Did you take any of the shots?' Eden asked.

'No. Acquaintances did all that.' Sue saw her facts did not please the two policemen. 'Tell me, the senior police officers on the list. Had they been under suspicion?'

185

Not a muscle flickered. 'Rumours, whispers,' Ashford said. 'You know how it is in any organization.'

'Was anyone on the list missed?' she wanted to know.

The superintendent weighed his response then, 'Only one. Ray Fletcher. He was not at home.'

Sue remembered the subservience. 'I think Sean Beck was afraid of him.'

'First time Beck's shown any sense,' Eden said. 'Fletcher's nasty and he's ambitious. Very nasty and very ambitious.'

'He's also an extremely wily individual,' Ashford added. 'The serious crime division have had him in their sights and he doesn't come under our remit – unless he links in with pressure groups or bomb-making equipment.'

'Just an ordinary criminal?' Sam asked.

'Come now, Mr Haddleston,' Ashford chided. 'You know as well as I do the line between terrorists and ordinary criminals disappears on occasion. A common arrogance, a shared disregard for the sanctity of human life. If they're ruthless and use the same levels of violence, greed soon overtakes every other consideration. After all, what is a terrorist but someone who uses a cause to excuse what they do?'

Ashford's questioning went on until midnight. After he left with Inspector Eden, Sam stayed on. Leonie, yawning convincingly, went to bed leaving Sam to his nightcap of a small Scotch and the chance of a quiet time with Sue.

'Celia and Peter keep asking after you, the children, too. They wonder when you're going to see them again.'

'And risk endangering them?' The evil which had spawned in the mind of the indulged child who had become Andy Passmore had spread like a fungus of death across so many lives. Sue would not take the chance of carrying that contamination to those she loved.

'Isn't it you who made the risk greater by chasing up

186

Beck and his associates?' he asked. 'Why didn't you tell me what you were doing?'

'It was nothing to do with the *Journal*.'

'That's not the real reason.'

Sue said nothing, merely offering him more whisky.

Sam shook his head. 'You knew I'd do all I could to stop you.'

'Yes,' she sighed, 'you're very good at getting what you want but I had to do it. I've spent too much of my life sitting in a corner like a frightened animal.'

'It's more than that. You still blame yourself.'

Sue was so tired. 'If they hadn't made the decision to kill me –'

Sam moved swiftly and caught her by the shoulders, shaking her with the strength of his anger. 'Then let them suffer, not you.'

'I've got to do what I can. I have to!'

'Oh, Sue!' Sam sat beside her, holding her as he would one of Celia's children. 'It's gone beyond Passmore and Gibson. The first bombs were them, I grant you, but can't you see? Since then, it's changed. It's different now – much too professional to be the actions of a couple of blinkered activists.'

'Then why is Ashford keeping Leonie here? As well as the teams who shadow us when we're on the move and the men and women who sit outside all night? If I'm no longer of interest to anybody, I'd only need a lock on the door to be safe.'

The phone ringing next morning was a klaxon warning of the world outside. Sue was heavy-eyed as she lifted it and heard her mother's cheerful voice. Rubbing her eyes to irritate them into wakefulness she countered questions.

'I know it's my weekend off and I'm sorry, Mum, but I promised to go shopping with Pippa.'

'Of course! I forgot it's the wedding on Wednesday. Where will you look for your dresses?'

187

'Kensington High Street, I expect.'

'Oh, how I envy you! It's ages since I had a good nose round there. Tell me, is that nice Italian restaurant still open? The one in Church Street?'

'I expect so. We'll go there next time you're in town.'

'I'll hold you to that, darling. Give Pippa my love and say I'll keep her present here until you can collect it.'

Sue put down the phone. 'Damn you, Andy Passmore. If you don't have a good reason for all this . . .'

Leonie knocked and carried in hot tea. 'First sign, you know.'

The dark silk of Sue's hair swung free of her face as she looked up. 'Of what?'

'Talking to yourself? And here's me thinking you're the expert.' She sat on the edge of Sue's bed. 'You OK?'

'I'm still alive – thanks to you.'

'Nah, not me, guv.' The cockney drawl was perfect, the curled lip copied from too many streetwise juveniles. Leonie sipped from her own mug. 'I doubt you're on anyone's agenda.'

'Ashford must think so, three of his best coppers on my bed or outside my front door.'

'Window dressing.'

Sue would have liked to believe it was so. 'Why are you all still here?'

'The super doesn't like to be left out of whatever's going down. You're his link.'

'Thank you very much! If I don't get blown up I get staked out?'

There was Mrs Naib's comparison with the tiger and the deer. Sue shivered as any living animal must do when tethered for its killer.

'Cold?' Leonie asked.

'Someone walking over the proverbial.'

'Hey! None of that. If you land up there I'm in trouble right up to my neck.'

Sue drank her tea. 'Special Branch looking out for me. Why not the Met?'

'Ashford had you first,' the girl answered quickly. 'He's a man who doesn't like handing over in the middle of a case.'

'It sounds plausible but I don't think that's the real reason.'

'The importation and use of explosives – it's our remit.'

'You're saying there's a foreign angle to all this?'

'Am I?' Leonie looked deceptively innocent. 'It's too nice a morning to argue semantics. Do you want the shower first?'

By the time an excited Pippa arrived her two helpers were ready.

Leonie was curious. 'What have you done with Ken?'

'He's gone into the office to clear some work.'

Sue caught her breath. So often Colin had done that if they were due to go away. He would arrive home in time for a quick kiss before changing office clothes for jeans and a sweater. Mentally, Sue shook herself as she hugged her friend.

'Come on. You can keep Ken waiting on Wednesday. We've some serious shopping to do today.'

'I'll order the flowers on Monday,' Pippa told her. 'We should know the colours by then.'

'Not if we stay here all day, we won't!'

Leonie held the door open for them, hoping they had not noticed her checking the contents of her handbag and making sure what she might need was easily reached.

Monday's early morning newsroom had a hum of activity which meant a fast-breaking story. Three children had disappeared on a Saturday ramble through woodland in Somerset. Search parties had gone out but only at lunch-time on Sunday had cries been heard, faint sounds from subsidence above very old mine workings. For the last two hours there had been silence.

189

Leonie turned away, determined no one should see her sadness. Like all police officers, she had often been the one to talk to parents. Few knew better the sight of the raw anguish of hopeless grief as well as the feeling of intrusion which was the lot of the bearer of bad news.

There was no time for mourning. Several topics were directed Sue's way and by the time the copy was ready for printing some hours later, she was physically tired, yawning as Kate approached.

'I could really do with an early night.'

Kate examined her critically. 'Yes, you could. Take her home, Leonie. Karin, drink?'

Sue hid her amusement as Karin accepted eagerly. Kate might be the opposite of everything Karin believed in but there was no doubt the girl was blossoming under all the attention and working with her was becoming much less of a chore.

Pippa was waiting for Sue. 'I phoned your mother to thank her for the present. She was so glad you went home yesterday.'

It had taken a little arranging but Ashford had agreed and there had been covert back-up for Leonie 'to be on the safe side'. Sunday lunch in the warm house in Dorking had been a segment of peace in an unpleasant world. Although they guessed Leonie's role, Sue's parents enjoyed the girl's company, inviting her to return.

Sue smiled at Pippa. 'I knew how much she wanted you to have it before Wednesday.'

The carving of a marble swan had been a good choice. The lines were clean, simple, the angles of wing and neck giving the impression of a bird settling contentedly on its nest. A child would want to hold it and, in doing so, would learn a little of beauty.

Sue was hugged. 'For your mother – in case you see her before I do.'

'Any more to get ready for the big day?' Leonie asked.

'Only the packing. After lunch on Wednesday we just get in the car and head for the Cotswolds.'

'Where's Ken now?'

'Guess.'

Sue groaned. 'Making sure everything handed over is complete?'

'You've got it.'

'Then come and have supper with us.'

Pippa protested until she was reminded that any visit Sue made to her parents resulted in an excess of food in Islington. During the meal Leonie was persuaded to talk of some of the more bizarre incidents she had encountered. Sue and Pippa were fascinated and although little wine was drunk because of duty, pregnancy, the need for a clear head in the morning, an impromptu party ended in gales of laughter.

In the morning reality had to be faced. The Special Branch personnel were on station when Leonie escorted Sue out to the car, and the *Journal* offices were reached without incident. Inside, the mood was sombre. Bodies of three children had been brought out of the collapsed mine at midnight.

'Why, oh why do kids do such stupid things?' Kate wailed.

Cary overheard her. 'Ask Sue. Something to do with the survival of the fittest?' he offered and went in pursuit of a new blonde trainee.

'Is that true?' Kate asked.

'In this case, I doubt it. Everything seems to point to a genuine accident.'

'And the survival business?'

'Nature's way. Thanks to vaccinations and antibiotics there's a massive overdose of young males. They compete, each one trying to outdo the other. It happens early so there's a weeding out of the least successful.'

'The ones unable to get across a rail track quickly enough when they play chicken,' Leonie added, remembering.

'He who survives all the rites of passage stands a better chance of getting a mate and spending his genetic material,' Sue said. 'That's the whole purpose of the exercise.'

Kate's cigarette arced a sliver of grey. 'No wonder today's girls won't marry if they can avoid it. Fancy being tied to someone whose greatest charm lies in the fact he can successfully behave more stupidly than anyone else!'

'That's civilization for you. In the old days it was hunting that killed off the boys,' Sue explained. 'Much more natural – but the outcome was the same.'

'Mm. You've given me an idea.' Kate walked back to her desk.

As she began typing Julian deserted his computers for the newsroom. Peering through his flop of curls he made his way to Sue with a report.

'Thought I'd better bring this one myself. It looked official.'

It was. A bird protection society claimed endangered species were being deliberately decimated by farmers. Dead lambs spiked with highly toxic pesticides were being left out for eagles and kites. The number of natural predators was dropping alarmingly but their possible meals of newborn lambs survived.

'Nature red in tooth and claw,' Sue quoted, 'And that's just the humans.'

'Odd?' Julian asked, his eyes dreamy.

'Not really. When conservationists try to adjust a balance, it's all too easy for it to be tilted the other way.'

'Then another group becomes endangered?' Julian thought the question through and, as he did so, Sue remembered a question she had for him.

'Julian. I wanted to ask about money.'

His eyes were blue and surprisingly sharp. 'Did you want some?'

'No,' she laughed, 'nothing like that. It's really the transfer of money electronically. Is there a way of tracing cash disappearing into several companies?'

He mulled over what she had said. 'It never actually disappears – but you have to know where to look.'

'Do you?'

'Perhaps.'

'You don't seem sure.'

'It's not that. Sam . . .' Julian gnawed a knuckle.

'Oh, I see. You can't use the *Journal* system for hacking.'

'It's not hacking!' he said and went back to his computers.

Pippa's wedding day went smoothly from the beginning. There was a hint of green in the cream chiffon which swirled to designer order around the bride and it was echoed in her flowers. Sue had chosen emerald velvet in a simple, long-skirted suit and Leonie was quietly stunning in a cream shirt with her black jacket and trousers, a string of carved amber beads adding a touch of the exotic.

At the registrar's office in Chelsea Ken was waiting with Bill Farnham and his wife. Ken was nervous, Bill fussy and Lady Jane bored. When Pippa arrived, everyone brightened and walked into a ceremony of gentle dignity. There was no doubt of Ken and Pippa's commitment to each other, and when a kiss sealed the moment the celebrations began.

'I'm not much good at weddings,' Sam murmured to Sue as they stood on the steps of the building and watched a photographer struggle for control.

She had no doubts. 'As long as those two are together, that's all that matters for today.'

There was time only for hugs, kisses, confetti, before a limousine swept the newly-weds to the reception. The subsequent scramble was less to do with hunger than a need to rescue cars from the threat of fines and clamping. Taxis were whistled up and in a remarkably short space of time, the steps were deserted.

The buffet lunch was a joyous affair. Fresh salmon and succulent beef were flanked by innumerable salads and the lack of formality allowed guests to mingle and chat. Champagne flowed and strangers became instant friends.

With Sue at his side Sam was happy and his wit sparkled, thawing even Bill Farnham's aloof wife, Lady Jane. Leonie had attracted a junior partner in Ken's office and the girl responded cautiously, wary of such a situation when she was on duty.

With the speeches over, the last toasts drunk, Pippa and Ken were waved away. Most of the guests were content to stay longer and order more wine but Sue wanted to leave. She had spent too many happy evenings with them all, Colin at her side. The memories still had the power to hurt and it was with a sense of escape she said her goodbyes, Leonie following.

Sam hurried to join them. 'I'm due back at the *Journal* for a meeting this evening.'

'Then you've time for some of Leonie's coffee first,' Sue said and watched delight flare in his eyes.

Together they walked behind Leonie to her car. It had been parked some distance from the restaurant and Sue was glad to stretch muscles and breathe cool air. For the first time in weeks she was at peace. Colin would have loved to see Pippa and Ken so happy and this time the thought of him brought only a gentle pleasure.

There was a sudden, dull thump in the middle of her back. Sue's arm was wrenched as her bag was pulled from her and she saw a skinny white boy race away with it, his roller blades carrying him faster than Sam could run. A dark bomber jacket, maybe blue, she thought. Black baseball cap with a white peak. He was wearing it back to front, the white peak twisting and turning out of her view.

Leonie had been knocked over by the boy and was back on her feet when there was a screech of wheels. As if in slow motion Sue watched two men run from the car in the middle of the road. They were all in black, ski masks

covering their faces and only a few patches of skin showing white.

In seconds one had hold of Sue. The other lunged at
Sam, wrong-footing him and knocking him against rail-
ings. The two raiders lifted a struggling Sue and carried
her to the car, its engine noisy as it was revved hard.

Leonie ran fast but could not prevent Sue being heaved
inside the vehicle. All the policewoman could do was to
cling to the car door and prevent it from being closed as
the driver sped away, carrying her along the street.

Sue saw no more. Something thick covered her head and
she could hardly breathe. The smell of dust and oil was in
her nostrils and she heard muffled cursing. The car slewed,
hit something, then stopped. She heard doors open and
angry voices. Her captors released her arms and Sue was
aware of action of some sort. There were yells of triumph
and a gentle hand lifted away fetid cloth.

'You're OK now, love.'

Through her hair Sue could see one of the men who had
spent so much time outside her flat. 'Is Leonie all right?
Sergeant Webley?'

A wide grin answered her. 'See for yourself.'

The toes of her shoes might have gone, immaculate
slacks shredded and torn, but Leonie's blood-stained foot
was firmly clamped across the neck of a miserable lump of
humanity. Handcuffs were being put into use and ensuring
there would be no more unacceptable behaviour.

A tousled, jubilant Sam was at the car. He helped Sue
out, enabling her to see Bill Farnham's Bentley with a
dented wing and a furious Lady Jane in the back seat. Two
more men were trussed and waiting for a police van, one
of them with a rapidly swelling jaw and enough residual
animosity to glare at Sam and mutter.

'What was all that about?' Sue wanted to know.

Leonie's smile was shaky. 'I think someone wanted a
chat with you.'

Chapter Eleven

Why are hospitals such depressing places, Sue asked herself? This one was bright, flowers in abundance, nurses quietly efficient, yet there was an invisible pall over it all. The silent screaming of fear echoed and was almost tangible. People around her in the casualty department, some of them children, sat mute, each terrified of what a doctor might find.

'Are you OK?' Sam asked for the thousandth time.

Sue released a breath. 'I'm fine.'

It would not help to talk of wrenched shoulders, aching arms, a banged knee. When compared with Leonie's, Sue injuries were slight.

Sam caught hold of her hand. In the ambulance he had held her while they watched Leonie's bleeding feet and legs checked by experts. There, too, screams had been silent. Sue leaned against Sam's shoulder. It was good to have him beside her.

'Mrs Bennett?' A stocky girl in dark blue called and it was Sue's turn to strip off and be examined.

From his very long name Sue guessed the young doctor must have come from Sri Lanka. He was short, already balding, with dark eyes, beautiful teeth and gentle fingers which missed nothing. He listed Sue's injuries for the record and told her she was extremely lucky.

'Leonie? Leonie Webley?'

The doctor was cautious, unprepared to commit himself.

'She was hurt looking after me,' Sue explained and he heard the desperation in her voice.

'Miss Webley will be fine. Her shoulders are very sore but her hands are losing the cramping. The main traumas were to her feet and legs. She was very badly grazed and it will take a long time for the skin to heal completely.'

'How long?'

'I can't say. A day or so and scabs will begin to form. She will be able to move about as she heals, although very stiffly to begin with.'

'Can I see her?'

'Of course – as soon as the nurse has finished her dressings.'

By that time Ashford was in the hospital, thrusting his way past NHS officialdom to make sure his sergeant was properly cared for and on the mend.

'Glad you're safe, Mrs Bennett.'

'Thanks to Leonie.'

'And Bill Farnham's precious car,' Sam said with a grin. 'If his chauffeur hadn't seen what was happening and pulled out at that precise moment –'

'Two of my men were right behind the abductors,' Ashford informed them. 'They'd radioed in the number of the suspect vehicle and other cars in the area were waiting for them.'

Sue thought of Lady Jane, inconvenienced for no reason. 'Have you told the Farnhams that?'

Ashford cleared his throat. 'Actually, no. I thought it best they believed they were instrumental in obtaining your release.'

'I doubt Lady Jane would consider my freedom worth a bent wing.'

'She'd better,' Sam muttered as Sue, followed by the superintendent, went into the cubicle where Leonie lay.

The girl began to sit up. 'Did you get anything out of the three arrested?' she asked her boss.

'Hired help,' Ashford said. 'The description they gave of the person setting up the kidnap would fit half the white

197

males in London. There's no name for that contact, let alone the man ordering it.'

'Nothing at all, sir?'

'Gallagher, one of the men picked up, he's a bit nosy and wanted to know why they were to lift Mrs Bennett – so he said.'

'Was he told?'

'Only that it was something to do with animals.'

Sue shivered. 'What about the boy who stole my bag? Was he part of it?'

'Highly likely,' Ashford said. 'Mick Gallagher has a young brother on the way to becoming real trouble. I expect it was him.'

'Who were the other two?' Leonie wanted to know.

'Trevor Cleary and Jimmy Coughlan. They're well known too and have records as long as Gallagher's. Specialists in strong-arm security on building sites.'

Something in his voice made Sue look at him closely. The lines in Ashford's face were deeper, his skin dry and tired. Only his eyes were bright, flicking from one to another as he gathered all he could.

'Is there a way to link them with Passmore and Gibson?' she asked.

The superintendent made no comment. As if by instinct, Sue followed his thoughts. 'The attempt to get me?'

Ashford nodded. 'Whoever wants you is the key to all this.'

'Animal Equality? It's hardly their style.'

'I agree,' he said, 'but there's big money circulating and Ray Fletcher may be running the show now. We have to consider his habits.'

'What about this man, Fletcher?' Sam asked. 'I can't see him as an animal lover.'

'I very much doubt he is, Mr Haddleston. First and foremost he's a professional crook – one who's seen a way of getting his hands on easy money. With their bombs Animal Equality set the pattern and engendered the fear. Once he guessed that, it's odds on Fletcher decided to take over as the financial manager and beneficiary of the enterprise.'

'Are you sure it's Fletcher, sir?' Leonie asked.

He did not tell her of the smell of fear arising in numerous interview rooms at the mere mention of Fletcher's name. 'Your guess is as good as mine.' Ashford had a tired smile for his sergeant. 'Just get well and help me nail him. In the meantime, we'll sort out a safe house for Mrs Bennett –'

'No! I won't be shut away again!'

Having to account for everything she said and did, her every movement watched and recorded, was draining Sue. Her greatest need was for fear of the unknown to be ended. It had all gone on too long.

Superintendent Ashford and Sam joined forces to persuade Sue to see sense but their efforts were in vain.

'Fletcher won't be tempted out of hiding if I'm in a safe house. You'll get him faster if I'm free to be followed.'

Sam was furious. 'You're not in a fit state to take it on!'

'By the time he's aware of me being back in my own home, I'll have had time to recover.'

Leonie supported her. She had come to know Sue's character, her resilience, even after major setbacks. The arguments continued for some time but Sue was adamant. Ashford eventually agreed, as long as Leonie stayed with Sue, her guard at night. Inspector Eden would drive Sue to and from the *Journal* offices.

'There must be constant back-up,' Sam insisted. 'Have you a problem with that?'

'None at all,' Ashford said. 'A Serious Crimes squad wants Fletcher very badly too. There'll be plenty of units available – for once.'

At that point Sue had an urge to giggle. 'Make sure they don't stick out like sore thumbs.'

'How was the wedding?' Kate asked.

199

'Great.' Sue summoned up all her energy to be fresh, cheerful.

'Come on, then – tell.'

Karin stopped reading to swivel in her chair. 'Where's Leonie this morning?'

The story had been rehearsed hours ago. 'She fell and hurt her foot badly. A few days and she'll be more or less mobile again.'

Kate's chuckle was rich, throaty. 'Too much fizzy pop, I'll bet. Poor girl not got the head for it?'

'Something like that.'

'It must have been a good do. How was Pippa?'

'Radiant, so was Ken. The idea of spending the rest of their life together put them on cloud nine. I doubt they'll ever come off it.'

'They will, darling. They will,' Kate insisted before trolling off to accost Cary and entertain the entire newsroom with her attack on the main subject of his latest column. 'I can't believe you can consider him one of the elite! A half-witted actor from Basingstoke who's not even good-looking, shacked up with a little scrubber from Poplar?' carried clearly to everyone within range.

'Anything come in you think we could use?' Sue asked Karin when at last there was peace.

'Not a lot. A grant by the EC to help restore breeding grounds of the bittern in East Anglia.'

'Someone boomed to good effect for once,' Sue punned. 'You could get it written up ready, two hundred words and a photo from the library. Expect it to be cut to fifty words – if it's used.'

Karin made a note on her pad and Sue settled to a write-up of Australian bandicoots loose in Swansea and then a project to give red squirrels the advantage over the grey variety.

Sandy arrived to discuss wind farms. Benefits were agreed and so were the disadvantages, the noise factor a major issue. Sue put forward the suggestion that more should be made of wave power, miles of coastline normally inaccessible to humans, with enormous energy guaranteed to be released upon it twice a day. She quoted a research project in Pembrokeshire on wave energy, wondering why the government had not raced down there to give it full support and backing with lottery money.

Karin joined in, her contribution surprising Sandy. 'She's not just a pretty face,' he commented before enlisting the girl's help.

Sue took the opportunity to find Julian. His room was quiet, tidy, the array of equipment impressive and paper stacked in orderly piles. He was at one with his machines and Sue had been at his side some time before he noticed her.

'Is there a problem?'

'No, a suggestion.'

Dreamy eyes became shrewd. 'To do with what we talked about the other day?'

'Money movement? Yes.'

'There's very little I can do here.'

She knew he would do nothing which could backfire on Sam. 'Of course not – but I have a contact who has a cousin.' Sue explained work testing the security of computer installations.

'Don't they – this person – have to get permission first?'

Sue nodded. 'She's acting on behalf of a group of insurance companies and the arrangement is that tests can occur any time.'

Curls bounced as Julian understood. 'You'd like me to meet her and see what we can find out?'

'Would you? I know you can carry out things like company checks –'

'But accessing bank records could cost the *Journal* in damages?'

'Exactly.'

Julian's fingers stroked the mouse beside his keyboard as he thought. He was in a world of whizzing electrons behind the screen of his computer, a world where innumerable connections promised excitement. Sue had offered

201

him the chance of taking those connections almost to infinity and anything was possible. 'Tonight?' he asked hopefully.

'If I can set it up in time.'

In a quiet stretch of corridor Sue used her mobile, aware Ashford might have had her phone extension bugged.

Anil's brother was delighted. 'Sunitra will agree, I'm sure. To work with someone who understands what she is talking about will give her great pleasure. Exactly what is it you want to know?'

'Everything must be legal,' she insisted before outlining her needs.

Anwar assured Sue of Sunitra's probity and asked for Julian to be at the main entrance of the *Journal* at six o'clock. 'Gauri is her brother and will take your friend to her.'

When the message had been delivered Sue thought longingly of coffee but she was thwarted by a grim-faced Kate slamming down a copy of the *Daily Press*. It was a tabloid usually filled with adverts mixed with scraps of London's news. A red-nailed finger pointed to a paragraph.

'A scuffle in Mallord Street, Chelsea, at three thirty. Wasn't that where the reception was yesterday?'

Sue read the details. They were blessedly brief.

'Did you see anything?'

There was a memory of stifling cloth and she could be truthful. 'Not really. Bill Farnham's car got banged and he was rather annoyed. I gather a certain amount of abuse was exchanged. The police arrived and dealt with it all.'

'Where were you when it happened?'

'I left before Bill.'

'That's your story and you're sticking to it?'

Sue smiled. 'Of course.'

'And Leonie ended up getting injured?'

'I suppose it was a day of small accidents.'

Kate's gaze held Sue. As a friend she expected the truth and Sue was clearly holding something back. She sighed.

They were both journalists and some secrets had to be kept.

'If you say so, darling. If you say so.'

Inspector Eden was waiting for Sue when it was time to begin the trek home. He rarely talked as he drove and all Sue's efforts to take an interest in his family life, hobbies, outlook, had been politely foiled. He did talk to his colleagues as messages reached him by radio but the codes were so cryptic Sue had no chance of understanding what passed.

As they drew up outside her home a car slid in behind them; from Eden's calmness Sue realized there had been extra protection all the way home. She was tired, and as the inspector followed her to her door she wondered if there would ever be an end to suspicion, fear and the need for a guard.

Eden preceded Sue into the flat, walking quickly and lightly as he checked the rooms. Leonie was stretched out on the couch. She took her hand away from the gun in her bag as she welcomed the inspector, widening her smile to include Sue.

'Good day at the office, dear?'

Sue's answer was to pick up a cushion and fling it.

'Any problems?'

She began to outline what had gone on at the *Journal*, glimpsing Eden shaking his head and Leonie relaxing.

'Is Sam sore from yesterday?' Leonie wanted to know. 'He certainly lammed Coughlan.'

'Sam's fine.' He had not only phoned Sue at regular intervals, he had dragged Gavin on a few circuits of the newsroom to check all was well. Sue had seen no obvious bruises.

Leonie swung her feet to the floor and stood up, her face a mask hiding pain. 'Supper?'

Inspector Eden excused himself, explaining he had to report to Ashford before going home.

'Your mother called half an hour ago,' Leonie told Sue as she returned from locking the flat door. 'I told her you were on your way home and was given a list of things to get out of the freezer.' She hobbled towards the kitchen. 'It'll be on the table in five minutes.'

Sue was concerned, seeing Leonie wince as she tried to flex her feet. 'Stop right there and tell me how you are.'

The girl swung her head towards Sue, knowing the truth had been demanded. 'A bit stiff still. Better after I had a very long, hot shower.'

'How did you cope with your bandages?'

'Fine,' Leonie said as she hobbled away, 'but you're almost out of clingfilm.'

Ashford arrived unannounced the following evening with more photographs of demonstrators for Sue to examine.

'Why do I still have to be so restricted?'

He took a long time to answer. 'Fletcher is determined to get you. We want to tempt him to try – but on our terms.'

'And you're stuck with me,' said Leonie with a grin.

Even after Ashford left the flat Sue could not shake off the idea that her safety was of secondary importance. The Special Branch team watching her was in place to pick up a trail to Fletcher. It was not a pleasant thought.

The days passed slowly for Leonie as damaged tissues repaired and itched. For Sue, work in the newsroom was hectic enough to make time fly by. It helped keep her sane but the private hunt for the bombers was made impossible by the total surveillance she endured.

Inspector Eden relaxed enough on their journeys to become Pat and talk of his wife, Ros, and the baby due soon. Sue discovered fishing was his passion and she listened to almost poetic accounts of river stretches holding the sparkling mystery of an underwater life so graceful a man could only envy.

'You won't be too happy with the new lobby wanting to ban fishing?'

'Lobby?' He dismissed the idea with a shake of his head. 'A pack of wannabes. They wannabe noticed, wannabe on telly.'

'There's more to it than that, surely?'

Traffic lights had stopped them and Eden routinely noted nearby cars. 'Fishing clubs help police the rivers and keep stocks safe. Do-gooders trying to stop all that will only increase the number of savages who dynamite a river and sell off fish blasted to death.'

'So only ordinary fishermen would be affected if the bans go through?'

Pat Eden slammed on brakes and sounded his horn at a driver pulling into his lane too slowly. 'If nobody's to hunt fish from a river or a pond, who's going to go round and tell all the kingfishers, cormorants, otters, owls ospreys –'

'OK, I get the message,' Sue said with a laugh.

'No, I'm serious. Sportsmen only take a tiny fraction of the fish in our waters and in nearly every case the animal goes back alive after it's been measured and weighed.'

'With hook damage?'

'Which heals. If you've ever watched keen anglers you've seen how careful they are taking out the hook. The fish has been their opponent and they've won – that's all they need to know. Remember, the men – and women – stand still. Fish can go in any direction.'

'Aren't there brutal fishermen?'

They were turning into the *Journal* car park and he did not try to speak until they were safely beyond the barrier.

'Brutality implies arrogance, a short temper. No good for fishing.'

On her way to her desk Sue reflected on the methods of Superintendent Ashford. He was quietly waiting, his lure cast, waiting for a man-fish to swim to it. There was a coldness across her back and she shivered. At least it made a change from being a deer or a goat.

The big newsroom was strangely quiet. 'What's happened?' Sue asked Beth, resplendent in a Richmond shirt.

'Jonah. A stroke.'

'How bad?'

Beth said nothing, her shoulders moving expressively.

'Poor old boy,' Sue said, half to herself.

'He was a damned good reporter.' Beth had already consigned Jonah to the past.

'He could be a good friend, too. I ought to go and see Evelyn.' Jonah's wife was thin, blonde, elegant. 'She was very kind to me when Colin died.'

'Sam's there. He wants us all to keep back for a while.' Her short, sturdy legs took Beth away.

Sue sat at her desk and wondered about Benny. He could answer so many questions but it was no use trying to find him. Only Jonah could do that and he was out of action.

'You've heard, then?'

Kate's grooming was as faultless as ever but Sue caught the whiff of fresh gin in the cigarette smoke and was worried for her friend. Kate usually waited until lunchtime before starting on the alcohol.

'Isn't it time you gave up that filty habit?' Cary demanded, pointing to Kate's cigarette. 'You pollute all our environments and kill yourself into the bargain.'

'The more you nag me, the more I worry, the more I smoke,' Kate retorted.

'You'll get wrinkles – and do you really want to go the same way as Jonah?'

Kate was surprised. 'Anyone would think you cared.'

'I do. Who will argue with me if you go off in a puff of nicotine?'

'Carbon monoxide, actually,' Sue told them.

'Sue! Haven't you anything even slightly amusing to cheer us all up?' Kate's hand was shaking as she fitted a fresh cigarette into its holder.

'Italian football?'

'What's funny about that?' Cary wanted to know.

Sue read from her notepad. 'Researchers found boys who play football more than ten hours a week have reduced chances of fatherhood.'

'There are quite enough Italians already,' Kate said dismissively.

Sue tried again. 'How about cold sores and tea bags – but they must be Earl Grey because of the bergamot?'

'I must tell Chloe about that,' Cary said, 'she does love her Earl Grey.'

'Probably the only satisfaction your poor wife gets these days.' Kate was in a waspish mood. 'Is that the lot?' she asked Sue.

'A report on an anaesthetic. Propofol. Women wake up afterwards faster than men.'

'Women take more drugs than men – they're used to them,' Cary decided but Kate was not ready to compromise.

'No way! It's because the slightest of efforts make men fall asleep on the job.'

'Are you talking from experience?' he asked, his words like silk.

'No, but it does explain why Chloe's consumption of Earl Grey's gone sky high.'

The two friends moved off, bickering furiously, and Sue was left in peace to wonder what direction her searches could take now the link with Benny had gone.

'For you, Sue. I haven't had a chance before.' A remarkably alert Julian was handing her an envelope.

She looked inside and was impressed by the mass of print-outs. 'You've been working hard on this.'

'I liked Anil,' he said quietly.

'So did I. How's it going with Sunitra?'

Julian's face was alight. 'Terrific!' He said no more, ambling to his room to sit and dream with electrons.

A swift look through the sheets he had given her made Sue realize that a visit to the library was a must. There, she spent some time checking through the City files and when

207

she was ready to go home she was tired, and her eyes ached.

'Bad day?' Pat Eden asked after informing a co-ordinator they were leaving *Journal* premises.

'Just busy.'

She relaxed as he drove, eyelids drooping as a one-sided conversation was punctuated by technical crackles. In a quiet stretch she sat up.

'Ray Fletcher.'

Eden's eyes never left the road. 'What about him?'

'Have you no idea where he is?'

'Confirmed reports of him being seen in Spain. That was a few days ago. He could be anywhere. Why do you ask?'

Sunitra and Julian had unearthed a string of companies, all apparently bona fide and all with a strange array of company directors, company secretaries and treasurers. One company secretary kept recurring, enough to make Sue curious.

'A name.'

There was a brief smile for her. 'From your secret team?'

'Sort of. Beatrice Norton.'

'Beatrice Norton? No, I don't know the lady. You're sure that's the name?'

'Positive. The address given is Ilford but she's not on the phone there or on the electoral roll.'

'I'll see what I can find out,' Eden promised as he stopped the car at Sue's home and saw her into safety.

In the warm and welcoming flat supper was ready, the table laid. Sue opened a bottle of wine and poured a glass for Leonie, watching her sip it appreciatively.

'Ray Fletcher,' Sue said. 'Tell me about him.'

Leonie inspected the colour of the wine. 'Why the interest?'

'I've seen photos of him but they don't reveal much.' He was on one side of the web of information, tugging it viciously to get at her. Sue wanted to know him, his methods, his habits.

'OK. Male aged forty-five, IC1, height five eleven, medium build, fair hair, blue eyes.'

'Thank you, Sergeant Webley. Now think like a journalist and give me some colour.'

Leonie lifted the wine bottle and served Sue. 'I watched him being interviewed once,' she said quietly. 'He sat quite still, totally in control of himself. Occasionally he smoothed his hair or fiddled with his ring. It's gold and set with a large diamond.'

'He's flashy?'

'No, that's what's odd about Ray Fletcher. He dresses expensively but discreetly and keeps himself well groomed. He could walk into any club in St James's and look at home. Until he opens his mouth.'

'The accent?'

Leonie shook her head as she twisted the stem of her glass and watched wine swirl. 'It's his teeth. They're irregular, yellowish – they spoil the whole effect.'

'Of passing as a gentleman?'

'He can do that – at a distance,' Leonie said and grinned. 'I wouldn't mind betting some poor little housemaid once got laid by the lord of the manor's son and a few generations later Fletcher inherited the boning. He looks well bred and he has had a go at improving the way he talks.'

'But he hasn't got it right?'

'Not quite. Then there's the aura of menace he carries with him. I know some women are turned on by that sort of thing but I'm not one of them.'

'Is there a wife?'

'Yes, the stupid cow.'

Sue was startled. 'That's not like you.'

'Well, how else do you describe a woman who lets herself be used like a dumb animal?'

'He beats her?'

'To a pulp. She must have the thickest file in NHS history, the number of times she's been turned the colour of liver and admitted to casualty.'

209

'For Pete's sake! Why doesn't she get him charged? Why does she stay?'

'Perhaps she loves him?' There was no doubt Leonie thought the woman mad if she did. 'I guess she knows if she resisted he might start on the children. A boy and girl, early teens. From what I've heard they're nice kids.'

'Pity they can't all get away.'

'Where would they go? They can't just turn up at a battered wives' refuge. Fletcher's powerful in his own world and would soon have them tracked down. Either his boys would go in and smash the place up or it would be petrol-bombed. He's quite keen on cleansing by fire.'

'You're kidding!'

'I wish I was. He plays for keeps – and Mrs Fletcher knows it.'

There was a silence in the cosy room. 'Girlfriends?' Sue asked.

Leonie nodded. 'Plenty. He's particularly fond of models.'

'That's strange. I've never seen any with him in photos, recent ones or those in the *Journal* records.'

'Photographers taking an interest get more than their cameras smashed – and they know it.'

'Does Fletcher react the same way to anyone curious about him?'

Leonie hesitated, wondering how frank she should be. 'If he gives an order it has to be carried out – no matter what the cost. He's very conscious of status. If that's threatened, he turns nasty.'

'Has he friends?'

'No. Associates, I suppose you'd call the people he deals with. They have to show a great deal of respect.'

It explained Beck's deference. 'The attempts to get me,' Sue said slowly, 'they're not likely to stop?'

'If he's put out the word to have you lifted and gave up on the idea it would mean you – and the police –

had beaten him. Once that whisper got around he'd be finished.'

By the time Pat Eden collected Sue next morning he had acquired an air of satisfaction.

'Your Beatrice Norton.'

'You've found her?'

'In the paperwork. Fletcher has an Auntie Beattie. Beattie Mower she was, his mother's sister. Like the rest of the Mowers she originated in Essex but not as upmarket as Ilford. Beattie married an electrician, Sam Norton, who handled a bit of stolen goods on the side. Nothing much. Both disappeared a few years ago.'

'Was Norton local to Ilford?'

'No, he came over from Jersey sometime in the '50s when their police had got to know him and his ways too well.'

'Jersey. Nice place for a holiday.'

Sue became interested in a small boy at a crossing. He was tugging at his mother's hand as they waited for the traffic to pass. She saw little and hoped Pat Eden had not picked up the click of a mental connection. What he had just told her tallied with some of Sunitra's findings.

It was difficult for Sue to contain her impatience, and when they reached the *Journal* she hurried from the car and towards Julian.

Education filled the main pages in all the newspapers and Sue's day was a little easier because of it, even if arguments around her were as noisy as they were meant to be persuasive.

Kate knew the answer to all the problems. 'Stop the benefits of parents who allow their children to run riot in the schools.'

Cary disagreed. 'It's the cane that's missing from the equation!'

211

The debate roared most of the morning and it was obvious from newscasts that the theme would fill the *Journal* the next day, vote-hungry politicians joining in. Sue thought how much simpler life was in a slow-moving tribe of great apes. As the babies grew and became adventurous older relatives helped, grabbing loose skin, swiping with a hairy paw, to keep boisterousness within bounds. By the time independence was possible the lessons of survival and living in a close society had been learned.

'Penny for them.'

Sue looked up to see Sandy and was cheered by his smile. She explained about the apes.

'Perhaps we'd all be better off living in a zoo.'

'As long as I'm not in the one in Athens!' Sue retorted. 'I'd have more respect for animal rights people if they cleaned up that place.'

'You're joking! No one in their right mind tangles with the Greek police. They're armed.'

'Is that why Britain's cornered the market in psychos? Because our police don't carry guns?' she asked.

'It must give the sub-humans in Animal Equality a sense of security. They're terrorists, just like Al Qaeda, the IRA and all the others. They feel safe as they kill, knowing they can't be shot down like the rabid dogs they are.' Sandy's mouth was a hard line, his jaw tight with anger. Because of two well-educated terrorists and their skills Sandy's children had nearly grown up without a father.

'They've got to be stopped,' she said quietly, wondering how surprised Sandy would be to count the carefully hidden side-arms protecting her each day.

He saw her distress. 'The police will get them in time, Sue, and the ones cashing in.'

'How many more deaths will that mean while we wait?'

Sandy took off his glasses and polished them. 'There've been no attacks since the chemists' shops. Maybe the police are closing in.'

Sue knew only too well how distant Ashford was from

212

his quarry but there was no point worrying Sandy, he had suffered enough. Left alone, Sue was haunted again by all those who had harmed her. All of them had seen her as a mere woman to be used and discarded.

She was cold, rubbing her arms to warmth which did not touch the chill inside her. She stared at the busy room, people intent on their work, knowing she must be positive, as they were. So many had helped her. Anwar and his friends working hard and easing their grief as they did so, Leonie, her feet scarred, and Sam who had been like a rock since the first bomb.

Miles had gone from her life because James needed his father. Sue wondered what it would be like if Sam went too. In an instant a deep ache inside her made her catch her breath. There was an echoing void, a sense of desolation which shocked.

'Are you OK, Sue?' Beth asked. 'I'll bet you've been drinking too much coffee.'

Shaking her head helped, Sue found. 'I'm fine, really. Have you come to tell me I've got to cut my paras on the activists taking on that college over the use of mice in labs?'

'No way! More power to their collective elbow. At least they've got the guts not to be anonymous.' Beth leaned on Sue's VDU, her scrutiny caring, not intrusive. 'I used to keep mice when I was little. Don't know how my mother stood it – she hates 'em.'

Beth ambled away carrying her sanity like a banner, and on an impulse Sue rang Leonie. 'How about going home this weekend?'

'To your parents? Marvellous idea. I'd better check with the super before your mother makes up beds and cooks for a regiment. Any special reason?'

'I've got the urge for fresh air. It might help me think things through.'

'To do with work?'

Sue pictured Sam at his desk, only yards away from where she was sitting. 'In a way.'

The air was fresh in Dorking although heavy rain prevented all but a quick rush to the car when it was essential to go out. Mr Lavin poured sherry and teased the girls while his wife whirled in the kitchen. Evenings were filled with gentle conversation and Scrabble alternating with quiet hours lost in good books. In front of a log fire Sue and Leonie were tranquil, the microcosm of threats and fear, radios and surveillance, belonging to a different existence.

Sunday evening loomed and Mrs Lavin boxed food for the freezer in Islington while Sue's father cut chrysanthemums which filled the car with the dampness of autumn nostalgia. No one had seen the discreet vehicles which changed every few hours as Ashford's people guarded.

'Did you get the problem sorted out?' Leonie asked on the way home after she had made sure the guards on duty were following.

'It wasn't a problem,' Sue murmured. 'More a case of accepting reality.'

Pippa and Ken gusted in. There was a small painting for Sue, a bright cushion cover for Leonie, trophies from the peace of honey-stoned Cotswold villages.

'I gather a good time was had by all?'

Sue was answered with enthusiasm and descriptions of places off the beaten track not to be missed. Stanton, Laverton, Buckland, all tucked into folds of the hills near Broadway.

'I know where I want to live when I retire,' Ken said.

'What about Devon?' his wife wanted to know.

'Wherever.' He looked at Sue, hesitating to say what was on his mind. 'Actually, the gardens we saw were so beautiful it made us think.'

'We knew we had to find somewhere with a garden for the baby,' Pippa explained to her. 'Will you mind very much?'

'You moving away from here? Why should I?' Sue knelt in front of her friend and hugged her. 'Haven't you told me often enough life doesn't stand still? We all have to move on – one way or another.'

Pippa gazed at Sue and recognized a change in her. For the better, she thought. 'You'll always be welcome, wherever we are.'

Sue grinned. 'Just make sure I get to help with the housewarming party.'

Sam was waiting at the door of the newsroom when Sue arrived. 'Did you have a good weekend?' he asked.

She was suddenly shy, hoping her cheeks were not as red as they felt. 'Yes, thank you. My mother stuffed us to bursting point and the rain meant there was no chance to walk it off.'

'Your parents are well?'

Sue nodded.

'What about Leonie?'

'A medical this morning. If she's passed fit she'll be back in here tomorrow.'

'Will she make it?'

'I think so. We'd hoped to do enough walking at the weekend for her to be sure –'

There was a fierce blaze in Sam's eyes, quickly shuttered. 'How's Jonah?' she asked.

'Still not able to speak. His breathing's ghastly, as you'd imagine, and he's not awake for long each day. But he's still with us.'

The day was busy and passed quickly. Before Sue went home she visited Julian for an illuminating chat and hasty notes. It made her later than usual leaving the *Journal* but Pat Eden was ready, his patience intact.

215

'Sorry you've had to wait.'

'No problem. Ros's mother's with her.'

'Then have you time for some information?'

He cleared a junction, making sure there was no car in pursuit. 'Useful?'

'Possibly. It's to do with the blackmail money which vanished.'

Eden's hands tightened on the steering wheel. 'Go on.'

'Money doesn't disappear, it leaves traces – if you know where to look.'

'Your mysterious friends again?'

'Some people are more expert than others with computers.'

'That weirdo in the *Journal*, was it him?'

'Julian? There's no way the *Journal*'s systems were used for tracking the money.' It felt good to tell the truth.

'And you can't reveal your sources?'

'Not done in the best circles.'

'OK. Let's have what you've got.'

Sue drew in a long breath. 'The blackmail money was all sent to the Caymans, right?'

'Right. Minutes before the end of trading –'

'So by the time it was possible to check out the destination, it was too late?'

'Agreed. By then the money had gone and there was no evidence of any transactions.'

'Wrong.'

The car hiccuped as Pat Eden's attention was caught and held. 'Nothing was found,' he said as the engine purred on again towards Islington.

'Maybe not by your experts but mine are something special. I don't understand it, I must admit. It's something to do with data in limbo.'

'You're kidding!'

'No. Data used and dismissed doesn't necessarily always leave the system. If you or I tap in we only see what appears on the screen because that's all we're looking for. Supposing you could call up what had been on the screen in the not-so-distant past and was thought to have been deleted?'

'Oh, my God! You've accessed cancelled information?'

'Well done, Inspector. Go to the top of the class.'

'Do I get details I can take to Ashford?'

Sue heaved a folder from her briefcase. 'I've a report of sorts – written on my own paper and not the *Journal's*, I might add.'

'I'd better get the super to come over.' Pat Eden reached for the radio. 'It could be a long night.'

He was right.

'Where's this report?' Ashford demanded as soon as he walked in.

Sue gave him the folder. The notes he read had been handwritten by Sue so no one else need be involved in any questioning. Ashford read fast.

'You realize whoever got this information for you probably broke every law in the book?'

'Not at all. I was assured everything came from sources available to the public.'

'Don't take me for a fool!' Knotted veins stood out on Ashford's temples. 'Our experts went over everything.'

'I expect they did,' Sue said calmly, 'but they only saw what was left for them to see. Supposing you could find what had been properly deleted?'

'It can't be done!'

Sue pointed to the papers strewing the coffee table. 'It was. Transfers were made from a bank in the Caymans to a group of shadow companies in various countries. From those accounts the money was moved several times, ending up in a consortium set up to hide cash transfers, this time nearer home. Whoever organized it all was a damn good accountant and a fairly good computer user – but not as good as the ones helping me.'

Ashford raised his hands, palms up in surrender. 'Your

notes only tell me the paths the money took and the names of the false companies. You're keeping something back.'

'The link is Jersey and a lady by the name of Beatrice Norton.'

The superintendent was puzzled. 'Who?'

Pat Eden was eager to help. 'You remember, sir, she's Fletcher's aunt. Retired to Jersey.' He waited for Sue to continue.

'Officially, she's the company secretary for a range of organizations, some of which bank in St Helier. All the money traced so far has ended up in one of three accounts there, all in the name of Beatrice Norton.'

'Auntie Beattie,' Pat Eden murmured. 'She lives in a bungalow two miles west of St Aubin. After something Mrs Bennett said, I contacted Jersey police and asked for all they could tell us about Beattie Norton. It took some time to get an answer out of them but from what we've heard now, I think we should ask them to pick her up, sir.'

'If I know Ray Fletcher, I doubt this female's been allowed near the banks since the accounts were opened,' Ashford snapped, 'but go on, get the old witch – unless it's better to keep her under observation for now.' He turned to Sue. 'You've done the sums. How much are we looking at?'

'It wasn't possible to find the amounts on deposit – that would have been illegal.' Sue risked a grin. 'All that could be done was to total the cash transferred into those accounts.' She took a deep breath. 'In the three banks there's at least six million pounds sterling.'

Chapter Twelve

'Mrs Bennett?' asked the voice on the phone.

It was Benny Rogers and Sue's stomach tightened against the nausea of remembered smells.

'Is there something wrong?'

'Mr Blackburn, how is he?'

Sue told of the stroke, the coma, pneumonia threatening lungs barely able to function.

'Poor old bugger,' came to Sue with a strange sincerity. 'Tell you why I'm ringing. If there's a chance he can't work again, has he got a friend who does the same sort of thing? Only I got a nice little story for them – if they're interested.'

So that was it. Benny wanted to make sure his payments from the *Journal* continued.

'I don't know,' she said. 'Some of the information you gave me wasn't up to much.'

Sue was tempted to cut the call but if Benny had passed on her name to Beck, or even Fletcher, Superintendent Ashford might be able to use the smelly little man.

'Mrs Bennett,' Benny cajoled, 'I couldn't tell you anything that might give you grief. Mr Blackburn, he wouldn't like that.'

'Instead, you took top whack for second-rate goods and sold me to Beck.'

'That's not nice – and you a lady! I told you I'd do you no harm.' Benny was very offended but he had more important things on his mind. 'Listen now, tell your bloke I got Charlie Marshall's address.'

'Who?'

'Before your time. You'd be in a gymslip when he was boss. Did a runner after a job in the Garden.'

'Hatton Garden?'

'That's right. He likes diamonds – big ones. Went to Rio to start with but his wife fancied Spain. He wants to come home but only if it gives the missus enough to be comfortable.'

'He's prepared to come back and face jail.'

'Beats getting your head blown off in your own bleeding swimming pool.'

Sue saw the force of the argument but she was only interested in how to get hold of Benny.

'See your guvnor,' he begged.

'First, I must have a number where I can reach you.'

'Ooh, now. I never really know where I'll be. I'll call you.'

'That's not good enough. No number, no cash from the *Journal*.'

'Don't be like that! Listen, Beck's girlfriend's a bit short of the readies now he's inside. She might sell you what you want – if you ask nicely.'

'She's been interviewed by the police several times.'

Sue heard Benny snort with disgust. It was an unlovely sound. 'They don't pay, she don't say,' he said and ended the call.

Dialling 1471 was no help, Benny had been too cautious, and there was nothing Sue could do except take Benny's offer to Jonah's successor. If Mr Rogers was lucky, his career as an informer for the paper might blossom again.

'Where've you been?' Leonie wanted to know when Sue returned to her own desk. 'We're needed in Sam's office.'

Ashford was in place, his bulk and stern expression discouraging.

'I need to know how you got the information you passed on to us,' he began, holding up a warning hand as both Sue and Sam protested. 'I know you like to promise confidentiality but there are times when the public good must come first.'

Sam was ready to debate the theme at length but Ashford waited for Sue's answer.

'Have you found any breach of the law on my part?'

'No.'

'Then I can't see any reason for breaking my word.'

Ashford sighed heavily and Sue realized he was older than she had first thought.

'What I say here is privileged information?' he asked Sam.

'If that's what you want.'

'Any bugs?' The superintendent's smile was a mere flicker of humour.

'Not one.'

Even then Ashford hesitated. 'It's on the cards there'll be a bombing campaign in the very near future by splinter groups of the IRA out to wreck what there is of a peace deal in Ireland. Security in London may have frightened them off so mainland Britain will bear the brunt of it.'

'You've had a tip-off?'

'The explosives have already been brought in.'

'How?'

'Some of it in the lining of containers for frozen produce. One of the names leaked to us has an interest in a big depot in Luton. Some Semtex arrived that way and a wholesaler not far from Luton has been stockpiling a large consignment of fertilizer.'

The office and its inhabitants were silent as the implications sank in. Undefended cities and towns around Britain at risk from the sort of carnage which had been endured where they were sitting.

'Mrs Bennett.' The policeman was normally as patient as a cat at a mousehole but not today. 'Time is running out. Is there any way your informants can help?'

Sue doubted Anwar and his friends would be willing to help the police directly but they had earned satisfaction from their activities. It was possible they might be prepared to carry on a little longer.

'I can put it to them but anything they do is independent of me.'

'Do what you can and as soon as possible. Enough people have been blown to bits already this year.'

'Then try working on Beck's girlfriend. I've had a tip-off of my own. She's holding out on you to get cash from the tabloids for what she knows.'

'Thank you, Mrs Bennett. Your informant's reliable?'

Sue chuckled. 'Hardly – but I think this piece of information's genuine.'

'What about Fletcher, sir?' Leonie asked. 'And Auntie Beattie?'

'There's been round-the-clock surveillance but she very rarely leaves the house. The husband's not mobile – he's waiting for a hip replacement.'

'That's odd,' Sue said. 'All that money in her official bank accounts and he's waiting for an op? It looks as though she hasn't a clue what's going on.'

Ashford's expression was bleak. 'It makes for good cover.'

'You mean Fletcher could pay for a new hip but he'd rather let the old man suffer?'

'If there was suddenly money for hospital bills, someone might get curious.'

Sam was intrigued. 'Why go to the bother of getting the money to Jersey? Surely it would have been safer to leave it in the Caymans.'

'I'd agree,' Ashford said, 'if it was a nest egg. Supposing it's a stake?'

'Six million? What for?' Sue asked.

'A helluva lot of drugs,' Ashford said quietly. 'That kind of input could take Fletcher from being a small player of the bully-boy variety. He'd get all of the profits and none of the hassle of street sales. At last he'd really be Mr Big.'

Sam followed the logic of the situation. 'So, when he got to hear about Passmore and Gibson –'

'Probably thanks to Sean Beck,' Sue added.

Ashford nodded. 'Fletcher saw his chance. He must have thought it was Christmas.' He turned to Sue. 'Your mysterious associates helped put paid to that. Thanks to them, Fletcher's a marked man.'

'It was Beck they wanted nailed.'

'Ah! They wanted the supplier of the explosives used in your car. If *Journal* facilities were used –'

'Anything I've done has been on my own,' Sue said, her chin lifting defiantly.

'Along with friends of Anil Naib?' Ashford pursed his lips. 'One of them's a high-grade computer expert.'

'There were lawyers too, making sure everything was done properly and Beck couldn't wriggle out on a technicality.'

'I still don't believe all the financial data was obtained the way you said,' Ashford argued. 'It's just not possible.'

Sue was patient with him. 'I went to a very good lecture once, on forensic science. Apparently, wherever you go, whatever you do, you leave traces. I walk into a room and it's empty. For your specialists, it's different. They can find fingerprints, dog hairs, dust of all kinds. A patch of oil on a cushion can be analysed. It may be fresh diesel, sun cream, old sump oil, perhaps it's come from a chip pan – and if it has they can even tell you how often chips have been cooked in it. Nowadays they can even get your DNA from the air you exhaled in the room.'

Leonie was trying to hide a smile as Ashford grew restless but it was Sam who intervened.

'You're saying it's the same with computers? A blank screen is like an empty room, hiding electronic fingerprints and dog hairs?'

Ashford was still not happy. 'I'm not convinced.'

'They said the same of DNA. Look,' she pleaded with the superintendent, 'someone in your office knocks the wrong key on the computer and a file is lost. What do you do – apart from giving them hell?'

Leonie hastily found a tissue and hid behind it.

It was Sue's turn to be impatient. 'You send for an

expert. I'd guess you sit and watch them play with the keyboard and the mouse and you probably think they're making a meal of it to justify their rate of pay, then bingo! The file's been reinstated. That's all Anil's friends have done. Sifted through electronic garbage.'

'Julian?' Sam asked Sue.

'Only in his own time and away from here.'

'You still insist the *Journal* wasn't involved?'

Sue confessed to using the library and Sam sighed with relief. 'Thank God!'

'I thought you'd be mad.'

Sam shook his head. 'When Animal Equality decided to bomb the *Journal* they took on all of us.' For a moment he relived the chill wind, the shards of glass, soft crying. He smiled at Sue. 'I didn't want our resources putting you in even more danger.'

Sue felt herself go pink as Ashford cleared his throat and Leonie carefully stowed the tissue in her bag.

'Off the record, Mrs Bennett, I'd like to meet this expert of yours,' Ashford said.

'Oh no, you wouldn't,' she told him with a smile. 'They charge a small fortune for services rendered.'

Sightings of Fletcher were still being reported from Spain. Leonie's feet healed well enough for her to resume driving and daily life settled to a routine broken only by visits to Dorking.

To Anwar Naib Sue delivered Superintendent Ashford's plea for help and occasionally her mobile carried a message in return. Names and addresses were passed on, mostly of people choosing a solitary life in the maelstrom of a big city. Ashford's air of satisfaction grew and Sue sensed that here and there amongst the data, along with anything gleaned from Beck's girlfriend, was enough to identify sleeping terrorists.

Miles called Sue at work and she heard a wistfulness in his voice, even as he delighted at James's progress.

'It's early days but the specialist does seem pleased with his progress. Poor little chap, he's so brave and cheerful, even when he must be feeling really rotten. The atmosphere in the ward is tremendous – so positive.'

'Give him my love.'

'I will. He asks about you – when's he going to see you again?'

'James has you and his mother. For now that's the whole of his world.'

'Later?'

'When he's better, he'll still need you.'

Switching off the phone Sue hoped her voice had not given too much away. A child's rights should be paramount, it was the only way. Natural honesty made Sue examine her own feelings. She had let Miles go out of her life. Could she have done it so easily if Sam was not with her at every opportunity?

Leonie continued to be amazed at the variety of topics arriving at Sue's desk. The two girls worked amicably, Karin joining in and puzzled only by the fact that Leonie's employers were willing to leave her at the *Journal* for so long.

Superintendent Ashford was consulted by Sam and the two men agreed to Sue travelling further afield as long as she was accompanied by Leonie and a back-up car.

'How does Ashford swing the cost?' Sue wanted to know as they drove back to Islington from Birmingham. 'There's been no sign of any wrong 'uns watching us since Pippa's wedding.'

The policewoman did not voice her own fears, that Sue was being allowed a wider range of travel to lure Fletcher into action. Instead, 'Maybe not but the super's been getting whispers about Fletcher. He's been seen on the Normandy coast.'

'Closer to Jersey. Are the French police involved?'

Leonie shook her head. 'Interpol. They've got a Russian

team under the microscope and Fletcher floats in and out of the picture.'

'Russians? What on earth are they up to?'

'You name it. Drugs, diamonds, nuclear warheads, chemical weapons. With a disintegrating army to do the looting and a police force unable to cope, the Russian threat's far greater than it's ever been.'

'What's Fletcher after?'

'My guess is drugs – and it's what the super thinks. Fletcher knows the set-up, even if he's only been on the fringes of it so far.'

'How did he get entangled with the Russians?'

'You found out he'd got six million to spend. I wouldn't mind betting they did too – and made him an offer he found it unwise to refuse.'

'You mean he was sold on by someone?'

Leonie nodded and Sue's thoughts raced. 'He's canny enough to see if Auntie Beattie's being watched. Once he knows she is, he also knows the money's stuck in the bank and he can't get at it.'

'What a pity,' Leonie said with a smile.

The morning drive to work was always as varied as Leonie could make it, never deciding on a route until they were settled in the car, the engine warming. Sue enjoyed the sense of security the tactic gave and she had come to know her police guards well.

'Who's on today?' she asked, pointing at the police car pulling out behind them.

'Paul and Glenys.'

'Did Paul's wife get the job she was after?'

'Must have done. He was off to do the shopping after he left us last night.'

'Keeping tabs on me must be the most boring job ever,' Sue chuckled.

'That's why it's known as the school run.' Leonie glanced at the dashboard. 'Damn!'

226

'What's the matter?'

'Petrol. I should have got some last night.'

She used her radio to warn Paul before drawing into the forecourt of the next garage. It was a cold morning and Sue wriggled as Leonie cut the engine.

'I'll do it,' Sue said, needing movement.

'No!'

'For heaven's sake! There's no problem. Surely, I can do it this once.'

'Ashford would have my guts for garters.'

Impatient, Sue settled back in her seat and waited. Leonie was very quick but as she started the engine, there was an exclamation from Sue.

'Batteries! My dictaphone's a dead duck,' she explained before sprinting towards the petrol station's shop, refusing to listen to Leonie's shouted warnings.

The purchase took a little longer than Sue expected, the man in front of her counting out very small change to pay for his paper and cigarettes. At last she was out in the cold air and walking towards Leonie.

From the roadway there was the sound of engines being raced, wheels screeching on tarmac. A van was being driven straight at Sue and she jumped back to avoid being hit. Shocked, she looked towards Leonie, seeing the girl shouting into her radio.

A movement to the left drew Sue's attention as a red Sierra was slammed against the front of the second police car. It trapped Paul in his seat and jammed Glenys's exit against a wall. Frozen to the spot Sue watched the driver of the assault vehicle run like a maniac away from the scene. It was all happening in slow motion, the man's back seared into her memory as he disappeared.

It had only taken seconds. In that time the doors of the van opened and two men jumped towards Sue. They were dressed in black, faces covered by ski masks. She had a moment of déjà vu before she was grabbed and heard herself screaming endlessly.

She had a glimpse of Leonie getting out of her car, gun

rock-steady. Quite clearly Sue heard the shouted warning of 'Armed police!' A burst of fire from the front of the van crossed the forecourt and Leonie dropped behind the shelter of the open car door.

Sue was heaved into the van, one man sitting on her as the other shut the doors behind them and the van careered away. There was the staccato whine of bullets from the van's driver, the sound of smashing glass.

Her mouth was taped and then her eyes. Hands were wrenched behind and secured. It gave Sue some satisfaction to lash out with her feet and make contact, hearing curses before her legs were dragged together and ankles wrapped tightly.

Breathing was difficult, Sue's struggles using air she could not renew easily through her nostrils. What air there was carried a smell of plaster, dust, putty.

Common sense made her quieten and Sue listened intently, trying to identify anything that might be useful. Almost as soon as she was used to the rocking of the van she was thrown across the floor as the vehicle slewed wildly round a corner. The bumping which followed meant very uneven ground and Sue could vaguely hear a sharp crunching noise as the tyres crawled over what she imagined to be very large ashes. Could clinkers mean an old foundry?

The van juddered to a stop and the back doors were opened. Hands clutched at her, grabbing skin with clothes. Sue was pulled out into the open air and made to stand upright before being dragged a short distance.

Words flung above her head were few and mostly cursing. Two of the accents had been acquired in the east or south of London, while the third, probably the driver, had the Scots of a tough part of Glasgow.

There was no time for more thought. Sue's head was pushed down as she was shoved into the back seat of a car. Her shins banged hard against the doorframe, making tears well up under the tape. Arranged like a package on the floor, she felt pairs of legs on either side of her then a blanket smothered. A final door slammed and they were on their way, a powerful engine eating up the miles.

Concentrating on breathing slowly and steadily took all of Sue's attention for some time. When she did start to think of other matters it was to realize there was no way Ashford's team could know of the switch of vehicles. All those weeks of shadowing her had been made useless in some out-of-the-way factory yard.

Voices above Sue were loud and complaining, the two Londoners not happy the Scot had used a gun. 'He won't like it,' was repeated at intervals until obscenities from the direction of the driving seat silenced the talking.

There were many twists and turns in the route, Sue flung around and ignored by the men.

'Will we make it in time, Tommy?'

'Course we soddin' will. I telt ye we would.' Tommy was the Scot and deeply resented being questioned.

There was silence in the car again as it travelled fast, occasionally stopping at lights. Sometimes roadworks held them, Sue hearing the sound of drills, machinery, as the car inched past in a queue. When the cramping became too painful Sue tried to relieve the agony by wriggling and stretching. Each time she was pushed down by an unfriendly hand.

Breathing continued to be a problem. She was not able to gulp air, increasing available oxygen, and her movements were limited as a result. Eventually, Sue managed to ease herself into a position which minimized discomfort.

'How much longer?' one of the Londoners asked. There was fear in the impatience.

'Half an hour,' Tommy snapped back. 'At most,' he added grudgingly.

It was impossible for Sue to guess how far they had travelled. For some time there had been no stops at traffic lights so London must have been left well behind. Unable to describe passing time in hours and minutes, she only knew the journey was interminable and, although she understood her chances of survival were zero, there was a longing for the bumping to stop.

When it did it was with a swift turn and the sharp crunch of gravel. Tommy cut the engine but none of the men moved. Sue heard footsteps.

'Problems?' The new voice was indistinct.

'Not really, smooth as silk,' Tommy assured. 'Barry get off?'

'You know Barry. It'd take more than the fuzz to stop him.'

'He did a guid job,' Tommy said. 'The police were cut off real well. We were away clean.'

'Not quite, Tommy. I've just heard a news flash. One shot copper?'

Even through the blanket Sue could sense unease, her captors in the back of the car moving feet as they rasped moist palms along their jeans.

There was a jolting as Tommy moved and opened his door. 'The cop had a gun, for Chrissake! What was I supposed to do?'

'You know what I like, Tommy. Keep things tidy.' Gravel crunched and another of the car's doors opened. 'Get her inside.'

The blanket was dragged away and Sue caught a moment of fresh air which held a hint of the sea before she was shrouded again. The tape at her ankles was sliced, the knife used nicking her skin. Such a small pain was lost in the agony of being forced to stand upright, then try to walk with muscles cramped and useless.

Gravel was underfoot. She stumbled on a metal grating. There was the harshness of coconut matting before her heels tapped on a bare wooden floor. Sue heard a chair pulled close and she was thrust down on it.

'Let's see what you've brought,' the newest voice suggested.

Smothering wool was heaved away, jerking and twisting Sue's head until she was aware of joints in her neck cracking. Fingers fumbled at her right temple and the

230

sticky tape was torn free. Pain seared through her and unwanted tears spilled.

When Sue could focus clearly it was to see Ray Fletcher studying her. Expensive yachting clothes were enhanced by an enviable tan but nothing could hide the power of his shoulders. They told their own story of the physical force propelling him from playground to importance.

Leonie had described him well. Meeting him in another place Sue might have considered him attractive, but she was unprepared for the chill of an ice-floe when her eyes met his.

'Interfering bitch!'

A hand whipped up and smacked hard against Sue's cheek, knocking her sideways. As Tommy hauled her upright in her chair Sue tried to stay calm and breathe evenly. It was a struggle with her mouth still sealed. Dimly, she saw the hand rise again and tried to move with it to lessen the impact. She hung sideways in the chair and felt blood trickle along her chin.

Under the cover of her hair she watched Fletcher twist his ring, the huge diamond flashing in the light from the window. He turned the sharp facets inside once more and, with dawning horror, Sue remembered Leonie's assessment of the man's deliberate cruelty, his enjoyment of causing blood to run.

Busy with her thought she missed Fletcher's nod to Tommy and was not ready when the tape was ripped from her mouth. Entangled hair was torn with it and she dug her nails into her palms, refusing to let anything but a low moan escape her. Fletcher's mouth tightened and Sue had a small pleasure in disappointing him.

'I want to know about you,' he told her, the words soft, caressing. 'You start asking questions and every frigging player on the pitch gets pulled in.'

Sue glared at him. 'Except you.'

'Ah. Friends in high places.'

'Still?'

There was a feral wariness in the pale blue flick of his

231

glance. 'One you don't know about, Ms Bennett? That was careless of you.' He leaned towards her and Sue caught the aroma of a classic cologne mixed with sweat. 'Come on, then. Tell me what you're really after – and don't give me that bleeding hearts bit about animals. I've had enough of that to last me a lifetime.'

Leonie had been right about his teeth. He really should have invested in a good orthodontist.

'I have to talk to Andy Passmore.'

'An interview for your boyfriend's front page? "My chat with the bombers."' Fletcher's eyes gleamed with amusement and there were nervous titters from Tommy and his colleagues.

'It's nothing to do with the *Journal*.'

'Pull the other one! The checking up on me wasn't done by the police – I know that for a fact. There's no way you could have done it on your own.'

Benny had been a busy little skunk, Sue decided.

'A girl like you with that kind of cash? Nah. It had to be a rag like the *Journal*.'

'No! It's personal!'

'Is it? Just because you had a sticker for the *Journal* on your car when you went to visit some toffee-nosed professor? Too easy to trace, you were – and a nice bit of extra publicity on the side.'

It took time for fact to become reality. It had been the press car which had attracted Passmore and Gibson's attention. Finding her name and using it had merely been a way of adding to the pressure on Professor Turnbull.

'Did they tell you that was why the bomb was put in my car?' Sue's eagerness was not lost on Fletcher.

'Maybe.' He was back to twisting the ring which could slice skin.

'I must see them!'

'You will. First, you've got to pay for costing me money.'

'Six million in Jersey banks not enough?'

His eyes flared wide, surprised by her knowledge, then they were shuttered from the inside. 'Yeah, but I was expecting double that until you starting messing me about. So, you bitch, I want to know who grassed and you're the one who can tell me.'

Sue began to understand why Fletcher had wanted her so badly. It was not only his need to be seen dealing with someone who had offended him. He genuinely believed himself important enough to have earned a major traitor, one which must be exterminated.

She gazed at him calmly, knowing her answer would annoy him. 'No one grassed. Some friends went fishing and you trawled up in the net.'

Sue saw a punch coming and twisted away but Fletcher was experienced in hitting women and it was the back of his hand which cracked against the side of her head. There was a ringing in her ears and she found it hard to focus clearly.

'I've no time for games. Business associates are waiting for cash I can't get to because of you. They're not likely to hang about and that upsets me. Now, I need a name to explain the delay. Who talked?'

'No one.'

There were more blows, more blood, and pain was a constant.

'Tell me who it was! Sean Beck?'

'No. He was being watched – and all his contacts. You were only one of them.'

'Who set it up? I know it wasn't the police, so don't try conning me.'

It was Sue's turn to smile, the pain worth it. 'You'd never believe me.'

His hand rose and fell. 'Tell me!'

She shook her head to clear it and glared at her assailant. 'People you'd never notice in a million years.'

'No? I can spot a busy a mile away.'

'I'm sure you can – and his price tag.' Speaking was becoming difficult as lips swelled.

Bruises were piled on bruises. 'The colour of raw liver' Leonie had said of Mrs Fletcher. Sue knew her face must be cut and swollen, eyelids closing as they flooded with damage fluids. With Tommy to make sure she was in position for the blows there was little Sue could do to minimize the beating.

'I'll know who it was!'

Sue shook her head slowly. 'You'd never see them because, for you, they hardly exist. In a bar, a restaurant, they come when you click your fingers.' Her words were mumbled, indistinct.

Fletcher was unsure for a moment, wondering what she meant. His puzzlement was the reward for her agony.

She straightened in her chair, vestiges of pride linking in her like an unseen steel mesh. 'Anil, the boy who borrowed my car and died, he has many invisible friends. They sell you your groceries, cook your food. They're the ones who work in the casinos you like to visit. From all those people came a lot of information on you and your friends in high places. Who was missed?'

'Devenish. Super in Catford.'

Fletcher's answer was offhand as his thoughts churned and Sue accepted that his revelation of Devenish signalled her death.

'You mean a bunch of . . .'

She tried to smile at his disbelief but her beaten muscles refused to move. In the wreckage of her face her eyes danced. 'Speak of them with respect, Mr Fletcher. They got the better of you.'

'Nah! The little sods are only good for pushing curry, that's all.'

His accent was reverting to its origins, she noticed as she prepared to twist the knife. 'Not clever enough to outwit you? You were only a side issue to them – unimportant. One of the little men,' she said softly and watched the message hit home.

Her fleeting pleasure had to be paid for and Sue was knocked backwards under a hail of blows. With her hands still taped she had no way of saving herself and skidded across bare boards.

'Pick the bitch up!'

The men did as they were told.

'She wanted to meet Animal Equality. It's about time she did. Take her upstairs.'

Sue was heaved upright. She had lost a shoe and limped as Tommy held her in a firm grip, aiming her up the stairs of the shabby house and into a bedroom. What she saw and smelled made nausea rise and flood violently and she tried to turn her head away. Ray Fletcher had followed. He bunched Sue's hair in a fist and forced her to look.

'They wanted equality with animals. Well, they got it. You can't get more equal to a side of beef than that.'

What had been Andy Passmore lay twisted on the bed, her open eyes still staring in terror. On the floor beside her was the shell of Dennis Gibson, battered until he only vaguely resembled a human being.

'Why kill them?' Sue asked Fletcher.

'They were no more use.'

'You mean you had the money you wanted?'

'All they could provide – you robbed me of the rest.' Sue's head was banged hard against the door jamb and this time agony and the smell in the room made her vomit, Fletcher crowing as he witnessed her humiliation.

'Will I leave her here?' Tommy asked his boss.

'No, take her down – and get rid of those two goons.'

Roped on to a chair she watched the men who had kidnapped her grab the money they were offered and run for the car. Tommy only realized his predicament after the noise of the engine had disappeared.

'Hey, what about me? How do I gae hame?'

'No problem,' Fletcher assured him.

The Scot relaxed, pleased with himself, but Sue read Fletcher's expression and her blood ran cold.

'You'd better give me the gun, I'll get rid of it so there's no comeback to you. It'll be somewhere safe when I've finished with it,' Fletcher said, his smile literally disarming Tommy. 'I do like things to be neat. Straighten her up, will you?'

235

Not only Tommy assumed the next bullet would be for Sue. She breathed slowly and prayed, Colin coming into her mind. He was there with her parents when there was the sound of a single shot and a body falling.

By turning her head she was able to watch Fletcher wipe the butt of the revolver then place it in Tommy's fingers, flaccid now in death. With an artist's care the body was arranged until there was the appearance of a suicide.

'Are you going to shoot me too?' Sue had tried to keep her voice steady, courageous. She hoped she was the only one to hear it shake.

'Oh no, not you, Ms Bennett. You'll take time to die and every second of it you'll regret crossing me. Pity I can't stay to watch but business calls.'

She thought of Ashford, Pat Eden, Leonie. 'You won't get away with it.'

He was smug, oozing self-satisfaction. 'I already have.'

'There's a block on the money in the Jersey bank accounts. You'll never touch a penny of it.'

'I won't have to. One day soon there'll be an accident. I plan to be scuba diving in Mombasa when I drown. After my grieving widow has had a suitable body cremated she'll collect the money and fly somewhere pleasant.'

'Where you'll be waiting to start again? Are you sure you can trust her after all the thrashings you've given her?'

Fletcher did not bother to reply, certain of his wife's loyalty and stupidity. He went out of the room and Sue heard him go to the back of the house before he began to climb the stairs. His tread was heavy as though he was carrying something weighty. Splashing sounds puzzled Sue until the first tendrils of vapour reached her. Petrol!

Footsteps quartered the floor above her where the two bodies lay. Another bedroom received the same treatment and then Fletcher started on the stairs, working his way slowly downwards.

'Goodbye, Ms Bennett. There's no one around to save you and no fire station for miles. Still, you'll have plenty of time to think of me before the house falls in on you.'

He tightened the rope which held her, making sure the knots were well away from her fingers.

'I'd really like to have watched you burn.'

Paper was twisted, Fletcher using a heavy gold lighter to get a flame which brightened the exultant gleam in his eyes.

'I don't like to leave a mess,' he said as he walked out of her life and closed the door of the room behind him.

There was a whooshing sound which travelled upwards. The slam of the front door. Hasty footsteps on the gravel. He was gone.

Sue fought desperately to free herself but Fletcher had done his job too well and she was forced to rock her chair to the window. She struggled to open her eyes but the left one remained swollen and closed. Only with her right eye could she see anything of Fletcher. He was running along a path which led to the sea and a jetty where a speedboat bounced. Anchored further out were the sleek lines of an ocean-going yacht.

Black despair threatened to engulf her. Fletcher had planned carefully and his callous disregard for life meant Tommy, the gun in his hand, would be the scapegoat for all the deaths as well as Leonie's shooting. No matter the house would be a burnt shell, forensic specialists would prove Tommy's guilt and find no sign of Fletcher. They would also confirm her identity.

She bowed her head and let her last thoughts linger amongst those she loved. There was an ache in Sue's breast as she dreamed fleetingly of the children she might have had.

Coughing racked her as smoke began to billow into the room. There was a crackling in the ceiling. The noise made Sue look up and she was hypnotized by a long line of flame moving steadily.

Consciousness was slipping away as the smoke thickened. In the distance she heard the sound of breaking glass and knew she had only seconds before the room above fell on her.

Shouts were in her imagination, then strong arms held her and she was lifted, still in her chair, and bundled through the gaping hole which had been a window. At a safe distance from the house Sue was deposited gently, the ropes and tapes cut away.

'I thought they only wore those caps on TV,' she croaked at her rescuers, navy blue flak jackets and diced baseball caps identifying them.

'Oh, we dress up now and then,' one assured her. 'Listen, love,' he said urgently, 'any more inside?'

'Three,' she told him through stiff lips. 'All dead.'

Superintendent Ashford was looking down as she slumped in her chair and she saw Pat Eden's anxious face. He was on his knees beside her, wrapping his coat round her. 'Who's dead?' he asked gently.

'Passmore and Gibson. I saw their bodies.' Sue remembered the smell. 'I think they must have been killed some time ago.'

Neither man wasted grief on the two who had destroyed so many lives.

'The third?' Ashford wanted to know, bending low to hear Sue's answer.

'Someone called Tommy. A Scot. He was the one who shot Leonie.'

At last tears came for her friend, a luxury Sue had denied herself while she must resist Fletcher. Salt stung her ravaged eyes and the wounds on her cheeks but it was an astringent for her grief. She was denied time to mourn, the upper floor of the cottage settling on the ground with a weird sigh. A gust of heat reached them.

'Fletcher escaped,' she whispered to Pat Eden, 'but he let slip there was another bent policeman.' Ashford had heard what she was murmuring and leaned close. 'Devenish, a super at Catford. Must have warned him about the raid.'

She did not see Ashford turn away and give crisp orders into his radio. Sam was there, arguing with everyone in sight. He was holding her, soothing her as he would a child, and she was grateful.

238

'Is there anything else you want to tell me?' Ashford wanted to know.

She ached and was so tired, but they must be told of the Mombasa plan and Fletcher's wife. Before there was time to begin an answer they were all distracted by a huge flash out at sea. In silence they watched pieces of the yacht dance in the sky while flaming timbers inscribed perfect parabolas. The boom of an explosion reached them.

'Damn!' Ashford was disappointed. 'I wanted that bastard in the dock.'

'That wasn't you?' Sam asked.

'Me?' The superintendent allowed himself a small smile. 'Highly tempting, but no. I knew he was playing footsie with the Russians.' He lifted a hand towards the burning flotsam. 'That's more their style.'

Sam was unforgiving. 'Pity it couldn't have happened before Sue was savaged so badly.' His fury was an entity in the field with them.

'It was meant to and we'd have succeeded if we'd been able to keep her away from him for another twenty-four hours. As it was, we only managed to trace her because of that list of second homes her little helpers passed on.'

'But by putting a block on Fletcher's accounts you knew the Russians would deal with him, didn't you?' he demanded to know from Ashford.

'Did I, Mr Haddleston?'

'It's why, when we did arrive here, you left Sue in that house and wouldn't let even your own men get close. How could you be so sure he wouldn't kill Sue before he left?'

'For him, that would have been kind. Ray Fletcher likes very slow deaths for his real enemies.'

'Likes fires,' Sue whispered but Ashford heard.

'Yes, Mrs Bennett. I had to take the risk. It was the only way to get you out safely. My people were ready as soon as Fletcher was out of sight. He had to get on that yacht.'

239

'And if there'd been no bomb in place?' Sam wanted to know.

'The navy was standing by at all times.'

The silence between the two men was grim, uneasy.

Sue had to know. 'Leonie?'

'Intensive care,' Ashford said. 'Her family's with her.'

Relieved, she closed her eyes, leaning against Sam as he buried his face in the smokiness of her hair. A girl in paramedic green tried to persuade Sue to lie on a stretcher. She resisted and Sam settled the budding argument by picking Sue up and carrying her to the ambulance. Wrapped in blankets she wriggled a hand out to Sam, needing him. A mask was moved near the wreckage of her face and Sue recoiled but the paramedic soothed patiently, letting mild anaesthesia reach her and suspend pain.

Sue breathed more easily and the darkness of sleep approached. Sam lifted her fingers to his lips. 'I'm so glad Leonie's all right,' she said, too tired to see Sam's tears.

With a sigh of relief, Sue let her senses slip away. The debt she owed Anil had been paid.